Give It Back

Danielle
Esplin

BLACK ROSE
writing™

The final approval for this literary material is granted by the author.

Second printing

This is a work of fiction. Names, characters, businesses, places, events and incidents are either the products of the author's imagination or used in a fictitious manner. Any resemblance to actual persons, living or dead, or actual events is purely coincidental.

ISBN: 978-1-61296-832-2
PUBLISHED BY BLACK ROSE WRITING
www.blackrosewriting.com

Printed in the United States of America
Suggested retail price $18.95

Give It Back is printed in Adobe Garamond Pro

To my twin sister, Chanelle.

Acknowledgments

My deepest thanks to:

Kirstin Price Bonney for reading every draft and always encouraging me with her amusing remarks and opinions—not to mention my messaging her in the middle of the night, just to share the latest ARC review. I'm thankful for her astute insights and unwavering belief in this book, and I'm forever grateful that I wrote *Give It Back*; otherwise I wouldn't have met her.

Nickolay for supporting me through this journey and for believing in me. Chanelle Esplin, my twin sister, who is thousands of miles away but never fails to be there in my time of need. My parents, Ada and Campbell, for checking in on me throughout the months.

Special thanks to Marietjie Hurter, who, unfortunately, has passed away of cancer since sharing her story with me. She's an inspiration to many. To Yelena Kondratyeva, for encouraging me. My beta reader, Mercy Pilkington, for her professional services. Dane from Ebook Launch for designing my book cover and being so patient with my requests.

Michelle Fambrough, who gave me her interpretations of the poems in the novel. And finally, my wonderful editor, Angela Brown, for sharing her professional knowledge and helping me cross the finish line.

Lastly, I'd like to thank Black Rose Writing for believing in my work.

To contact me or leave feedback regarding the novel, please visit at www.danielleesplin.com. I'm looking forward to our next writing-reading endeavour together, and I wish you all happy reads until then!

Give It Back

Ella

Thursday, June 25, 2015
Evening

My phone vibrates, and my arm swings out, propelling my glass to the floor. The shatter echoes throughout my apartment as red wine trails along the grout lines of the kitchen tiles. It looks just like the blood that seeps down the victims' bodies when I force my blade into their skin. I grab a towel to stop the wine from reaching my beige carpet in the next room. My eyes move back to my phone. Guilt slithers through me as my sister's name flickers on the screen. I should've called, asked her how she's doing.

"Lorraine," I say. "How are you?" There's silence. "Lorraine?"

"Hi, El." She's breathing deeply on the other end.

I tiptoe around the kitchen bar to avoid stepping on the shards of glass and slicing up my bare feet. "Are you okay?" I ask. Another pause. "Can you hear me?"

"I need you."

I swallow hard, my eyes dashing around as though I'll find an excuse in my apartment. "The au pair is still there, right? The one from London?" This could be a replay of the night she called to tell me what the doctor had said. I've known about her diagnosis for eight months, and I haven't visited her once. A good sister would've made the short flight from San Diego to Seattle to support her, but I haven't.

"Yeah. She's here."

"Great," I say, then fall silent as she starts to sob.

"Please. Come to me."

I clench my teeth. The last time Lorraine begged, I lied. I told her I couldn't take time off from my new job because when I asked, my boss threatened to fire me. Not long after, the nightmares started. Many nights I'd lurch awake, drenched in sweat, panting. In my dreams, she'd die. My subconscious kept reminding me of reality, the brutal truth. It haunted me, and I couldn't shake the guilt anymore, which made me retreat even more. And then I stopped calling her altogether.

Part of me wants to postpone this once more, but I'm afraid that if I do, I'll never get to see her again. "Of course," I say, almost choking on my words. "Yes," I tell her, this time more assured. "I'll come as soon as I can." I want to say "only for a few days" because I know seeing her like this will kill me.

"Thank you," she says, her voice almost breaking into a relieved chuckle. I want to tell her I love her, even though I have a shit way of showing it, but instead I say good-bye and end the call.

Startled, I stumble to the barstool. I pour another glass of wine, and then I swill it down my throat. At least I'll have something to do this weekend other than spending it in the laboratory, burning myself out, and working when everyone has gone home as a single light burns on the corpse I'm dissecting.

I once read a quote: "You can't stop the waves, but you can learn how to surf." After I read that, I decided to loosen up, work fewer hours, and live a little, just to find myself in my apartment with more empty hours to fill.

I lower my glass to the counter and wipe my forehead with my free arm. The blazing sun beats down on the windows throughout the day, making my apartment ridiculously hot at night. It takes me back to the days when I'd make fun of Lorraine when she had oily skin as a teenager.

"We could fry some eggs on your forehead you know," I told her once, as we walked side by side in the California sun.

She always took it a step further: "Scrambled eggs and pus coming up! Want a hamburger patty with that, ma'am?"

We were gross, filthy-minded kids trying to make each other laugh to an impractical extent. Lorraine was more reserved than I was, a habitual taciturn teenager, utterly reticent about her personal affairs, but as soon as she felt comfortable with you, she'd transform into a verbose storyteller.

My mind races through the years: the days at the orphanage—Lorraine was six, and I was barely two when we became orphans; our caregivers, Miss McBeth, school, college; her leaving me in San Francisco to live in Seattle, tagging after Craig; the announcement of her first pregnancy; Logan's birth. She was at her happiest when she had him. Before I can continue with these thoughts. I think of what I have to say about my thirty-three-year-old-self: work, study, work, and more work. No boyfriend, kids, or even pets. I've been alone for so many years.

And now, suddenly, I'll take off on a plane to Seattle, unfamiliar territory, possibly saying my last good-byes to my beloved sister. *My* sister, the only friend I've had for as long as I can remember.

Lexy

Friday, June 26, 2015
Morning

Does she know? I wonder. First I focus on Lorraine's sallow skin, then on her hazel eyes, which are losing their colour. The ends of her thinned, dark curls curve into her sunken cheeks as though they're peeking into a desolate gorge. Ever since her diagnosis, she's been fading like a light bulb with cancer's hand on the rotary dimmer.

A shaft of sunlight strikes the sliding door behind her, casting a shadow across her face. Her fingers run along the edge of the newspaper. The rustle of a single page turning breaks the silence. An incongruous calm sound, opposing the restlessness ripping me from within.

I'm well aware that she's not reading but merely scanning the paper, looking at the pictures. If she had eyes on the top of her forehead, she'd think I'm a bloody stalker. The screech of a chair makes me snap out of my gaze. Logan plants himself next to me.

"Why aren't you dressed for school?" I ask, as my eyes track down his long legs, which are still clothed in pyjama pants.

"It's the last day," he says, his light-brown hair pointing in different directions. "No one's going."

Lorraine slams the newspaper on the table, her sharp tone cutting through me. "What did you just say?"

"Mom, just keep reading," he says, and laughs. A few weeks ago, I might have shared the moment with him, but not today. Lorraine sighs, and before I can set him right, she gets to her feet.

To maintain an authoritative stance against him isn't for the weak. I wasn't hired to look after a sixteen-year-old. I'm primarily here for Sam, Lorraine's eight-month-old son. Logan is six years younger than I am, but he could've been one of my university mates back in London. He's bulkier and taller than half the men I went to class with, who ironically shared some of his boyish qualities. For most students living in residence halls, the transition from high school to university involves nothing but work, binge drinking, and sex.

Lorraine hauls herself across the kitchen, clumsier than ever. I dash to her side and grab her arm. She flinches and steadies herself against the counter. "Sorry," I say, noticing a red imprint of my hand on her skin. She smiles subserviently at the floor, her eyes compelling mine to follow her gaze. "Please," I say, "go lie down. I'll bring you breakfast in bed." She doesn't thank me, nor does she seem pleased with my offer, which makes my heart thump against my chest. She merely nods, her face blank. I glance at Logan; his well-defined shoulders are curved forward, the smile wiped from his face. My eyes shift from him to Lorraine, who's a few inches taller than I am, and then I help her up the stairs, step by step.

Lately I've been running this entire household. I'm not only an au pair anymore—I'm also a caregiver, or at least that's what they call me. *Oh, and this is Lexy, Lorraine's au pair and caregiver,* followed by that god-awful tilt of their heads, and the *aww* sounds that emit from their rounded lips. Oh, God, and the whisper when I walk away: *You know…she's just helping out,* like I'm some petty twenty-two-year-old who needs them to explain the situation I'm in.

Once we're in Lorraine's room, she staggers into bed. "My sister is visiting this weekend," she says in an even tone. There's no more chitchat; she's straight to the point, conserving her energy for pivotal moments.

I met Ella once, right after Lorraine gave birth to Sam. Despite the fast "Hello, good-bye," I immediately picked up on some stark differences between the sisters. In addition to Ella's vanilla-malt hair, smaller body frame, and decent posture, she speaks with an assertive firmness. She's a woman you definitely don't want to argue with.

At the doorway, I turn to give Lorraine a polite smile, but she doesn't reciprocate. I break eye contact, trying to hide my suspicion. *Perhaps she knows*, I think. *Or maybe she's just tired.* But if the second one's not the case, I'm a dead girl.

Ella

Saturday, June 27, 2015
Morning

The cab driver hurls my luggage into the taxi, and it flies like only a light packer's bag would, striking the back of the trunk with full force. I wince, trying to catch his eye, but he doesn't seem to care. "A bit more careful next time," I say, knitting my eyebrows together. He nods as his face breaks into a smile, and then he says something in a strong Spanish accent.

Once I'm in the car, a call comes through. The judder grows stronger as my fear sets in. An unknown number from Washington urges me to answer. I stare at the screen as I try to calm myself down. Perhaps Lorraine's calling from someone else's phone. Maybe she forgot to ask me to bring her something from California, or she forgot what time I'll arrive. It rings for a few more seconds before I answer.

"Hi," I say, forcing the word out.

"Hello," a man says. I wait for him to say, "Sorry, wrong number," but then I break out in a cold sweat as he continues. "Ella Jensen?"

"Yes." My eyes glance down the road as the car shifts into motion.

"This is Tim Beaker. I'm a nurse at Westbridge Hospital in Seattle. I'm calling to inform you that your sister, Lorraine Davis, was admitted earlier today." He says this in an utterly formal manner, callously cold. There's silence. He's waiting for a reply. I can tell he's done this many times. For him, it's routine, just another day at work.

"Miss Jensen?"

"Yes…yes, sorry." I pause. "What happened?"

"The cause of the accident isn't clear." My body goes rigid. "At the moment she's very—"

"Accident?"

"Yes. The police are waiting for a report from us to assist with the investigation." He falls silent. "They haven't reached out to you?"

"No. This is the first I've heard of it." I straighten my back against the car seat. "Is she okay?"

"Right now she's quite confused and distressed. We're running some tests."

"Where did you find her?" I ask.

"She called for an ambulance from her house."

"Where was her son? And the au pair?"

"Her son is fine. He's with his fath—"

"And the baby?"

"I just told you…he's with his father."

My stomach flips. Something's not right. "I meant the sixteen-year-old, Logan."

The nurse clears his throat and says something away from the phone that I can't make out. "No, ma'am…I'm talking about the baby, Samuel. There was no sign of anyone else in the house. That's all we know."

My hand glued to my forehead, I thank him for informing me. "I'll be there soon," I say, and then hang up. As I stare at the back of the driver's head, my heart feels heavy, agonized by the image of my unresponsive sister lying on the floor with no one to help her.

I call Logan's father, Craig, but no one answers. I try again, but it goes straight to his voice mail. My hand drops to my lap, and I let out a barely audible sigh. This will be the longest flight of my life.

Afternoon

Seattle looks different from last year in October. A few days after my nephew was born, I walked into the most depressing atmosphere I'd ever encountered. At least in snow you can picture kids throwing snowballs, teenagers skiing, and moms making hot chocolate. No, it was nothing like that. The sky was dark gray, filled with clouds, and the roads were wet. It felt like Washington's sorrow was weighing on my shoulders, trying to oppress me with its aura.

But today, in the midst of summer, I'd prefer to live in Seattle than in San Diego. Now I understand that the nine months of drizzling rain are, after all, worth it. When Lorraine moved here with Craig, she sent me an e-mail, saying, "The forests intertwine with the pristine lakes—the mirror of nature." I burst out laughing because it's typical of her to become poetical about it. "Seattleites explore hiking trails as their skin soaks up the filtered sun, which beams down on them through the branches. They wander into the meandering mountains with many possibilities awaiting them," she wrote. Back in San Francisco, I didn't get it, but now I understand why Lorraine moved here. It's magical. I want to smile, take it all in, but I can't, not after the phone call I received this morning.

Throughout the flight, thoughts consumed me: *Where was Logan? The au pair? Where are they now? Maybe Lorraine stood up too fast or she didn't eat enough?* One of her brain tumors could've been responsible, but I refuse to believe that. I tried to use the Internet on the plane to see if any of her friends had posted on Facebook about what happened, but the Wi-Fi service wasn't working. I then concluded, *Yes, she has low blood pressure. That's it. That's definitely it.* But I'm wrong, I think.

Now my eyes race through the hospital waiting area. The walls are dull, with lighter streaks where they were cleaned. There's plenty of room to move around but nowhere to get comfortable. An occasional request for Dr. Anderson blares over the loudspeaker. Family members anxiously hug and greet one another. Feet tap the floor as faces are buried in hands. A woman to my right wrings her hands as we all wait for a doctor to come around the corner to fulfill our hopes or rip our hearts out.

The smell of iodoform reminds me of the first time I held Sam. Except back then I also detected the scent of lavender and Ivory soap on his skin. When Lorraine handed him over, my stomach knotted and my pulse quickened. He looked like a little boxer after a fight, puffy eyed, his mouth twisted into a grimace. As he twitched, my damp fingers melted into his soft, chubby legs. Lorraine laughed at how unnaturally silent I grew as I stared at him. It was the first time I saw my sister smile in a long time. It was a magical, precious moment, and I thought, *If only all hospital visits could be this heartwarming.*

As I glance at the wall clock, a nurse walks in a half circle from behind the desk to take me to Lorraine's room. The hairs on my arms rise. I'm cold and afraid. Food carts, machines, wheelchairs, and beds are being pushed up and down the hallway. A doctor and a nurse rush from behind me into an elevator. I take a deep breath—I have no idea what to expect.

The nurse slows down, and my heart speeds up. She beckons me to a room with plastic-covered gurneys, surrounded by curtains hanging from metal tubes.

My eyes meet Lorraine's, and she casts me a forlorn look. Her body is covered with a bundle of white sheets. I scan the area; the room feels empty. There's no one nervously watching her heart monitor, no flowers on the end table or letters wishing her to "get well soon." The area around her bed appears untouched, lonely, dead. My heart drops as my eyebrows pull together, and then I rush to her side to embrace her.

I lean back and place my hands on her shoulders, my fingertips resting along her collarbone and shoulder blades. She feels small, bony. Mascara streaks down her face, the black lines contrasting with the white bandage that's wrapped around the top of her head.

"What happened?" I ask, as another tear trickles along her nose.

Her chest hitches. "Lexy peered into my room while I took a nap. She said something about Logan wanting to go somewhere. I felt so sick—I told her it was fine. You know, I trust her." I nod as she falls silent. Her lower lip starts to tremble, and she lets out an anguished wail. "Well, I shouldn't have!" She covers her face with her hands. I stare at her, unsure what to do. I let her cry for a few seconds, but it only grows more frantic.

"Lorraine! Listen, I can only be of help if you calm down and tell me what happened." I wait for her response, but she says nothing. "Did Lexy hurt you?"

"No," she says, her voice straining. "They didn't come home!"

"What do you mean? How did you end up here?"

"They never came back, El."

Evening

I'm still not sure how Lorraine ended up in the hospital. The test results aren't back yet, and she was too distressed and weary to tell me exactly what happened. From what I can make out, it seems like Lexy and Logan are missing. I had to let Lorraine rest, and before leaving, I did a foolish thing: I promised her I'd find Logan. That's when reality struck: I might be in Seattle much longer than I initially planned. It's my job or my nephew, and today, I chose my nephew.

She gave me the keys to her house and car after she told me that Samuel is safe at his father's house. She then gave me Robert's address and asked me to check up on them. She trusts no one with her baby, except the au pair, as they seem to get along pretty well. I wonder if anyone has reached out to Lexy's parents in London, the au pair agency, or her friends. Perhaps she has a boyfriend?

I take my phone out of my handbag to call Craig again. He'll probably be able to bring more to the table than Lorraine, but again no one answers, and now it's not giving me the option to leave a voice mail. I realize I don't have Robert's number but decide to head to his place anyway. I request a ride using my Uber app.

After a few minutes, a Prius pulls up, and the driver waves his hand, gesturing for me to get in. The GPS estimates that the drive to Kirkland will take eighteen minutes. On the way to Robert, Sam's father, I keep mulling over possible scenarios. *Maybe Lexy went to a friend's after she dropped Logan off, or if she has a boyfriend, she might be with him. Logan probably was just being a teenager, staying out later than he should have. Maybe they're waiting at Lorraine's place. Maybe this is all a big misunderstanding.* I wonder if the police will search for them before the mandatory twenty-four-hour waiting period. *And why are the police involved with Lorraine being in the hospital?* The car comes to a halt. The driver tells me we've arrived, and I realize this is the first time we've exchanged words.

I step out the car, tugging my bag from the backseat, and then he drives off. I turn to the apartment building, an eyesore gray cement box. For some reason, I assumed Robert lives in a house. Now I remember Lorraine told me he's "not quite settled" and "he never planned on having kids, ever." She also said, "He'll never abandon Sam, but he doesn't mind not having custody." A heedless man with a live-and-let-live attitude. Lorraine was attracted to his "carefree lifestyle"—she boasted about it like it was some kind of achievement. It wasn't until after she got pregnant that she realized he's too much of a boho to support their child financially or to be emotionally involved in his relationship with her. Needless to say, it didn't last long between them.

I walk closer to the apartment complex and place my hands around my mouth to project my voice. I yell his name repeatedly. After my fourth attempt, a young blonde pokes her head out the window, her hands covering her breasts. She leans back inside, and a thin man with a scraggly beard appears. His eyebrows furrow. "Who are you? What do you want?"

"I'm Lorraine's sister!" I shout, wondering if he can hear me. He disappears back into the apartment, and I decide to wait it out. My phone vibrates in my pocket; it's Craig. *Thank God.*

"Hi," I say, cautiously avoiding the "How are you?" part.

"Yes, who's this?"

"It's me, Ella."

"Oh. If you're wondering why Lorraine isn't answering her phone or where she is, she's in the hospital," he says.

"I know that. Thanks for sugarcoating it, *Craig*." Pissing me off requires no effort on his part whatsoever. After what he's done to Lorraine, I struggle to fight the urge to wring his fucking neck. I'm like an on-off switch when it comes to him. Perhaps I'm too overprotective of my sister, which seems odd, because I'm four years younger than her. But as cliché as this might sound, you really don't know what you have until it's gone. And Lorraine, according to her doctors, is almost gone.

"Well, then you probably heard about Logan and the nanny?" he says. I hear the television playing in the background. From his nonchalant tone, I wouldn't have guessed his son was missing.

"I went to the hospital today and tried to talk to Lorraine, but I couldn't get much information about what's going on." For a moment I believe everything will be all right, like this is just one big mistake.

"You know, she's going through a lot of turmoil. I'm pretty sure Logan is caught up at some party. He's a smart kid. This kind of thing has happened before."

"Oh…really?"

"Yeah. It was my week with Logan, and right after we learned about his mom's cancer, he became…well…more rebellious. I gave him some space. Lorraine would've freaked out if she knew I waited two days for him to return. *Two days*, no calls, text messages, nothing." He chuckles.

"Why are the police involved then?"

"They believe it's something to look into. With Logan and the nanny gone, they think something might have happened inside the house. Lorraine…uh…she's not the same since the cancer spread to her brain."

She's not the same? How would he know? They barely spoke during the last few years of their marriage, and he acted like a stranger around her.

"Sometimes she can't remember things." Craig falls silent for a moment. "And she did say she blacked out, fainted. Maybe she had a seizure. I'm not sure."

Seeing Robert approaching me, I tell Craig I'll call him later before hanging up. Up until now, I've only seen Robert in photos. He's taller than I imagined, and he looks thinner than he does in his Facebook profile picture. He doesn't even look like Lorraine's type. She was never attracted to men with long skinny arms, sloping shoulders, glazed eyes, and hipster beards. What the hell did she see in him?

"Where's Sam?" I ask without greeting.

"Upstairs, sleeping."

"You left him with a stranger?" I frown, wondering if it would be illegal for me to take Sam home without Robert's consent, away from his father. *Father*…that sounds too dominant, too stern or Mufasa-like—he's a coward, a low-budget, hand-fucking coward.

"She'll head out soon," he says, flashing his teeth.

"Well, I'm taking Sam. I don't care if you're done with your fuck fest or not."

"Sure," he says, jumping at the opportunity to hand over his son. My face is twisted in an expression of unmistakable disgust, and my eyes beam through his shallow head. I don't suffer fools, and I can't tolerate idiots. That's also, mainly, why I'm still single.

As we walk upstairs to his apartment, he rambles about random topics I couldn't care less about. I'm revolted by the combined stench of urine and dust, leaving me with an even grimmer expression. He swings the door open, smashing the handle against the wall. It must've scared Sam, because now he's crying frantically.

The girl yells from the bedroom, "Come finish me up, babe!" She clearly has no idea I'm inside the apartment. I'm so infuriated I feel like kicking the bedroom door off its hinges and breaking my foot off in her ass. Although I have no kids of my own, the family I do have is gold, and you'd better treat them right.

I scoop Sam up in my arms and cradle him tightly to my chest, trying to calm him down. A pit forms in the bottom of my stomach, the same one that always comes whenever I hold him. I swing him back and forth, trying to read his cues, rubbing my hand up and down his back. He stops crying, but he still whimpers. I gather Sam's things—his diaper bag, fold-up crib, blanket, and pacifier. Looking like a packed mule, I walk out without saying good-bye, and I notice Robert already has returned to his lover.

Lexy

Tuesday, November 11, 2014
Morning - 7 ½ Months Earlier

As I open the casement windows above the sink, the silence in the kitchen dwindles as the birds greet me with their enchanting melodies. I spot an American robin on the highest branch of an incense-cedar tree that blocks half the house across the street. A house I believe to be empty, for there's no sign of curtains, cars in the driveway, or even lights gleaming at night.

Redmond is a gorgeous city, nestled between public parks, hiking trails, Lake Sammamish, and forest evergreens. I did some research before moving here; apparently 34 percent of the residents of Redmond were born outside the United States, which contributes to the fact that I barely suffer from culture shock. However, some mornings I flip my eyes open, startled by the accents resonating through the house, but I never really feel out of place here.

A thumping sound on the stairs makes me swing around, facing Lorraine. She trundles to the chair and stares at the baby monitor at the end of the counter. I guess it's my cue to assure her that the device is on. Samuel isn't far away—I'll hear him even when the morning news blares on the telly—but when it comes to Lorraine's kids, it's like paranoia is her biological father. Yesterday she snatched Sam away from her own shadow, and then she forced a laugh that went on for longer than usual.

I signed up with aupairworld.com a few months ago. Families contacted me from all over: Australia, Italy, Turkey, New Zealand, and of course the United States. My profile description was a total sham. I claimed to have had many hours of childcare experience; I said I'd bathed infants, played with them, and filled their bellies. When Lorraine Skyped me, I had to bite down on my smile because I didn't even know what the job entailed or how many kids she had. I only knew she lived where I wanted to be.

I moved here the first week of October, just before Samuel was born. Lorraine wanted me to settle in and familiarise myself with the neighbourhood.

I fell even more in love with the idea of moving to Seattle when I heard weed had been legalized in Washington. I had to remind myself that eating the whole brownie would lead to more than just saddlebags. Not that I'm a pothead, but I enjoyed an occasional smoke after my ex-boyfriend and I broke up, to mollify my nerves and angst.

Two weeks into my stay, which is a month ago, Lorraine gave birth to Samuel. The anticipation killed us. Not knowing when *it* would happen was a tad too much for me. I kept thinking, *God, I hope it doesn't happen in the middle of the night.* Being jet-lagged made me love sleep even more. It was a ten-hour-long labour—yes, in the middle of the night. Weary eyed, consumed by the awakening hours of the day, we rushed to the hospital. I slumped back on a perforated metal bench while a nurse pushed Lorraine in a wheelchair around the corner. Her veins popped out from her neck as her screams echoed, bouncing off the walls down the hallway.

Sitting in the waiting room felt like an eternity as I wondered if I was still supposed to go to Craig's the next morning. Fortunately, Logan had spent the night at his dad's place. He would've been pissed off if we'd had to wake him for the birth of his half brother. "Just tell me about it in the morning," he would've said.

And then, almost four hours into Lorraine's labour, Robert made his mortifying stride into fatherhood. He was slurring, making me turn my head to avoid the pungent scent of vodka and cigarettes from crawling down my throat. I was on the verge of telling him to fuck off, but instead I pretended to be sick, expressing how awful it would be if Sam got his first flu from his dad. After I repeated myself, he stumbled away…*two* seats to my left. *Two.*

Lorraine's voice jars me from my memory. "There's some pasta and chicken in the fridge. Help yourself. I shouldn't be too long." She gets to her feet.

I nod as my eyes track her movement across the kitchen. "Everything will be okay," I tell her.

She forces a smile. "I hope so."

"Don't stress yourself out. I'm sure you'll be fine." I wish I knew for sure, but something isn't right. She's been in bed the last few days with a swollen belly and drugged with pain meds, and yesterday she vomited several times.

She shrugs. "It's just a checkup," she says, and grabs her bag. I fake a smile, because something tells me we're awaiting bad news.

Saturday, November 15, 2014
Afternoon

Lorraine's car hums in the driveway. She just came back from her doctor, who gave her the results of her tests. I bounce Sam on my hip, exciting him for his mommy's arrival. He giggles, flapping his arms around. I stare at the door, but no one shows. After a few minutes, concern sets in. I put Sam in his rocking chair and strap him in.

The floor creaks as I make my way outside. Lorraine's head is lowered, her chin tucked against her chest. She turns the engine off, and then her shoulders bounce as she starts to cry. Without a second thought, I rush to the passenger's side. I grab the handle, but the door's locked. My stomach tenses, and for a moment I hesitate. This is, after all, none of my business. Our eyes meet, and she stares at me for a few seconds before the pin pops up from the leather interior. I get in without taking my eyes off her. I stretch my arm out to touch her shoulder, but she moves it away.

"Where's Sam?" she asks, jerking her head up.

"Strapped in his rocking chair. He's falling asleep."

She swallows, wiping away the lighter streaks in her foundation. Then she turns her head away, gazing out the window. "We need to get him to latch on to a bottle."

"Sure," I say, wondering what that has to do with anything. "I can try tonight."

"Earlier," she says. "Next feeding. It needs to happen as soon as possible." Silence settles in as I wait for her to continue; part of me can already tell what she's about to say, but my head refuses to accept it. "I'll start with chemo soon," she says, and I give her a glazed look. Adrenaline surges through me, but before I can say anything, she jumps out of the car and hurries inside.

Sunday, November 16, 2014
Evening

Logan's girlfriend, Carmen, came over tonight. They've been dating for more than a year. She looked sweet with her petite figure and blond braids, but she was so obsequious around Lorraine that I excused myself from the dinner table and came to my room. She seemed to have no opinion of her own and agreed with everything Lorraine said, even on matters we've discussed in her absence. I cringed for Logan's sake.

I sit cross-legged on my bed, sinking into the memory foam mattress, my elbows resting on my knees. For the first time I can Google "choriocarcinoma" without being on edge. She hasn't broken the news to *them* yet. By "them," I mean everyone else.

My fingers dance over the keyboard, misspelling "choriocarcinoma" on the first attempt. After I hit "enter," a paragraph pops up at the top of my screen. I reread the first line: "A malignant, trophoblastic cancer, usually of the placenta." My muscles tense. One day Sam will understand what this means. I really hope that he won't take it to heart and that he won't encounter assholes, inducing undeserved guilt. Of course, he's not responsible for any of this, but the thought of being here, alive, at the possible cost of someone else's life is heartbreaking.

My throat dries out. I won't sleep tonight. I stare off into space. Derealisation…I think it's my mind's way of shutting itself down, subconsciously blocking itself from painful emotions.

Friday, November 21, 2014
Evening

On Wednesday, I dropped Lorraine off at the hospital. They implanted a port—which I also Googled; it's where they inject the drugs underneath her skin, so she can start chemotherapy soon. When I brought her home, I didn't expect her to be in good spirits. In fact, this entire week she pretended like nothing's wrong. If she didn't offer compliments, she baked muffins, hummed tunes, or played with Sam.

In a way I was relieved because I had no idea how to comfort her. What do I say to her? "I'm sorry"? Tell her I'm here for her? Make her laugh? Be serious about it? I'm just glad I don't have to deal with it right now.

I barely worked this week because Lorraine did everything she could for the kids. Every morning she cooked Logan breakfast, packed his lunch, dropped him off at school, and did his laundry. She had Sam in her arms all day while I sat in the living room, channel hopping.

I watched some of my favourite shows—the ones I used to watch with my mother in Croyden, London. Every night after school, we ate dinner in front of the telly, watching *Game of Thrones, Arrow, Grey's Anatomy, The Good Wife*, or crime documentaries. The thought of it makes me miss home. I've been in the United States for almost two months, and I haven't had the chance to Skype with my mum. We keep in touch via WhatsApp and Facebook, though. Every photo I upload gets "liked" by her, and she occasionally comforts me by sharing photos of our cats. I miss them jumping onto my lap, cuddling and purring all through the night. It's all about that cosy, homey feeling, the one you leave behind when you travel across the world. Lorraine has tried her best to make me comfortable here, but nothing will give me the feeling that my own home does.

The au pair agency refers to Lorraine as my "host mother," but with the fifteen-year age difference, she feels more like a friend. We're still getting to know each other, and I tell her more about my life than she'll ever share about hers. I've been wondering what happened between her and Craig, but she won't talk about it. Sometimes I repeat statements as questions, but I guess she's picked up on it. So I've just assumed they weren't a good match. My desire for knowledge has me feigning boredom sometimes, just to lessen my evident eagerness. The other day someone mistook my curiosity for "a youthful effervescence," but the compliment made me feel good, because it's a sign that I'm finally transforming back into my old self, into the Lexy I know.

Sunday, November 22, 2014
Early morning

In the living room, Logan sits across from Lorraine and me, waiting for his mum to tell him why she asked him to come down from his room. He has no idea what's coming, and from his expression, he's expecting good news.

"What's up?" he says, glistening with excitement for his football game later today, but his grin disappears when he sees Lorraine tearing up. "Mom, what's wrong?" His eyes are soft, *vulnerable*, but his jaw is tight.

"Honey," she says, with a dreadful nasal tone, "you know I've been sick lately, right?" He nods, wringing his hands. "Well, the doctor did some tests, and he told me I have cancer."

The color drains from Logan's face as his lips part. The tips of his fingers press the bridge of his nose. He leans forward, not saying a word. Instead he blows the air out of his lungs, his head moving from side to side, uncertain what to do.

"Nothing will change," Lorraine says, and he swallows hard, placing his hands on his parted knees, looking as though he's preparing to leave.

"Is it fatal?" His voice cracks a little as he fights the need to look away. I don't see a kid anymore. I see a broken young man who's about to lose his mum.

"They can't tell. It all depends."

"What kind of cancer?"

"A gestational trophoblastic disease," she says, and it's clear he doesn't understand what she's talking about. "It happened in my womb."

Logan's eyes fall on Sam, who's asleep in the rocking chair. He clenches his teeth and gives a painful chuckle as a tear escapes his eye. Lorraine stands to comfort him, but as soon as she approaches him, he jumps off the couch and storms off to his room.

Morning

I don't have to work today, but sometimes I go to Logan's football games to support him. I don't earn a fixed salary; Lorraine pays me more when she thinks I deserve it. Small things count, like supporting Logan's passion for football, driving him to a friend's house, or taking out the rubbish. I try to do a little extra here and there, and so far she hasn't failed to acknowledge it.

I lean sideways with my ear pressed against his door. "Logan?" I jump as he swings the door open, storming past me. He's miserable, troubled. He's still wearing his Seahawks shirt and shorts, making it clear that he won't be playing football today. I follow him downstairs but stop when he heads outside.

"They won't be expecting him," Lorraine says, as her fingers glide onto the white keys of her piano. I wonder if she thought it would give the foyer a grand appearance, as it's the first thing you see when you enter the house. My first impression was that someone temporarily placed the instrument there to be taken away, since it's consuming the little space the foyer has to offer. It's like getting Honey Boo Boo's mum to fit on a Twister mat—it just doesn't work.

I break my stare as Lorraine speaks. "I'll take him to Craig's tomorrow. I'll have to tell his father about my diagnosis."

My mouth opens to say something, but she cuts me short. "Don't worry. I asked Carmen to look after Sam. I know you have plans." Her fingers press down on the piano keys, and I smile as her hands dance around with grace.

Every other week, when Logan's at his dad's place, my work starts there at 7:00 a.m. Usually Craig's wife, Martha, leaves the house first, depending on how long she takes to write out my to-do list of *favours.* Once, she asked me to run errands for her but in a tone that elucidated that I should feel honoured to serve her. Ever since it became a habit of hers to shunt me around, I try my best to avoid her. After she leaves, I see Craig off to work, and then I make sure Logan goes to school.

I'll pack him lunch like he's a little boy and drop him off at Martin Jefferson High School. When I asked him why his parents treat him like he's twelve, he told me he sometimes skipped class before I was hired. "They don't trust that I'll go to school," he said with a mischievous smile, and I shook my head, laughing. At least I get a short break from taking care of Sam, so it's a win-win situation.

Lorraine

Sunday, November 23, 2014
Afternoon - 7 Months Before Disappearance

It's like I'm in a high-energy vortex, tunneling me down into a dark pit, a solitary place of hopelessness, anchoring my feet to nothing, steadily casting them sideways to the spiraling wall. It's disintegrating my flesh by the second, crippling me, killing me. The pendulum keeps swinging. *Tick. Tick. Tick.* I'm running out of time.

"Be strong," they say, but that seems counterintuitive. Be strong against what? Myself? Against my *own* body, which turned my cells cancerous? It's haunting, as though someone's reminding me of my diagnosis every day, without my being reminded by anyone. The thought keeps sneaking back up. As I wake, it overpowers me, devouring my day; having cancer is just goddamn awful. Sometimes I want to scream, and then suddenly I go numb. It's like I'm on a roller-coaster ride, but I'm not allowed to get off. I'm strapped to the seat, and within eyesight the unfinished twirl of the track swirls into the air.

My second most-engrossing thought: Craig. Yes, my ex-husband. Pathetic, I know. It dawns on me that I might die alone. Of course, my two boys will be with me, but that's different. I love and care for them, but they don't reciprocate. Sam's a baby, and Logan's a teenager—that's just how it is. My sons won't be able to fathom how much I adore them until they father their own children.

I'm worried about Logan. He didn't seem like himself this weekend. I don't want to cause my child grief or distress, but unfortunately it's inevitable. I'll have to tell Craig, for Logan's sake. I'll do it tonight when I drop Logan off at his father's place, even though I don't want to see Craig, and I don't want to set foot in that house again.

Danielle Esplin

Evening

Earlier, Lexy passed me on her way out. She looked stunning, and I thought I should also make an effort with my appearance for a change. I decided to wash my hair and do my makeup like in the old days, when I had someone to impress.

I park my car and stare at the house. The one I designed. A modern home with a raised foundation. Three tiny steps lead to the entrance, with a metal sheet suspended from the sliding wooden wall. Craig hated it—he still does—but I insisted, because there's nothing better than hearing every raindrop breaking its own fall.

I wonder whether my full-length mirror is still leaning against the master bedroom's wall, the one I stared at when I found out I was pregnant with our child. Craig stood behind me. He lifted my top and politely placed his hand on my stomach.

"This is the product of our love," he said, gazing into me, his twenty-year-old girlfriend. God, we were foolish, young kids. But oh, we were in love, so smitten with each other that he put a ring on my finger right before we welcomed Logan into the world. Some said he proposed because it was "the right thing to do," but I know he loved me.

Or so I believed.

Earlier today, I asked Logan if he wants to join me when I tell his father about my cancer. Predictably, he said no. He'd rather go upstairs to his room. Secretly, I hoped he would join us, to serve as a distraction, so I wouldn't have to look at Craig for too long. Now my eyes will dance around the living room, reaping memories I'd hoped to forget.

I set foot on the cobblestone driveway that runs out toward the attached two-car garage. Logan strides over the small lawn to my left as we make our way to the entrance.

As I ring the bell, I think about how it never crossed my mind that one day I'd wait for someone to welcome me into my own house. Perhaps I can try to get Craig to come outside, speak with me on the driveway. Footsteps creak on the hardwood floor as someone approaches the door. It's not him. I want to turn around, get in my car, and drive off, but I'm too late. Martha opens the door and stands aside for Logan to walk in. She turns to face me, fiercely staring me down. I look at my feet like a dog that's being shamed for eating the cat's food. I'm a coward. I did her no wrong, and it's supposed to be the other way around. I think of my brave little sister, what she would do. My eyes glide up, meeting her light-blue stare. Her blond hair is perfectly styled in soft waves, hanging above her shoulders. She squints, and with a valiant effort, I glare harder as a cold sensation shoots through my body, numbing me. We're the same height, and I can't help wonder if Craig sometimes thinks of me when he holds her tight at night.

"What?" Martha snarls, overemphasizing the *t*.

"I'm here to speak to Craig, regarding my son."

"Yeah, of course, you're here to speak to my husband," she says with a smirk. It's obvious Craig told her about my pleading episode when he left me. Why wouldn't he? He definitely wasn't worth my giving up my dignity, but love makes you do stupid things. That was two years ago. Our divorce was barely finalized when he hastily married Martha. She didn't even bear his child; he just wanted *her*.

She lets go of the door and walks into the house. I stretch my arm out, preventing the door from slamming into my knee. "Darling!" she yells. Déjà vu. It's sickening. Craig is in his study, like most Sunday evenings, planning his week ahead.

Logan already ran off to his room, evading this awkward situation. I amble toward the living room, waiting for Craig to come down from the second floor. I glance at the TV stand: a modern, rich, white art piece with a hollow-core surface and a tail-end storage drawer. They must have sold the old one. It probably wasn't elaborate or ostentatious enough for her. My mouth is dry, and my throat burns. I need a glass of water, and of course Martha won't offer me one. I sit down with my hands on top of each other, my palms facing the ceiling, resting on my lap.

Craig prances down the last step. He doesn't see me, and he's walking toward Martha. He grabs her around the waist and pulls her in, giving her a kiss while smiling. It's odd. He's in a good mood. He reminds me of the Craig I was married to for the first five years, the one I searched for during the eight after. If only my feelings could have dimmed, like his smile did, throughout our thirteen years of marriage. I divorced a stranger while still longing for the Craig I'd fallen in love with.

"Hi," I say, interrupting them, trying to accelerate the meeting. He turns and our eyes lock. He pushes his glasses up the bridge of his nose, the black frames disappearing underneath his pepper-colored hair. He glances at Martha as if we're up to something, and then she heads to the kitchen, raising her eyebrows while flattening her thin lips.

"I came to talk to you about something regarding Logan. Well…it's affecting Logan," I tell him.

"Sure," Craig says. He sits down on the opposite couch with his legs wide apart, facing me diagonally. He leans back into the backrest, his arms straight out to the sides, resting on the pillows.

I hear a knife beating the cutting board, and I can sense Martha's glare over the kitchen island. The kitchen where I spent hours preparing Craig dinner, where he made love to me for hours on end. The kitchen where I caught Logan stealing candy when he was a little boy, where we'd bake cakes together and have food fights. Many nights Craig and I sat on the barstools, drinking tea as we discussed our future, where we'd retire, when we'd be ready for another child, or where we'd like to go for our next vacation. And now, the kitchen where the "love of his life"—as he posted on Facebook—stares his ex-wife down.

The bashing in the kitchen makes me anxious as the sound grows louder and louder. It becomes disturbingly arrhythmic, which makes me blurt it out: "I've got cancer. I told Logan." The beating behind me stops. My eyes shoot up, and I find myself doing it again: searching for a hint of concern on his face, a hint of compassion. There's none. Instead he looks at Martha. The silence stretches out, filling the space between us, the whole house.

"It's apparently…quite fatal…this type of cancer," I say, but he doesn't even blink.

"Thanks for sharing," he says, and I find myself staring at nothing. There's a sudden sting in my chest. Suddenly I feel foolish. I try to swallow down the painful lump in my throat as I fight back the tears.

"Pleasure's mine," I say, and give him a faint smile.

"You tell me if you need anything," Craig says, and continues when he sees the confusion on my face. "For Logan." He falls silent for a moment. "I mean, if your cancer gets severe, and…if you're no longer around, I'll take good care of him."

I stare at him for a few seconds, trying to find the words. "Good. That's all then." Struggling to find my balance, I get to my feet. I try my best not to dart for the door. The last thing I need to do is to make a bigger fool of myself. *What was I thinking*?

Craig doesn't move. He's anchored to the couch.

"Good luck," Martha says, retreating from her abhorrent behavior. Without looking at her, I walk pass the bar counter and out the front door as she continues to beat the cutting board with the knife.

Ella

Sunday, June 28, 2015
Morning - 2 Days After Disappearance

I barely closed an eye. With the sublime awe of mothers, I got up twice in the middle of the night to feed Sam. A third time to change his diaper and a forth to comfort him. He's developed enough to identify loved ones, and of course, I'm not cutting it, but I need to try for my sister's sake.

My face is buried in the pillow. I feel like sleeping all day, but I can't. I want to get Lorraine out of the hospital, find Logan and Lexy, and get back to work in San Diego.

The baby monitor faces me on the nightstand, taunting me. Snores drift through the speaker, and I dread the moment Sam wakes up. I feel awful about it, but I'm not cut out for this type of lifestyle or perhaps I'm just not used to this.

I drag myself out of bed, throw my robe on, and head downstairs. The kitchen is a mess. *Did the police even search the house?* I wonder, but I guess they would've done so if they thought it was necessary. As I reach for the dirty plates, reality strikes: there's no one here but Sam, and I can do whatever I want.

I dash upstairs to Lexy's room and head straight for her dresser. An empty pink box has been left open on the top, with a book next to it, titled *The Shit No One Tells You: How to Survive with an Infant in the House*. I pull the drawers out one by one. My hands rummage through piles of clothes, searching for *something*, a lead, a hint, or a clue maybe. I don't know. But I find nothing.

I cross the room toward her closet. Next to her laundry basket are boxes stashed in the corner underneath hanged dresses and jackets. My knees drop to the floor, and I scoot closer. Inside the first box is a camera, placed on top of an empty wooden picture frame, some tangled cables, lingerie, and a small black case.

The camera is a Canon PowerShot, which is in good condition. I press the power button, and a message appears on the LCD panel: "Battery low." After I slide the batteries out, I position them in the charger and rush to the wall outlet to plug the device in, and then I head back to the closet.

I peek inside the black case and see what looks to be a food scale. As I pull the scale out, a silver blister pack falls to the floor. Most of the aluminum foil lids are broken. Tucked inside the cavities are blue pieces of pills with "Zoloft" engraved on them. It's a portable milligram scale, a drug scale. Nothing too unusual. Many people suffer from depression. Perhaps Lexy was tapering off Zoloft?

I pull another box toward me; it's heavy and hard to move. I scoot closer and lean forward. This one is filled with papers, magazines, books, and journals. I place several issues of *Cosmopolitan* on the carpet as I carefully unpack the box. I take out a piece of paper and unfold it. As my eyes scan the document, I raise my hand to my mouth. I wonder if Lorraine knows about this. All this time we've been worried about Logan—what about Lexy?

Evening

I just came back from the hospital. I had to ask Lorraine what's going on. I had to find out if she knew.

"How are you feeling?" I asked her. Sipping water, she sat on the bed with Sam propped on her lap. The white bandage was still wrapped around her head, and I realized for the first time how much weight she has lost.

"Better than yesterday. Of course I'm still worried sick."

I placed my hand on her forearm, which looked like a ruler, long, and sharp around the edges. "Ray, let's try again," I said, and she gave me a tentative smile. "Did the detectives come around yet?"

"Yes," she said, shifting her weight back on her arm, "They asked me all sorts of que…questions. They're searching for them."

"That's good to know. Do you mind telling me again what happened Friday?"

"I'll tell you what I can remember…Like I said, I was tired from chemo, and I took a nap. Lexy had Sam, so I wasn't worried about him and—"

"What time was this?" I asked, trying to jot down the sequence of events.

"Just after four. So later I woke up. Lexy was peering into my room, whispering that Logan wanted to go somewhere." She waited for me to write it down. "I think it was a friend's party. I trust her, so I said she could take him…or drop him off." She shrugged.

"Did you get hold of this friend?" I asked.

"The detectives said there were two house parties in the neigh…neigh…" She blinked fast, her chest expanding as she inhaled a gulp of air.

"Neighborhood," I helped, and it hit me: *She's not the woman I visited eight months ago, not anymore.*

Lorraine lowered her head, her eyes fixed on Sam. "No one saw them or recognized them from the pictures. The kids were from other schools." She took another sip of water. "They'll have photos of Logan and Lexy on the news tonight."

"I hope so. It's been a day and a half," I said, glancing at my watch.

"Anyway," she continued, "after I said it was fine, Lexy came back into my room and put the baby monitor on the side table."

"Sam was sleeping in his crib?"

"Yes, that's where I found him when I woke up. He was still fast asleep."

"So after Lexy left the room the second time, did you go back to sleep?"

"Yes," she said. "I heard the car doors slam. Then, after a few minutes, I fell asleep."

"What time did you wake up?" I realized I wasn't asking anymore; rather, I was interrogating my own sister.

"Just after seven p.m."

"So if Sam was still sleeping when you woke up, they probably didn't leave too long before that."

She sighed. "It's hard to say because he sometimes naps for twenty or forty minutes or even more than an hour."

I nodded, staring at the useless few things I'd written in my notebook. My eyes moved back to her. "Did you talk to Craig?"

She froze. "I called him, once."

"And?"

"He reas…sured me that everything will be all right. He said he'll conduct a search by tomorrow." She moved Sam over to her other leg. Her eyebrows tensed. "I wish I could do something. I feel so helpless, El."

"Don't worry about that," I said, bobbing my pen in the air. "I'll do everything I can, okay? You need to rest."

"I trust you," she said, and inhaled deeply as she rubbed her collarbone.

Sam started to fuss, and I took that as my cue to show Lorraine the piece of paper from Lexy's closet before his wails could fill the room.

But before I could, she said, "Robert sent me a text," and my eyebrows lowered. "He said you weren't 'too stoked' to see him." She made air quotes with her fingers.

"Sounds like Robert."

"I guess you're okay with having Sam then?" Her eyes shifted between mine.

"Sure. No problem. When will you be released from the hospital?" I asked carefully.

"About that…" She fell silent for a moment. "I asked the doctor if I could stay here for a while."

"Why?" My voice rose a little.

"My tumor is in…inoperable."

"Since when?" She didn't say a word. "What about radiation?"

"It's not working." Her gaze held mine. "I wanted to tell you earlier, but I just wanted a normal conversation with you…for once." I ground my teeth, and my fingers tightened around my pen.

She's right, though. Whenever we've spoken these last few months, it's been about cancer or chemotherapy. I can't remember the last time we had a normal conversation like in the old days, when we'd call each other just to share an experience at the grocery store. *Oh, man, this weird woman behind me had this deep conversation about the meaning of life. When I turned around, I realized she was talking to herself.* And: *Oh, I just wasted two hundred dollars on a gym membership, which I didn't use…even once. My shorts are getting shorter. Lately I've been looking like a slut—unintentionally of course.* I miss those useless, empty conversations with Lorraine. I guess we're all guilty at some point of failing to appreciate the small things, because when we use a broad brush to paint our exemplary lives, we splatter ourselves with ignorance.

"So what are the next steps?" I asked her. "How serious is this?"

"Stage four," she said, but she held up three fingers, and then she slowly straightened her index finger.

"So now what?"

"Well, it's incurable. So I guess the doctors might try something else."

"To what end?"

"I'm not sure. To…prolong my life?" I sensed her discomfort. She broke eye contact. "What the hell do you want me to say?" she yelled, and for a moment it felt like I didn't know her. The sudden outburst was disturbing. I stared at her, and then Sam started to cry. Startled, I changed the subject—I had to—so I mentioned the document I'd found in the box. She wasn't pleased that I'd raided Lexy's room, but someone had to do something.

"Yeah, they're expecting. She told me…two days ago…or was it yesterday?" She stroked Sam's head to calm him.

"You didn't think of telling me?" I asked, shaking my head.

"She told me not to. She still had to tell her mother."

I nodded, pursing my lips. "Who's the dad?"

"Wayne, her boyfriend. Who else?"

"Oh…I didn't know she had a boyfriend." I flipped a page in my notebook and stared at the blank paper. Then I sighed and stood. "Did you know she's on Zoloft?"

She looked away. "Yes, but I couldn't tell anyone because she would've been kicked out of the program. The au pair agency would've—"

"You protected her."

"Yes."

"Why?" The conversation was going fast.

"She's been good to me, El. She's helped me when *no one* else has!"

I snickered. "You *paid* her!" This seemed to cut her to the core. She fell silent. "Think about it, Ray. She's pregnant and had to stop taking her antidepressants. The girl must've gone crazy," I said, pacing up and down the room.

"That's just an assumption." There's a pause. "It's pure spec…specu—"

"If Lexy didn't taper off completely before learning she's pregnant, she had to go off antidepressants cold turkey. The withdrawal symptoms can be severe."

"Well, she had no choice."

"How did her boyfriend react to her being pregnant?"

She shrugged. "She planned on telling him this week."

"Did you tell the police she's pregnant?"

"Yes. They tried to locate Wayne, but he's out of town." She barely finished her sentence when a nurse came in to tell me visiting hours were over.

I tried to force a smile, but I couldn't. Lorraine and I barely fought as kids. In fact, I can't remember the last time we argued. Whenever we have, I've always initiated it; it's never the other way around. My arms reached out to take Sam, and I planted a kiss on her forehead. In the doorway, I turned to look back. Lorraine smiled slightly as her eyes welled with tears. "I'll see you soon," I said, then left, plodding down the empty hallway.

I decided to get as much information about Wayne as possible. I don't care if I have to call him—I'll do it. I need to find out if Lexy told him. It might have changed everything, given him motive. But what about Logan? Maybe he shouldn't have been there. Perhaps it wasn't part of the plan. Or maybe none of that happened, and Lexy and Logan were in a car accident? What if they're lying in a ditch where no one can see them?

Back in Lexy's room, I swill a glass of wine as my eyes scan through papers, but they don't seem to contain anything significant. I pick up a thin leather journal. "Thoughts" is engraved on the front with a navy background, accented with a solid pewter button and a rawhide cord fastener. Poems cover the first page, the second, and the third. I'm too tipsy to read them, or anything in-depth for that matter, so I place the journal in my handbag to read later.

Suddenly I remember: *The camera!* I jump to my feet, almost losing my balance, and rush toward the charger. The light is green—a good sign. I slide the batteries into their compartment and switch the camera on.

There she is, Lexy, standing in the middle of the picture on a bridge, her back to the lens. Her dark, wavy hair runs along her back, layered and intertwined toward her waist. She looks like a goddess, dressed in a soft-blue flowing skirt and a crop top, accentuating her hourglass figure, as she admires the inland ocean gliding underneath her.

I remember when Lorraine told me about Lexy, how gorgeous she is. Her friends sarcastically asked if she ever wanted a man for herself again, knowing the young au pair would move in soon. Lorraine didn't seem to mind; she said that she clicked with Lexy when she interviewed her and that she was comfortable with her.

As I scan through the images, it becomes clear she was at Deception Pass Bridge, which connects Whidbey and Fidalgo islands. Then I pause at a picture of her with a man. Both of them have perfectly straight teeth. It must be Wayne. She's glowing, smiling wide, cradled in his arms. There are a few photos of them together. In the last one, he's looking down at her, kissing her forehead. He has broad shoulders and short brown hair, and he's at least eight inches taller than her.

Sam shifts in his seat, making grunting noises. I tiptoe toward him and place the pacifier in his mouth before I rock his chair on the floor. I'll strap him to my chest when I help Craig with the search tomorrow.

The picturesque mountains, pristine lakes, and lush forests in and around Seattle don't seem as enticing anymore. In fact, they've turned our desperate attempt to search for Logan and Lexy into a full-scale nightmare.

Lexy

Sunday, November 23, 2014
Afternoon - 7 Months Before Disappearance

I lean toward the mirror with my hips pressed against the bathroom counter. I've been trying to master winged eyeliner for years, but it's either too thick or too thin. Either way, the raven black accentuates my green eyes, and I like it. I extend the end of my lipstick and glide the nude pink over my lips, puckering them slightly.

I'm wearing black leggings, an off-white Oasis vest top, a Reiss long-line blazer, and black platform shoes. I don't have a lot of clothes, but the ones I own are good quality. My mum prefers it the other way around. She'll buy tons of outfits that wear out in months. She's a seasonal buyer, but in the end, it comes down to the same amount subtracted from our accounts.

I've gone through this routine many times before. After a few weeks in Seattle, I joined an online dating site. There's an undeniable thrill about meeting a stranger and spending a few hours together, indulging in each other's lives. It's that spurt of saying whatever you want and leaving it behind with someone who'll never look at you and think of it again.

My first date had the perfectly coiffed mien of a man straight out of a lad mag, but he led a roguish, uncertain existence. He said everything a girl would want to hear. He reminded me to be wary of strangers, but more so, he galvanised me. Of course, after our date, I didn't reply to his messages. I'm not interested in him—I'm only interested in the thrill, the idea of him.

The two men after him annoyed me. They were either too serious or trying too hard to amuse me. It was one of those dates where I constantly felt obligated to laugh at the guy's lame jokes. I almost deleted my profile, as it became tiring and tedious, when I checked my inbox for the last time. That's when Wayne's name popped up. I don't want to make assumptions yet—I've learnt my lesson—but wow, he's attractive: 185 cm tall, with dark-brown hair, tanned skin, and light-brown eyes. Tonight will be my second date with him. Maybe this time he'll rip my clothes off.

Evening

Wayne made reservations at Canlis on Aurora Avenue North—Seattle's most exclusive restaurant. I'm a little underdressed, but they let me in. He's wearing a black, midweight, woven-wool suit with four decorative button cuffs and a single chest pocket. His tie is a soft blue-grey and tied with an impeccable, effortless dimple that cuts his sleek white shirt in half. His trousers are elegant and simple—a perfect match for his blazer. His attire is finished off with a pair of polished Balmoral shoes.

"That's actually incorrect," Wayne says, while we share a bottle of champagne. "Single-sex schools are manifestations of patriarchal societies." He's speaking fast, as if the words are jumping from his mouth and running a race to my ears.

"Fair enough, but I think these days, with kids on their cell phones all the time, it can become a distraction," I tell him.

"How will they survive in college? Oh, a dick, a dick!" he says, his hands waving from side to side.

"So you slept around in high school?"

"No. I went to college a virgin."

"Don't lie."

He tilts his head. "What? That's a bad thing?"

"No…I just…never mind."

"What?" He leans back as the waiter places a small plate with cutlery on the white tablecloth.

"I'm having a hard time placing you," I say.

"I need to fit into a category now?" he asks, his eyebrows raised.

"Well, everyone fits into some category, right?"

His eyes glimmer as they reflect the candlelight between us. "Okay, then. Let's play by your rules. How am I doing?"

I smile. "You're…I don't mean this in a bad way, but you're like a very good-looking semi…nerd."

Wayne laughs. "Let's just say I'm interesting," he says, lifting his champagne glass and taking a sip.

"Okay, so at college you lost your virginity, right?"

"Yes. I saved it for a cute girl."

"How'd that go?" I laugh. "Is she waiting for you back home?"

"She cheated."

"Ah, same old, same old." I shake my head. "So *then* you became a player?"

"Not all men are players, Lexy." He looks down and smirks. "Okay, fine, I got a bit out of hand, but I never *used* girls."

I snicker. "Knew it."

"I've never cheated on a girl before," he says, as though it's an achievement. "I believe the wheel turns."

"You don't really believe in karma, do you?"

"Yeah. I do."

"Oh come on…"

"What?"

I smile again. "Well…hopefully karma won't come around and bite me in the ass."

"What ass?"

I grin, and then I bite my lip. "You're saying you've been eyeing my ass, Mr. Cooper?"

"No, I couldn't see it," he says, and winks.

"Oh, fuck off." I flick my hand in the air, and his smile gives his eyes crow's feet.

"This is crazy," he says. "It's like I've known you forever."

"Don't get ahead of yourself now."

"Feisty—I like it."

"Or perhaps I don't like you."

He slumps back in his chair, pressing his lips together to keep himself from smiling, his nostrils flaring. "We'll see," he says, smirking, and then he flags the waiter to bring him the cheque.

As he pays the hefty bill, I look away, taking in the scenery from the large picture window. The moon is hovering over the I-5 bridge, which stretches out over Lake Union. Seattle glows in front of Canlis, rolled out like a glitter carpet.

The receptionist thanks us as we walk toward the entrance. I follow Wayne, intrigued by his suave yet peculiar mannerisms. A wintry swirl bites my face as we step outside, colouring my skin in red. Fingers entwined, we head to my car.

"Want to come over to my place?" he asks, as a cloud of air whirls from his mouth. *Condensation,* I think, and I can hear my biochemistry professor saying it back in London as he points his wooden stick to the graph he drew on the chalkboard.

"Yeah. That would be fun," I say, unlocking my car. "So I'll follow you?"

"I took a cab here. Hope it's okay if I join you."

"That's not a question."

He smiles. "Ms. Wright, may I hast the honour to be transported by thou?

"Never doeth that again," I say, then break out in laughter. "Getteth in."

He guides me to his place, counting down every foot before the turn. "I know how far half a mile is," I say, glancing at him from the corner of my eye. "Do you know how far in miles half a kilometer is?"

Wayne clears his throat, the corner of his lips lifting a bit. "All right. Let's do it your way. In…um…shit, this isn't easy." He chuckles.

"Come on…quickly!" I grin.

"Shit…um…in 0.8 kilometers turn left."

"What's the street name?"

"North Fiftieth."

"We already passed it." I laugh. "You have no idea, do you?"

"No," he says, chuckling like a little boy.

After ten minutes of bantering, we finally arrive at his place. I grab my handbag and lock the car before I follow Wayne to a security gate to our right. It's dark out, and I can't see the entire building, since most of the streetlights don't seem to be working here. He holds the gate open for me and slams it shut behind us.

"No elevator?" I ask, as he swings a door open to a staircase.

"Nope," he says, skipping a step each time.

"How the hell did you move all your furniture?"

We exit to a hallway with a dark-green carpet. "Movers," he says, as he comes to a halt in front of a door with "32" in golden numbers on it. He fumbles with a bunch of keys before the door to his apartment creaks open.

"Looks better in here than it looks outside," I say, finishing my sentence with a wink.

He blinks fast, almost as though he's reevaluating his decision to bring me here. I look around. A bunch of coupons are on the kitchen counter; his couch looks flimsy; and the TV is resting on milk crates. "Not really settled in," he says, studying my face.

I'm not materialistic, but I can't help wonder if he uses paper plates while watching the telly. "What do you do for a living?" I ask.

"I'm a bartender at Grenley's." I try to hide my surprise as guilt surges through me. *Did I give him the impression that I need to go to the best, most expensive places?* I wonder. *Why did he take me to Canlis*? He rubs his hands together. "Still searching for a more decent job, though. Been looking at sales." He gestures for me to sit before he pours and gives me a glass of Shiraz.

Wayne joins me on the couch, and I lean back into his arms. "Which one are you reading?" I ask, pointing at the books covering his entire coffee table.

"This one, this one, and that one," he says, his index finger wagging in the air.

"Three? At the same time?" I sit up to lower my glass to the table, and he nods in approval, allowing me to place it on the books. "Told you you're a nerd."

"Just well informed."

"Whatever you want to call it," I mutter, and he turns my head with his fingers, politely pressing them against my chin. He tilts his head in, his cheeks almost touching mine. His eyes move to my mouth, and then our lips touch. It's soft and sensual, sending a strong pulse of desire through me.

I barely know him, but it feels good, the illusion that someone cares, so I go with it. The void inside me starts to fill, but my heart has holes, and whatever it holds will run out, leaving me empty once again.

His hands find their way underneath my top. They're strong against my back, pulling me to him. I lean forward to taste the wine on his lips, sucking them softly. He sits up, pushes me against his upper body, and gets to his feet. He carries me into his bedroom, where he throws me onto his bed. He moves his hands along his shirt, pushing the buttons through the holes, one by one, without taking his eyes off mine.

A familiar sensation sparks inside me, the one I had a few years ago, the one that hurts because it's dangerous and overwhelming. Knowing how it is to truly love someone is torturous. You try to bury that feeling. So you become lonely, deprived, and when you sense anything remotely like it, the emotion comes back to haunt you. It's one sick fucking game. I know this isn't love, but it's about the idea. Isn't it? So it feels good.

For now.

Ella

Monday, June 29, 2015
Morning - 3 Days After Disappearance

It's official. Lexy didn't show up for work, and there's still no sign of Logan. Craig looks incredulous as we stand on a small platform, overlooking hundreds of volunteers who are waiting for instructions.

Earlier, while I gobbled down a bowl of cereal, I watched the KOMO news, which gave a classic missing-persons report. One of those where you glance at the pictures, shrug, then go on with your daily routine. After I strapped Sam into the backpack carrier, I decided to drop him off at Brighter Horizons Day Care instead, realizing I might kill my one nephew while searching for the other. I'm no skilled rock climber, and I'm pretty sure Lorraine would appreciate me being responsible with her child.

I was shocked when so many eager volunteers came flocking in. Instead of being thankful, I became suspicious, questioning their presence and motives. *Are they trying to prove their innocence in this case? Don't they have jobs?*

Bullhorn in hand, Craig announces to the crowd, "We don't know what either of them wore the night they disappeared. So I ask that every piece of clothing be handled as evidence." He pauses. "If you see or find *anything*, please don't touch it. Flag us down, and we'll have the police deal with it." His eyes appear lifeless, circled with a deep gray. He searched a small area with some friends yesterday but came up with nothing.

Then he went home to spend the night posting online with Martha. They shared a photo of Lexy's work car, a 2005 silver Honda CR-V, which is now circling among strangers on social media. There's also a support group on Facebook, with 307 "likes," called "Hand-in-Hand search for Lexy and Logan."

We have no idea where to start, but at least the fire department gave us detailed maps of the Seattle metropolitan area and east Seattle. We'll take it from one side and try to cover as much ground as possible, marking the areas on the map with a Sharpie.

The crowd starts to disperse in different directions. Martha hands out flyers, asking five volunteers to post them in prominent locations. My contact information, along with Craig's, is neatly printed underneath two recent pictures of Logan and Lexy.

I stare at Martha, swallowing my pride. I don't really know her, but I've heard enough from Lorraine to know what type of woman she is. The kind of woman who takes pride in things she hasn't even achieved, and who wants the perfect life, or at least the image of a perfect life. But this isn't the time or place to mull over their problems; I have more important things to attend to.

I turn and gesture for a group of people to follow me into Marymoor Regional Park, which is roughly 640 acres. My hopes are low that we'll come up with anything, because dogs roam this area all day long and probably would have detected anything suspicious by now, but we'll search the area anyway.

Afternoon

My legs prickle. I need to sit down. Everything bothers me. I can't look at the lake without dread, without wondering if Lexy and Logan are anchored to the bottom. I've dealt with many homicidal cases, dissected hundreds of bodies, and I never thought of the victims as someone's nephew, mother, or brother. I've done a decent job of distancing myself from such thoughts.

People often ask me why I decided to be a forensic pathologist. First of all, chemistry and biology are my strong suits, and if they know me, they know I like a challenge. Not to mention the pay is quite good.

I turn my back to the lake. We combed through every inch of the park, followed extensive trails, and asked dog owners if they'd seen anything suspicious, but we came up with nothing. So what's there to investigate? Traces…of nothing?

The inner battle of wanting to find them but also not wanting to is killing me. I honestly don't know how I'll react if we do find something—clothes, shoes, or an item that belonged to Logan or Lexy. Will it be a step closer to closure? Toward the hard truth? Or just a step toward more confusion?

My phone vibrates in my pocket. Without looking at the screen, I answer, hoping the caller is responding to one of the flyers.

"Ella Jensen?"

My shoes crunch over dead leaves as I take a few steps away from the volunteers. "Yes."

"I saw your poster," a man says.

"Sorry…who is this?"

"It doesn't matter."

"What?"

"They found the car abandoned in Seahurst Park."

Seahurst Park. I went there on my previous trip to Seattle. The name says it all: a forest at the beach on Puget Sound with many unstable slopes. One of the worst places to conduct a search.

"Are you shitting me? Who is this?" I pace through the forest, searching for Craig.

"Ella, it's the car on Facebook. The Honda CR-V. I saw it with my own eyes." I start to run. "The area is cordoned off by police now." Trees sweep past as my eyes dart around.

"Listen, this better not be a sick joke," I tell the guy.

"It's not," he says. "I hope you find them." He hangs up.

I approach a few men scouring through some shrubs. When I stop to catch my breath, Craig appears, making his way to me.

"El, a detective just called. He said they have bad news."

Evening

The police said it'll be useless for us to go to the site, because no one is allowed near the car. Some volunteers pursed their lips as we thanked them, and then we made our way out of the forest. I stared at my feet as I trudged over the gravel in the parking lot.

Now, at Lorraine's house, I reek of sweat. My shirt clings to my back, and my hair is damp. In the bathroom, I take off my clothes and slide into the tub. I stare at my toes emerging from the water as I dissect how the last few days went wrong. First Lorraine collapsed; then her son went missing with the au pair; her cancer got worse; they found Lexy's car abandoned; and here I am, in the middle of it all. It's been two and a half days since they disappeared. Sixty mysterious hours—plenty could have happened—and I'm acutely aware that this is only the beginning.

Lorraine

Friday, December 19, 2014
Evening - 6 Months Before Disappearance

This past week, I've been feeling much better. Less nausea, dizziness, and fatigue. Perhaps the chemotherapy is working or my body is getting used to treatment. Either way, I feel like myself again. The intense weight on my chest feels lighter by the minute. It's like someone gave me a bunch of keys to free myself from this cancerous cage, and I just need to find the right one to use.

I'm not in remission, though, not yet. The doctor said, "It's better not to get your hopes up," but hope is all I have. So I decided I'm allowed to be happy, even though it's not a good idea. God, if I'd known how much joy being healthy would mean to me one day, I would have appreciated it more throughout my life.

Lexy helped me pull through the first month of chemo. When I couldn't get up in the morning, she brought me breakfast in bed. She even got up in the middle of the night to comfort Sam so I wouldn't wake up in a drug-induced daze. Not only did she keep her head high when my spirits were low, but she also injected life into me. She's been prancing around the house, sometimes whistling joyful songs. I could tell she'd met someone, and I told her I'd like to meet him, so she invited Wayne over for dinner.

Right after she called him, I jumped into a pair of tight jeans—something I haven't worn in months—and pulled my curls back into a messy bun. *Hip.* Then I went grocery shopping. As simple as that, and it was as though I'd undergone an exuviation. Renewed, I stacked the shopping cart with goodies.

When I came home, Lexy and I prepared dinner. We made a pot roast smothered in carrots, onions, celery, and leeks, with a hint of garlic. She suggested we add some butter, which I know will taste great.

I glance at my watch; it's 6:20 p.m. Wayne will be here any minute. I turn to Logan. "Can Carmen make it?"

He shrugs. "Doubt it, you know her parents. They need to know what she's doing two days ahead of time."

"Well," I say, arching an eyebrow, "that's how it's supposed to be."

Logan's father lets him get away with too much, and then he tries the same things at my house, which I won't tolerate. A few months ago, I received a phone call from Martin Jefferson High School. They said Logan hadn't been at school for three days. Turned out he'd been skipping class and playing video games at his father's place. Craig then stayed at home until Logan left for school, but now that Lexy's here, it's not a problem anymore.

"I'll call Carmen," he says, then grabs the receiver from its base before heading upstairs.

I turn to Lexy, who's setting the table. "Thanks for helping me with dinner," I say, grabbing the salad bowl and placing it in the middle of the table.

"My pleasure. Besides, I miss cooking with my mum back in London." I watch her align the forks and knives, perfectly spacing them alongside the square dinner plates.

A car pulls up on the driveway, and Lexy's head shoots up, her face breaking into a smile. As she moves over to the front door, Logan trudges down the stairs, shaking his head. "No, she can't make it," he says before he clicks the receiver back into its base.

I quickly remove the fifth plate and its cutlery, and then I wipe the creases out of the tablecloth. A dark-haired man appears in the doorway, clutching a bunch of red and white roses. Lexy courteously touches his elbow as they approach me with wide smiles.

"Lorraine, this is Wayne. Wayne, this is my host mother, Lorraine."

He stretches an arm out, and I place my hand into his. His grasp is soft, and polite, and his gray shirt sets off his tan on his forearms.

"This is for you," he says, holding out the roses. I stare at his light-brown eyes, giddily smiling, since I can't remember the last time someone gave me flowers.

"Thank you. Wow. Lexy, have you been in on this from the start?"

She shrugs then winks as I take the flowers from Wayne. They turn their attention to Logan while I grab a vase tucked deeply at the back of a cupboard. I've always loved roses, almost as much as geraniums. My eyes slowly move from the stems up to the petals, and then I inhale a long breath through my nose, taking in the sweet fragrance.

"Please, help yourselves," I say, carrying the pot roast to the table. Wayne and Lexy lean over to serve themselves, while Logan sits at the end of the table, typing something on his phone. "Honey," I say to him, "not now."

He glances at me, then slowly slides the phone into his pocket. "Carmen says hi," he says, propping his elbows on the table.

"Too bad she can't join us," I say, sitting down and taking the salad bowl from Lexy to serve myself. I really like Carmen. She's respectful and always prepared to help. I haven't met her parents—from what I've heard, though, they seem a bit stuck-up. The Roths. Logan says they always want Carmen to do better, achieve more, be at the top of her class. They're not really fond of the idea of her dating him either, especially since he's from "a broken family."

Wayne and Lexy tell me how they met, teasing each other in the process. Wayne speaks then pauses to take a mouthful as Lexy takes the story further. Logan eats in silence as the couple babbles about their time together.

I nod at the right times, thinking about the days when first dates gave me butterflies in my stomach. When I received flowers from romantic partners and when I had no worries other than meeting my assignment deadlines in college.

We talk for hours—Lexy and Wayne sipping wine, Logan drinking soda, and me refilling glasses of water. I tell Lexy about some tourist attractions around Seattle: Chihuly Garden and Glass, the art museum, and various ferries, with Wayne promising that he'll take her.

"Thanks, Lorraine. Dinner was delicious," Lexy says, pushing her chair back. She takes my plate and stacks it on top of the others.

"Thanks to you, dear." I get to my feet to help her with the dishes. As I pack the dishwasher, I glimpse at Logan. He's tapping away on his phone, ignoring Wayne, whose eyes are wandering around the room as his knee bounces underneath the table.

Lexy disappears upstairs for a few minutes then comes back down with a couple of blankets. She beckons Wayne to follow her outside to the deck. The agent sold me on it, on the "multilevel dark-red wooden deck with the built-in barbecue." There are red and white geraniums next to the steps leading to my small backyard, which now looks like mire and mud banks. The outdoor sofa and loveseat, placed around a low table, have cream cushions with black upholstery, providing a warm, cozy setting.

I find myself staring at Wayne and Lexy through the sliding door. For a moment I feel awful for envying her, for wanting *that.* For a while after my divorce, Robert made me feel better. I knew it wouldn't last, but it was good. I had days when I forgot about Craig and Martha. I had little spurts of happiness. I had *someone.* I'm not sure if I'm upset about ending things with Robert or if I'm just lonely. Either way, the happiness I felt earlier today is short-lived. Here I am, staring at my gorgeous au pair, who's sitting on her boyfriend's lap as she plays with his dark-brown hair, and once again, my failed marriage gets its way and ruins my evening.

Saturday, December 20, 2014
Morning

My head hurts and my mouth is dry. Stomach acid crawls up my throat, making me retch. It's been more than a month since I drank alcohol, so yesterday I poured myself a Jack and Coke…or four.

I had my first one as I sat across from Logan at the dinner table, staring at Lexy and Wayne. Then I drank my second one after I checked on Sam. My third when Logan left me alone at the table and my fourth as Lexy and Wayne came back inside. I immediately sensed the tension when she opened the sliding glass door. They walked past me toward the entrance of the house without saying a word. *Something happened*, I thought. Lexy's smile had vanished, and I wondered *why.*

She said good-bye to him then glanced at me and said she was tired. She headed straight to her room. I heard Wayne struggling to get his engine going. His car started up on the second try, and then the rattling sound grew imperceptible as he drove off.

I sat down at my piano, staring out the window. Lights glistened in trees, and houses sparkled from the outside, except for mine and the empty one across the street. When I was a kid, I always went all out for Christmas, trying to cheer my sister up, but I never succeeded. Now, more than twenty-five years later, I hate it as much as she does.

I've thought about calling her, inviting her over, but I know she won't come. Ella is someone you'd want as a sister but not as a friend, because she doesn't care about you unless you have her blood in your veins. She's shown a lack of compassion for others since she was a little girl. Let's just say she has rough edges. They weren't polished off like mine by the presence of our parents, who passed away in a car accident when she was an infant.

We grew up in an orphanage in San Francisco, battling for attention, always trying to please our caregivers. Ella never knew what it's like to have parents, because no one wanted to adopt us. We were "one too many."

We meant nothing to most of our caregivers. Either they were irritated by us or they fled as soon as their shifts were over. But there was one lady, Miss McBeth, who adored Ella. Even though I'm the older sibling, I occasionally turned to my sister for comfort and advice, and she turned to Miss McBeth.

My sister was a tough one to get along with, and the other girls didn't like her. I always knew where to find her. Miss McBeth would be braiding her hair or they'd sing songs underneath a tree in the backyard or build puzzles and read to each other. Late at night, she'd get tucked in, and in the mornings, Miss McBeth would wake her to have breakfast together. It was their little routine, their ritual.

One cold winter morning, a day before Christmas, Ella lay in bed, waiting to be fetched by Miss McBeth for breakfast. All the other girls already had gone downstairs to eat, and I told my sister she needed to come with me. She leaned back on her arm as she stared at the hallway to the right, anxiously waiting. A young man - someone I'd never seen before - instead entered the room and sat down on the bed. He must've been Miss McBeth's boyfriend. I was so certain that she asked him to tell Ella she wasn't coming in to work that day. Words can't describe how devastated my baby sister was when he told her she'd died of cancer. We never even knew she was sick—it was her well-kept secret. It was a guillotine blade ending. *Quick*, or so it seemed, but it was actually a slow and painful death for Miss McBeth.

For months and months, Ella wouldn't get out of bed. She was inconsolable. She became overprotective, calculating, and rebellious. Whenever the kids picked on me, she'd jump right in, ready for a fight. In her mind, I was all she had left.

As an adult, she once told me, "I couldn't help that circumstances molded me into the person I am today. But I'm glad I couldn't help it, because if I could, I would've stopped it, and I would've been a vulnerable, powerless human being."

Ever since Miss McBeth died, Ella taught herself a stoic acceptance of suffering, and since then, Christmas has never been the same.

Lexy

Thursday, December 25, 2014
Morning - 6 Months Before Disappearance

I miss my mother today; I've always spent Christmas with her. We'd decorate our living room with snow blankets and place Christmas figurines on the shelves. In the early morning, I'd make us hot chocolate. The radio would play jubilant carols in the background, and we'd have a great laugh at our two little wrapped presents, neatly placed next to each other on the coffee table.

I called her earlier this morning. She cried, but she tried her best to sound content. I guess she was worried she'd upset me. I feel sorry for her because she's spending the day alone. At least I'll be surrounded by people. By the time we said our good-byes, a tear ran down my face. Christmas will always be *our* day.

Today has been a total fuckup at Lorraine's house. *Logan.* Where would he spend the day? At Craig's or Lorraine's? He chose his dad's place because last year he celebrated Christmas with his mother. It seems fair, but then again, Craig did break up their family, and now Lorraine can't spend all her "special family occasions" with Logan. I try to keep myself out of it, but doing so is hard since I'm (suddenly) the one Lorraine confides in. Although she's said next to nothing about Craig before, today she has plenty to say.

She told me how they'd spend Christmas together and how Craig always found a way to ruin it. It seemed a little melodramatic, but what do I know? As she went on and on about every Christmas day throughout the years, I thought, *Why would this year be any different?* But who am I to judge? I've always had wonderful Christmas celebrations with my mother, so I heard Lorraine out for an hour or two.

Evening

I smile over the top of my champagne glass. Wayne is standing at the end of the room with his hands in his pockets, smirking. He's discussing politics with his dad, which bores me, so I decided to swing by the snack table. In an attempt to be polite, I try my best not to stuff my mouth with food. I've caught his mum glimpsing at me from time to time, examining me from hair to shoes. It's clear that she doesn't approve of me. I already can hear her: *Oh, Wayne, can't you just get a girl from here?*

I'm surrounded by his family: aunts, uncles, his dad and mum, and *their* mums and dads—it's a feast, and I hate it. His mum adored his ex-girlfriend, Tammy, and here I am, the disappointment. Not only did Mrs. Cooper's beady eyes look down her nose when Wayne introduced us, but she also made a few short, snarky comments before she walked off. The worst part was that Wayne didn't even notice.

He then tried to get the attention of his dad, an older clone of himself, who was speaking to a man whose belt was almost losing the fight against his stomach. But I excused myself before having to face yet another scrutiny.

I guess parents have incredibly strong, usually accurate instincts when it comes to their children. I won't say his mum is completely wrong, but whether she likes it or not, I'm sleeping with her son, and there's nothing she can do about it.

Wednesday, December 31, 2014
Afternoon

Everyone in Seattle flocks to the fireworks display from the Space Needle, and I'm following the trite movement. When I saw a video of it back in London, I told myself that I *will* see the show this New Year's Eve.

Wayne is going to meet me at Monty's Bar and Grill so we can fill our bellies before switching to alcohol. I'm sure the bar will be packed, but I'm still amped, ready to end the year on a good note.

I take the 169 exit toward Mercer Street, hoping the traffic will be better. I dial Wayne's number and put him on speakerphone.

"Hey, where are you?" he asks. "I ordered you a drink. Hope that's okay."

"I'm stuck in traffic. I'm almost there, though. Give me five more minutes, maybe ten. I'm sure parking will be a nightmare."

His voice is muffled by the buzz of the crowd. "Some friends of mine want us to join them at Claret tonight. Should I tell them we'll come?"

I hesitate. My car comes to a halt at a traffic light. "Well…"

"It'll be fun!" he yells over the roar of the crowd.

"Can't we all go somewhere else? Closer to the fireworks?"

He chuckles. "I don't expect twenty people to change their plans for us."

Pursing my lips, I take the turn onto Fairview Avenue. "Sure," I say, forcing the word from my throat.

"Sweet, see you soon then." He hangs up, and I slap the steering wheel.

"Fuck!"

Evening

At Monty's Bar and Grill, I tried to persuade Wayne that we should go straight to the park to get a good view of the Space Needle, but I couldn't convince him. He actually made a valid point: "The farther away you are, the more you can see, Lexy. The Space Needle is hundreds of feet up in the air. You'll want to see all of it."

So here we are, on our way to Claret. I dread every step I take toward the club, and I hope they won't let us in. *Sorry, you look like a dog. Go home.* Wishful thinking. If I'd known it would come down to this, I would've worn flip-flops or *anything* that went against their dress code.

After standing in line for fifteen minutes, we finally reach the front. "ID," the bouncer insists.

I fish my passport out of my purse, hoping they won't accept a foreign ID. He shines a flashlight on my photo as his eyes scan for details. Without saying a word, he flicks my passport back into my hand. Then he reaches out to take the next person's ID.

We step inside. Wayne's face breaks into a smile as his friends approach him. I put my hand in the air, awkwardly trying to direct my wave to the middle of the bunch, but no one reciprocates. *Oh, how nice of them.*

I slip away toward the bathroom. I open the door but quickly shut it and remain outside. It smells like someone took a shit on lavender flowers, with a dead rodent not far away. My hands are moist, and my eyes dart across the area, hopping from face to face. My chest tightens as I take my phone out of my handbag.

I open my Facebook app. I need to see it one more time. Maybe I read it all wrong. *Hopefully* I read it all wrong, but as my phone loads the profile, it's clear I didn't. *He* will be here tonight.

That's what it says on his Facebook page.

Ella

Tuesday, June 30, 2015
Evening - 4 Days After Disappearance

I had to go to Seahurst Park. I couldn't stay away. The silence killed me. I had Sam with me when I approached a detective this afternoon. It felt weird to push a stroller around, struggling through the mud. It felt wrong.

The detective directed his gaze from Sam to me, then held a hand out to introduce himself. "Eric Baldwin," he said, and I couldn't help stare at his shaved head, red flaky cheeks, and deep wrinkles.

"We've searched this area twice," he said, flattening his hand against his eyebrows to block the sun.

"And? Any progress?"

"None." We both gazed into the forest. "Sorry. I didn't get your name. You are…?"

"Ella." He caught my eye, examining my face. "I'm Lorraine's sister, Logan's aunt."

He squinted. "Sorry to hear that. I had a few interviews with Lorraine. She seemed confused. Did she—"

"Everyone says she seemed confused," I told him, louder than intended. "How exactly, Detective Baldwin?"

"Call me 'Eric,'" he said, turning back to the foliage among the trees. "Well…she told me one thing, and the next day she said something else."

"She hit her head when she fell."

He glanced at me from the corner of his eye. "I'm well aware of that." A long silence transpired as we watched the officers step high over logs and dirt. "Do you mind coming to the station tomorrow?" he asked, and without hesitation I agreed to meet him.

It was a short conversation, but it was all I needed. I want to contribute as much as possible. I want this all to end, and I want my sister to be happy.

They towed the Honda CR-V to an impoundment lot for further investigation. I'm sure Lorraine has been informed by now, since the story is all over the news. This clearly rules out my accident theory, leaving me with chilling thoughts.

Now, in Lorraine's car, I pull Lexy's journal out of my handbag to make copies of her poems, because I'll have to hand them over to the detectives to investigate. Perhaps they have an English genius in their department. I hate reading poems—school made me hate them. I'd spend hours interpreting one, just to read the memorandum and realize I'd be fucked during exams. I remember making a little asterisk next to every question I struggled with, and at the end of the paper, I'd realize I was looking at the fucking Milky Way.

I start the van's engine and drive to the nearest FedEx Office. Inside, I make three copies of each poem, ensuring I won't lose them. *Poems almost always say something about the poet's personal life*, I think. Especially when someone writes them as a hobby in a journal that was stashed away in a closet, hidden from the world. Perhaps Lexy wrote them out of boredom, but she doesn't strike me as someone who gets bored easily—all her photos indicate that she's adventurous.

Sam jerks in his seat as the copy machine roars to life, his eyes wide. I move over to him and tickle his cheeks. He smiles, and then he blows bubbles from his mouth. I stare at the saliva tracking down his chin and wonder if I'll ever get used to this.

As the machine spits out the pages, I notice a faint, washed-out image printed on the last one. I flick through the journal until I see it. A business card is firmly nestled in the fold of the journal. "Torkaz Law Firm, P.S." is printed in cursive underneath a white number on a thick blue line. I glance at my phone; it's 11:26 pm. I'll call the firm tomorrow.

Back at Lorraine's house, I put the kettle on the stove and make myself a cup of tea before I read the first poem, "The Full Blood Moon," which covers the first page in black ink:

Kindled stars in our eyes, pearly gates to our divine abode, crepuscular rays radiate through our wide blue yonder.
As the cerulean-blue background dwindles, the full blood moon beckons, and the fervor grows.

Paroxysm of pules as dusk rapidly falls.
The brevity of the Full Moon is daunting.
I hear the click of a crossbow, and a bolt whirs, coring the moon.
Death gestures toward an open grave.
Unorthodox, derelict quietus(es).

A kindled star in my eye, locked gates to my divine abode, tenebrous wild black yonder,
As the cerulean-blue background dwindles, the crescent wanes, and the fervor grows.

What the fuck did I just read? I read it again, this time slower, but nothing comes through to me. I have no idea what to think. It's boring—that's all I can make of it. The sketch, however, fascinates me. The one at the bottom of the page. It's of a couple standing in front of a swing set. They're on a beach, staring at the moon. Far in the background, on the side, trees curve along the seawater; the scene looks tropical. The woman is wearing a layered dress, and the end flutters in the air from a gush of wind. The man holds a bow in his one hand, while the other hand reaches for an arrow from the quiver on his back. There's no date, so Lexy could've written this many years ago or perhaps two weeks ago.

I flick through the pages. There are two more poems and some artwork. The rest of the journal is untouched, blank.

Wednesday, July 1, 2015
Afternoon

I called the law firm this morning; the woman on the other side said it's confidential information, and she can't provide me with details why Lexy consulted an attorney.

"Ma'am, please," I said, "this is my sister's son. She's on her deathbed, and you can help us."

There was silence. I could sense her hesitation, but sometimes you only have to unveil the slightest hint of compassion.

"She came in a week and a half ago," she whispered. "That's all I can tell you. I'm sorry." She cleared her throat.

"Sure, I understand. Please call me if you have a change of heart," and before I could say anything else, she hung up.

Now I'm waiting in the corridor of the police station, sitting on a chair with a garnet cushion, stained dark on the side. My knee bounces as I try to warm myself up. It's hot outside but uncomfortably cold in here, and I wonder how much taxpayer money goes toward their electricity bill.

As I page through my notes, I realize I haven't looked into Logan's matters. I immediately jumped at Lexy. *She must be hiding something*, I'd thought. Maybe my nephew isn't innocent after all. Teenagers can be foolish; everyone knows that. Then I think of the blonde I saw in one of his photos. *Did he have a girlfriend? Who's the petite blonde Lorraine mentioned?*

"Miss Jensen," Eric says, as he lowers his head to walk through the doorway. "We're ready for you."

As I rise from my seat, my notes almost fly to the floor. I quickly clutch them to my body before I awkwardly enter the interview room in a fucked-up-question-mark posture, walking as though I'm ten shits behind. A woman in a uniform snickers at the sight of me, making her curved stomach tremble. Dark strands of hair that didn't make it to her rubber band frizz in different directions. It looks like someone tried to put a fire out on her face, using a fork. I guess pitted acne scars are a bitch.

"Detective Aliya Winters," she says, raising her hand.

"Ella...Ella Jensen." I'd shake her hand if they had the decency to help, so instead I nod.

"Please have a seat," Eric says, gesturing toward a metal chair.

"Thanks for dropping by," Aliya says, ignoring my struggle. "Any information you have about your sister or the incident is appreciated."

"I don't know much," I say, sitting down opposite them. "I just arrived in Seattle on Saturday." I place the papers on the table, wiping the creases out.

Eric leans back in his chair. "How did you find out that your nephew was missing?"

"Lorraine told me. I received a call from the hospital. It was...you know..."

"Unexpected?" Aliya says, and my eyes move back to her, shamelessly staring at the craters on her face.

"Yes."

"Tell us about your hospital visit," she says.

"Which one?"

"All of them," Eric says, and I finally force myself to look away from Aliya. "We need to know what your sister told you. We just want to build a strong investigation so we can find your nephew and the au pair."

"Right. On the first visit, Lorraine was hysterical. I couldn't get much out of her. The second one, we had a decent conversation. Mostly about the au pair."

"What about her?" Eric asks.

"Well, I…I found some papers. Blood results showing she's pregnant…and she's on Zoloft." Aliya glimpses at Eric, and she shuffles in her chair. It's hard to tell what's going through their minds, as they seem unfazed.

"How do you know these things?" Aliya asks, her eyebrows knitted.

"I searched Lexy's room at Lorraine's house." I push the papers across the table. "Here, this is what I found." Neither of them says a word. "It's copies…of findings," I say, realizing how ridiculous I sound.

"And this?" Aliya holds the lawyer's card in the air.

"I found it in her journal," I say, staring at the back of the card, which is a bright sky blue, contrasting with the colorless room.

She rifles through the papers, scanning them. "Thanks," she says, and then she chuckles, almost as though she's dismissing their importance.

"Would you say your sister has been acting any differently from the last time you saw her?" Eric asks.

"Well, not really. She's distressed…so I guess she might seem a bit on edge, but that's about it."

Their eyes meet again, and my posture stiffens.

"We're well aware that your sister has brain cancer," Eric says. "Would you say these tumors make her say or do…odd things?"

My face flushes. "You don't think my sister has anything to do with this, do you?"

"We said nothing of that sort, Miss Jensen," Aliya interjects. "We've dealt with many cases, though, and anything's possible."

"This was the first time I saw Lorraine since her diagnosis."

"And why's that?" Eric asks.

I move around in my seat, not wanting to discuss the matter. "I have a job. I have to earn a living, right?"

"Don't we all?" Aliya says, scoffing.

"Like I said, your sister made some contradictory statements," Eric says, folding his arms. "We're trying to rule out any misleading data."

There's silence. They let the statement hang in the air before Aliya asks,

"Were there any reasons your nephew might run off?" His question lingers, firing off a lilt of nerves.

"Not that I know of, and besides, it's highly unlikely."

"Why's that?" she asks.

I frown. "His mother has cancer." I stare at him, not connecting in the least. Like the prerequisite for fathoming that simple statement was to assemble a fucking jigsaw puzzle.

Eric clears his throat. "Unless he did something that's beyond repair. In that case, he might be scared to come home. Maybe he doesn't want to deal with a confrontation, with all the questions regarding *why* he left."

"I doubt that," I say.

Aliya points at the papers. "Lexy wrote these poems?"

"Yes…or at least that's what it says." My eyes shift between them. "Listen, my sister has been through a lot. Whatever she told you, I'm pretty sure she didn't mean to confuse you."

"We're aware of that," Eric says. "But it's protocol to start with the person who saw the victims last."

Victims?

"You're doing the right thing," he assures me.

"But you probably knew most of this before I got here," I say, pointing a finger at the stack of papers.

Aliya presses her lips flat, shaking her head slightly.

My mouth dries. "Lorraine said she mentioned to you that Lexy's pregnant."

"She did?" They frown in unison, looking puzzled.

"You didn't know Lexy's pregnant?" I ask.

Aliya pokes her tongue into her cheek, blinking rapidly, a curled finger pressing against her chin, and before I can say anything, Eric cuts the conversation short. "Right, that's enough for today. Thank you, Miss Jensen, for your help." He stands up, preparing to leave.

"What have you been doing all this time?" I ask as a streak of pain sprouts through my jaw from clenching my teeth.

"Listen, it's hard to move forward if your sister keeps lying to us," Eric says, his voice echoing through the room.

"I asked you a question, *sir*," I say, but he ignores me and strides out.

Evening

I stormed out of the room. In the hallway, Aliya grabbed my arm, stopping me in my tracks.

"I know this is hard, but we need you to cooperate," she said.

"I'm trying."

"I know." She gestured to the doorway of her office. "Please. I need a few more minutes from you."

After I apologized for making a scene, she made me a cup of tea and asked me to write down everything I know. I started from the moment I placed foot in Washington up until my interview. She then asked me to call her if anything unusual or suspicious happens. She thanked me for my cooperation, and then I left to pick Sam up from the day-care center.

Immediately after arriving home, I log into my Facebook account. I type "Lexy Wright" into the search engine and click on her name. Two mutual friends: Lorraine Davis and Logan Davis. There's also a public post from Craig & Martha Davis—a combined profile—on Lexy's wall. It's a status Martha posted to update others on their findings. There are no other posts relating to Lexy's disappearance. I browse through her pictures. Not many of them have been taken since she arrived in Seattle.

The photos taken at Deception Pass Bridge aren't on her timeline. She probably didn't have time to upload them. I hover my mouse over a picture of Lexy with a dark-haired man. The tag appears: "Wayne Cooper." I stare at him and bite my lip as my eyes narrow. This isn't the man on the pictures taken at Deception Pass Bridge.

This is a face I've *never* seen before.

Lexy

Wednesday, December 31, 2014
Evening - 5 ¾ Months Before Disappearance

Wayne holds me in his arms, his chin resting on my head. We're surrounded by thousands of people. We left Claret earlier than expected, which is a huge relief. Wayne's friends will join us soon, but I doubt they'll find us among the crowd, and I don't mind if it's just the two of us.

The Space Needle shoots out from the crowd into the sky. Parts of it are blocked by kids on top of men's shoulders. The faces blur as I spin around to look at Wayne. His eyelids droop, and he's slurring his words. He takes my face into his hands to kiss me.

"Not yet, silly!" I say, tapping his stomach. "I want my *New Year's kiss* at twelve."

"Then…" he says, stumbling a step back as he tries to find the words, "I'll kiss you again."

I giggle, pointing my index finger in his face. "It should be completely separate…a distinct New Year's kiss."

"Well…we have two minutes till midnight." His body sways a bit as he puts a palm in the air. "I won't touch you until then." He winks, giving me a wolfish smile.

Suddenly the horde swallows me. Jackets brush against mine, shoving me forward. Wayne crouches. "What are you doing?" I ask.

"Climb onto my shoulders!" he yells, as people bump into him.

I hesitate, imagining the possible outcome: us reeling forward, crushing kids. "Are you sure?" I ask, and the crowd roars, "Ten, nine, eight…" Wayne grins, and I swing my legs around his neck, resting a palm on his head. As he stands up, the crowd shouts, "Three! Two!" and I join in. "One!"

Wayne kisses his hand and brings it up to my face. I press his palm against my mouth, and the sky lights up. The buzz of the crowd dwindles as streaks of light explode into sparkling flowers. It's a dance of colours, leaving me in awe.

Monday, January 5, 2015
Afternoon

My year is starting off well. Lorraine gave me a bonus. Not much, but a little extra. I stashed the money in my pink box on my dresser, saving it for later—perhaps for a special occasion.

Robert came to visit for the first time since Sam's birth. It's probably a New Year's resolution: be a better dad. *Pathetic.* In five days, Sam will be three months old, and he's seen Robert twice. I know how it is to grow up without a dad. My situation was a bit different, though.

I was two years old when my parents went on a road trip to Paris. On the ferry, my dad made his way upstairs, and my mum followed. When they reached the top, he seemed weary. He told my mum he had some pain in his upper back, so she sat him down. She left to buy them soup—my parents always ate soup on the ferry; it was their little tradition. Five minutes into the ride, he started to gasp for air. He grabbed his chest and collapsed from a heart attack. I don't think my mum ever went back to Paris again.

I'm startled from my daze as Logan slams the front door. "Lexy, do you mind taking me to my dad's place?" he asks as he approaches me. I'm almost done for the day, so I don't feel obliged to be here when Robert leaves.

"Yeah, sure," I say, grabbing my car keys.

Evening

While I'm in the shower, my phone buzzes on the bathroom counter as a message comes through, interfering with the music jamming from my phone. It's probably Logan messaging me about earlier, or Martha.

When I dropped Logan off at Craig's house, she walked across the driveway toward my car. I almost floored the accelerator, thinking she was about to ask me for another "favour." But instead she invited me inside to join her for a drink.

She sat opposite me at the dinner table while Logan watched telly in the living room. The house has an open layout, offering little privacy. Craig was on his way home from the city, where he works, so it was just the three of us.

"So…how do you like Seattle?" Martha asked with a direct, probing gaze.

"It's good."

"Yeah? I heard you already have a boyfriend, huh?"

"You can call him that," I allowed.

She glimpsed at herself in the mirror behind me, her face filled with pride. "So how's work?" she asked, and I immediately sensed where this was going.

"Good, thanks."

"Is the baby doing okay?"

"Yeah, Sam's sweet," I said. "Growing fonder of him by the day."

"Weird name, though…Samuel?" She raised her eyebrows as she gazed into her glass, and then she swigged the wine in three gulps.

Our eyes met. "How do *you* like it here?" I asked, and I felt like smiling.

"What do you mean, sweetie?" She pulled her shoulders back.

"In this house." I gestured around me. Logan turned down the volume of the telly. I guess he must've heard me.

"It's wonderful." She gave me an affected smile and continued in an incongruously joyful tone. "Living the dream, wouldn't you say?"

Yeah, which you stole from someone else, bitch.

She didn't wait for a reply. "What do you do when you're not working?" she asked.

I stared at her for a few seconds. "I spend time with Wayne." Martha said nothing, waiting for me to elaborate. "And sometimes I write."

She raised an eyebrow. "Oh…can I see your writing sometime?"

"No," I said, faster than intended. "It's personal."

"Oh…a diary?"

"Yes."

She broke eye contact with me, and I shuffled in my chair. "Would you like more wine?" she asked, and I noticed my glass was empty.

"No, thanks," I said, flattening my palm over the rim of my wineglass. "I need to get back to Lorraine."

"How's she doing?" she asked, jumping at the opportunity to discuss her.

"She's okay. She feels better."

"So I've heard. Poor woman…she must be so alone." There was silence, and by now the telly was on mute. We held each other's gaze for what felt like a lifetime.

"Please excuse me," I said, before I could scratch her eyes out. I left for the bathroom, where I took a few minutes to calm myself down. I didn't stay long after that; I didn't feel like playing her game. Before I left, she asked me to let her know when I got home, which I didn't do.

I get out of the shower and towel myself off before I put on my pyjamas. I head to my room, and then I check my phone. I have three text messages—one from Logan and two from Wayne. The first one reads:

> You are a legend. That was hilarious.

I chuckle and reply:

> Wasn't sure if you were listening. Did she say something?

Curiosity kicks in—as if I don't have enough shit going on in my own life. I open the message from Wayne:

> Who is this?

And the second message:

> LOL. Wrong number

I reply:

> You seriously need to save your contact numbers, Wayne. ;)

Every time his phone rings, a string of numbers appears on his screen. When he answers, the voice on the other side is almost always his mother's, calling from the same phone she's been using for years.

As I climb into bed, another message comes through from Logan:

> No, she made me dinner then went to bed. Sometimes she'll say things without thinking it thru. But what you said was classic.

I swallow as a small wave of regret moves over me. Perhaps Martha's just extremely tactless. I knew a girl like that in London; everyone hated her. She always managed to say something inappropriate, but she never meant to hurt anyone.

I check my phone one last time to see if Wayne replied, but there's nothing. I send him a text saying good night, and then I find myself staring at the ceiling.

Lorraine

Friday, February 6, 2015
Evening - 4 ¾ Months Before Disappearance

Cars hum in the distance while birds chirp their delightful songs as they fly above the city. The lake reflects the violet-rose colors of the sky, and Mount Rainier swallows the sun, which emanates dispersed pinks and blues through the feathered cloud beds.

Kerry Park is my go-to place when I have to make pivotal decisions or when I need time away from home. My sporadic visits started a few months before I learned about Craig and Martha.

Several years ago, Barson Designs had their year-end function. I received an award: Architect of the Year. I was proud of myself since I was climbing the ladder to success. Craig couldn't make it; he said he had to work. Before heading out, I left him dinner on the kitchen table—bourbon chicken—neatly covered with aluminum foil.

After the event, I proudly frolicked into the house and found the glassware scattered among the chicken on the floor. A few months later, I learned that Craig had sex with Martha that very night. She pushed the dinner I'd made off the table as she positioned herself for my husband to enter her. They became arrogant about their affair: *Let's leave this mess for the witless wife*. He came home after 2:00 a.m. and fell into bed as though nothing had happened. The next evening, I went to Kerry Park. I felt sick to my stomach, but I ignored my instincts since I blindly trusted Craig.

My visits became more frequent after he filed for divorce. As I stood there among strangers, like I'm doing tonight, I'd stare at the scenery and think about my life. Somehow it subdued my loneliness, and it made me feel better…for a while.

When we moved to Seattle, Craig worked for an investment company. After a year, he decided to carve his own road and start his own business. For three years, I kept us going—we could barely afford dinner. During the fourth year, he had a breakthrough. His company was delivering outstanding investment results, and they had consistent returns on equity, which meant the company consistently delivered to its shareholders. That was when I designed the house he's now living in; we moved in shortly before I gave birth to Logan. Throughout the years, I supported Craig emotionally. I understood when he couldn't make Logan's games, when he came home in a bad mood, when he snapped at me, and when he had to work through the night. I stood by him, and now Martha is sharing his success.

My arms rest on the black rails as I lean forward, gazing at Mount Rainier in the distance. Sam is sleeping in his stroller, parked next to me. Tonight I'm trying to accept what the doctor told me. He did an ultrasound, a CT scan, and an MRI to determine why my body isn't responding to the chemotherapy. I knew something was wrong because I've had a persistent headache for a couple of weeks. He discussed the results with me this morning and said my cancer is officially in stage four.

He located three tumors in my brain. First he gave me the bad news: the tumor in my temporal lobe is inoperable, and he'll have difficulty removing the entire tumor in my occipital lobe due to possible neurological damage. Then he gave me the "good" news: he *might* be able to remove the tumor in my frontal lobe to relieve some of my symptoms. He also gave me a radiation plan for after I recover from surgery. With my having gone through a full-term pregnancy—as well as how much the cancer has spread and the number of drugs that didn't work—I'm categorized as a high-risk patient.

After he told me this news, I immediately called Ella. She wanted to book the next flight to Seattle, but she couldn't. She recently moved from San Francisco to San Diego for work, and taking time off this early in her new job won't be possible. There was a moment when I thought she was lying, because she stuttered just enough to make me wonder. But I gave her the benefit of the doubt; I'd like to think my only sibling would want to be there for me in my time of need.

This leaves me with Lexy. I owe her. I don't know what I'd do without her. She offered to take care of Sam when I'm in the hospital. If the au pair agency finds out how many hours she'll be working, they'll remove her from my house. I'll pay her more if I have to, as long as my baby is in good hands.

Thursday, February 12, 2015
Morning

I'm petrified. My doctor explained that he can't confirm that I have secondary brain cancer. He has to do a biopsy to verify that the cancer has metastasized from the primary site. He went over the procedure with me. I didn't understand a word he said, except for the part where he rotated his hand as he told me he'll be drilling into my skull. I submissively nodded, signed the papers, and wished it could all be over soon.

Now the lights on the ceiling pass me one by one as a nurse pushes me on a gurney. I try not to think about the possible outcomes: loss of vision, paralysis, infection, bleeding, seizures, or brain damage.

My mind blocks out the rattling sound of the portable bed as my hands squeeze the sheets. My mind shifts to my boys. *I need to be strong for them*, I think, as we enter the operating room. My heart quickens, and the gurney comes to a halt.

Before I can say anything, an anesthesiologist hovers over me. "Count to ten," she says, a grin planted on her face. She places a mask over my nose and mouth, and the sweet taste of it fades as I pass out.

Lexy

Friday, February 13, 2015
Early morning - 4 ½ Months Before Disappearance

I couldn't sleep, so I came downstairs and made myself a cup of coffee. It was my first night alone with Sam. It felt scary, different. I kept checking on him. *What if he stops breathing?* Even so, the responsibility of having someone else's life in my hands is somewhat thrilling in a weird way. I felt powerful, but I won't say that out loud.

I'm out on the deck with a fluffy blue blanket I took from my room. I cup my hands around my coffee mug, relishing the warmth radiating into my body. It takes me back to my coffee-addicted days in university and the Starbucks visits with my mum. Even though my last year at university was the worst year of my life, I have some heartwarming memories.

I mull over so many what-ifs. Did I make a mistake coming to America? What if I'd finished my degree? What if I'd made different decisions? My mind drifts off to those days. To the competitive students who hated the ones doing better. To my university boyfriend. I wonder what he's up to and if he ever thinks of me. If he regrets it, feels guilty, or if he's forgotten about it all, about us.

Thinking back makes me want Wayne, a distraction. If my day starts off like this, it's usually not a good one. I know I should stop living in the past, but it's hard to get rid of the heartache and the guilt. I stare at the steam of my coffee swirling in the air, and then my vision blurs as my eyes well up with tears.

Afternoon

I thought my day couldn't get any worse, but I was wrong. This morning, at the hospital, I forgot about my problems for a moment. When Logan fell into his mum's arms, my knees weakened, and I had a sudden need to sit down. He hanged over Lorraine's bed, his face buried in her neck. The IV drip came into view as she extended her arm to hold him close to her chest. Noticing a tear trickling down Logan's face, I decided to give them some space.

"Everything will be all right," I told him as we drove to Craig's. I tried to touch his shoulder, but he pushed my hand away. Through the entire ride, he stared out the passenger window, clenching his teeth. After I dropped him off, I fetched Sam from the day-care centre before meeting Wayne at Lorraine's place.

"Martha invited us over for dinner tonight," I tell him, and smile when I notice the grocery bags in his hands.

Wayne steps inside. "Sure. Why not?"

"Well…I'm not sure how Lorraine would feel about it."

"Lexy, you're looking after Sam day and night without complaining—what more does she want? You're not on a leash." He heads to the kitchen, where he unpacks the bags. It's a huge turn-on to see him walk into the house and immediately take control.

"You're right," I tell him.

Lately, Lorraine barely compensates me for my extra work, but I can't blame her. I saw her searching for financial support on her laptop the other day. She had a fright when I came around the corner; perhaps she was embarrassed.

"All this shit between Martha and Lorraine is between them. It's not your problem," he says, opening a can of beer. "Here, take one. It's been a long week." I don't like beer, but on days like this, I'd drink any type of alcohol.

Evening

I'm standing next to Wayne, holding a bowl of potato salad, with a diaper bag hanging on my left shoulder and my handbag on the other one. Wayne's carrying Sam in the car seat, which makes him look even manlier. I knock on the door and wince as I remember that Sam's asleep.

When Craig opens the door, an infusion of fragrant herbs swirls up my nose. My stomach growls, and I realise all I ate today was a BLT.

"Make yourself at home," he says, after shaking Wayne's hand.

The house feels different, warm. For the first time, I feel relaxed walking into Craig's house. Perhaps it's the few beers I drank before I came; perhaps I'm relieved the day is coming to an end—whatever the reason is, the place feels cosy.

Martha smooths her white blouse out with her hands, like someone who's just won a fight. "Martha, this is my boyfriend, Wayne." Her face lights up as she approaches us, but her expression fades when she sees Sam, making her stop in her tracks.

"Welcome," she says, staring at Sam, her eyes filled with concern…or anxiety; I can't tell. Wayne glimpses at me, probably questioning my opinion of her. I told him that I don't like her, that she has some nerve.

The dining table looks like a picture cut out from a wedding magazine. I don't know if I should feel sorry for her trying this hard or if I should be impressed by her work. Either way, I just want to stuff my mouth with that baked salmon…and the sushi. Did she make all this herself?

I avert my eyes from the table. "Wayne, would you mind helping me take Sam's portable crib out?"

He stares at me for a few seconds before it clicks. "Oh! Yes. Yes. Of course." We unfold the crib, which looks like a laundry bag, and I lay Sam down without waking him. I catch Wayne giddily smiling at the baby, and I bite my lip as I stare at him with admiration.

Logan thumps his way down the stairs, gazing at the floor. He approaches the dinner table, takes a glimpse at us, purses his lips, and slightly flicks his head back, nodding in disapproval. Everyone accepts his behaviour: *The kid is going through a hard time. Give him some space.* He slumps into his chair and throws pieces of salmon onto his plate with his hands.

I look away, catching Wayne's eye. "Logan!" Craig growls, sending a shock wave through the house.

Finally.

Logan pauses, his arms still hovering in the air, his face growing pale. There's an unspoken understanding between them, and he immediately withdraws his hands from his plate.

There's silence as we all sit down in unison. "Wine, anyone?" Martha asks at last.

"Yes," I say, a little too desperate, "please."

She moves over to me, but first she fills Wayne's glass to the brim.

"Oh." He chuckles. "Not for me—I'm driving—but thanks."

"We have more than enough space for the two of you to stay here tonight," Martha offers, "and I see you brought Sam's diaper bag too."

"Thanks, but that won't be necessary," I say. Tonight I want to go home; I want to have sex, feel close to Wayne. *The illusion of being close.* I carefully take the wine away from him and slurp it, making Craig laugh.

I glance at Logan; he looks distraught. His eyes appear lifeless, as if he hasn't slept for days. I know how it is to mask pain with anger. For me it did more harm than good, and unfortunately, I learnt that the hard way.

Martha leans over the table to serve us. "Thanks. Everything looks delicious," I say, as she places my plate in front of me. I flake the fish with my fork and take a bite. The salmon dissolves in my mouth, a buttery sweet flavour reaching my palate. "Wow…it *is* delicious," I tell her, and Martha's face lights up again, her eyes dashing around as though she's checking to see who heard the compliment. She straightens her back, and her lips part to say something, but Sam interrupts as he starts to fuss.

"It's okay. I've got it," Craig says, and Martha's eyes shoot at him. I catch him glance at Sam every time she looks away. He thinks no one sees him, but I do.

"Are you sure, *Craig*?" She forces the sides of her forearms into the edge of the table as she clutches her knife and fork, then gives me a faint smile.

"Oh, no, please, it's fine." I jump to my feet and rush to the baby. No one says a word, and the clinking of cutlery fills the house. Sam grunts, but he's still asleep. I return to my seat. "False alarm."

Martha's smile has been wiped from her face, and everyone eats in silence. I feel like requesting a match with a different family—to leave this drama behind and move on—but I might get sent off to a family far from here, like in New York or somewhere in the Southern states. For now I'm stuck in this mess. I don't know what to do anymore. Part of me wants to run, but if I keep running every time shit hits the fan, I might end up lonelier than ever, if that's possible.

"Lexy, Lexy…sweetie," Martha says, and I snap out of my daze. "Will you pass me the tartar sauce, please?"

Our eyes meet, but nothing comes through to me. Wayne grabs the bottle and passes it to her before I can respond. "Are you okay?" he asks, placing his hand on my back.

"I'm just tired. I had a long day."

"Must be exhausting with the little one, huh? Isn't Lorraine violating your contract?" Craig asks.

"Well, yes, but I offered."

"You're a good person, Lexy," he says, bobbing his fork in the air.

"Yes, you are," Wayne says, then kisses my cheek.

I fall silent while Martha and Craig ask Wayne about his job. I watch Logan from the corner of my eye. His movements are fast, almost disturbing. He eats faster and faster, stuffing his mouth with second helpings. Something feels off, but I'm not sure what exactly.

Sam grunts again, and I excuse myself from the dinner table once more. As I pick him up to comfort him, he starts to wail. His ear-piercing screams penetrate my bones, and a sheen of sweat plasters his hair to his forehead. He's probably hungry, *again*.

"We have to go," I say, and before they can protest, I add, "Thank you so much for having us over."

Craig looks at Martha, who's faking a smile. Wayne gets up from his chair, his plate still half full, then moves to the living room. He folds Sam's crib and takes the diaper bag, glancing at me from time to time, his face filled with sympathy.

I turn to Craig and Martha. "We'll see you tomorrow," I say, and Logan makes a salute from his eyebrow with two fingers, a get-the-hell-out-of-here-already gesture.

Wayne and I thank them once more and make our way to the front door. As I trudge over the cobblestone, I let out a heavy sigh. Sam is still screaming, and I'm not sure why.

Midnight

I fed Sam some formula, and he immediately calmed down. We played for a bit in the living room, and then I placed him in his crib. I'm impressed with Wayne. He made me tea and cleaned the kitchen. It's been three months since I met him, and we've only had one fight. It was about a bloody text message, which turned out to be a misunderstanding. To me, it's sort of odd that we never really argue, but I'm not complaining; I think I just got used to drama.

Wayne's standing at the end of the bed, his body a black figure against the moon, which shines in from the window behind him. His silhouette makes an upward V from his hips to his shoulders. As he turns sideways, my eyes run along his body. His chest bulges out, and for the first time I truly study his figure. All of him. He takes out a rubber as he slowly moves over to my side of the bed.

I've been waiting for this all day long. *Wanting*…

Monday, February 16, 2015
Evening

Sam is lying on his play mat, grabbing and pulling his toys toward his face. His motor skills are quite developed for a four-month-old. I wonder what will happen to him if something happens to Lorraine. I almost want to say, "Make me his godmother!" I mean, I'd definitely do a better job than Robert, and perhaps I can change *someone's* life.

I had a great weekend with Wayne. Valentine's Day came and went. We didn't do much; we mostly spent our days wandering around the house, watching films while cuddled up under a duvet, eating pizza, and taking sugar-dipped naps.

I haven't heard from him since yesterday. He seems quite occupied whenever I'm not around. So I sent him a text a few hours ago, thanking him for the weekend.

Now I'm in bed, staring at the ceiling. I can't sleep, so I check my phone, but there's no reply. My fingers float over my Facebook app. I know I shouldn't, but I can't resist. I load his profile, and my body goes rigid. My breathing stops and my face falls slack. It's the first time I've seen him with another girl. Her black hair is cut in a straight bob, her fringe touching her thinly shaped eyebrows. I tap on her face, and her name pops up: Maria Ivanova. A Russian girl. *Fucking bitch*, I think, as I glare at them with a condescending sneer.

Tuesday, February 17, 2015
Evening

Wayne sent me one text message today after I sent him two. I don't want to be the "needy girlfriend," so I've decided to stop reaching out, to stop working at our relationship. Instead I'll wait for him to text me first, as childish as that sounds.

I'm on my way out to Claret. I'll go crazy if I don't get out of the house. I need alcohol and a good dance. I want to get drunk, throw my head back, daze off into space, and forget about everything and everyone.

Earlier, I called Logan's girlfriend, Carmen, and said I'd pay her if she'd look after Sam for the night. She hesitated. "I don't think that's a good idea," she said. "Last time when Lorraine dropped Logan off at Craig's place, she asked me to babysit for her. But then she arranged for the neighbour to stop by and check up on me. It was ridiculous; I babysat Sam, and this woman I'd never met before reported back to Lorraine."

A long pause transpired. "Well, it's either that or I'll tell Lorraine I found condoms in Logan's room," I said, which was a lie, but then she confirmed my suspicion.

I wondered when I would come across bloodstained, sperm-spattered bedsheets. I know how it goes—I've been groped since I was thirteen years old. When my mum had "the talk" with me, she said, "Men can't think with both heads, and they can't use the shallow one, right?" She adored my dad. He set the standards high for her, and she had a hard time finding a man equally intriguing, so she remained single after he died.

Carmen eventually agreed, and when she entered the house, she said, "Oh…wow. Lexy, is that you?" She's used to seeing me with my shower-hair bun and dressed in sweats. Since Sam puked all over a top my mum bought me as a going-away present, I started wearing outfits that even hillbillies wouldn't take as seconds.

"Okay," I said, ignoring her indirect compliment, "don't stay up waiting for me." She nodded, and then I left her with Sam.

Now, as I step out of the car in my crimson, strapless Bodycon dress, my curls bounce at my waist, drawing attention away from my cleavage. My black heels click-clack their way to the bar. The club is quiet, but it'll fill up soon. I know it will because the event starts in twenty minutes. I looked it up online: it's the eleventh-anniversary celebration of Paradigm Fig, the company Maria Ivanova works for.

"Four tequila shots and a double gin and tonic," I say. The bartender looks around, compelling me to do the same. "Oh, no…it's for me," I say, and laugh.

I stand sideways at the bar, leaning on my arm, with my eyes on the dance floor. A couple is sitting at a table to my right, gazing into each other's eyes, while a silver-haired old man on a tall chair pours whiskey down his throat.

The barman flips the tequila bottle over and runs it along the shot glasses, filling them one by one. Adrenaline slithers through my body.

They'll be here any moment.

Ella

Thursday, July 2, 2015
Morning - 6 Days After Disappearance

"Where have you been?" Lorraine asks. I keep my eyes on the floor. They removed the white bandage from her head, and I barely recognize her. Her long black curls are cut into a bob, and there are bald patches where she had surgery. "It's been…fi…figh days."

Four, actually, but I don't say that.

"Where's Sam?" she asks.

"At the day-care center."

"You dropped him off at Brighter Horizons?" Her eyes are wide.

"Yes."

There's silence. "But—"

"I took care of the bill," I say, studying her face. When I took him there the day we searched for Lexy and Logan, they refused to take him in. After a ten-minute argument, I paid the outstanding bill. "Why did you drop him off at a day-care center if you had an au pair?"

Her eyes shift away from mine, as though she's embarrassed. "I took him there once when Lexy went on vacation…two or three months ago."

"And you never paid them?"

"I couldn't," she says, almost whispering. I look away, guilt overwhelming me. I never even asked if she needed financial help. "Is Sam okay?"

I nod, and then I lower my head to hide my shame as my hands rummage through my handbag in search of my phone—a distraction. "Who's this?" I ask, sitting on the edge on the chair next to her bed, pointing to the picture I saw on Facebook yesterday.

"It's Wayne," she confirms.

"Do you have his number? Or…any contact information for him?"

"I don't think so." She pauses. "Lexy might have used my laptop once to send him an e-mail."

"Can you access it from your phone?" I ask her.

"No. It's only..." She sighs. "Only from my computer. One of those Microsoft Office accounts," she says, then tells me her password.

"Thanks. I'll search for it." She blinks slowly, as though her eyelids are heavy. I hesitate for a moment, but then I say it. "I saw her with another man."

"You saw her?" Her voice rises a little.

"No. No. Sorry. On a photo on her camera. It was taken at Deception Bridge."

"Jesus, El."

"Well. Was she seeing another man? Did you see her with another man? Do you know anything about her trip to Deception Pass Bridge?" I ask.

"No. It's probably a friend," she says, waving it off. "Where have you been all this time? What have you been doing?"

"Craig and I conducted a search."

"And?" Lorraine tries to push herself up the cushions, but exhaustion takes over.

"They haven't told you?"

"What?"

"The police found Lexy's car."

Her face lights up, and then it transforms into a frown. "What?"

"They found the Honda CR-V abandoned at Seahurst Park."

Her face is blank. No tears, nothing. Just pure disbelief. "It's not the car," she says.

"It is. The faster you accept thi—"

"No," she says. "Last time I checked, the car was still in the driveway."

"But you said they drove off in it."

Our eyes meet, and she frowns again. This time she looks out of it, like she's not with me in the room but somewhere else.

"Ray, people keep saying you're not making sense. The detectives said you're lying. It's clear you're having trouble speaking. Are you sure you know what happened?"

"Yes...yes, the car is still at my house." Her eyes wander off, slowly moving across the room as though she's not registering that I'm here.

"What do you mean? Where's your doctor? I want to see him."

"I told the police everything I know."

"No, you didn't. They didn't know Lexy's pregnant."

"I told them," she repeats.

"They seemed shocked to hear that, Ray."

She blinks hard, her eyes focused on me, and then her face fills with fear. She gasps for air. "They did?" She bursts into tears. "I don't know what's hap…ha…happening."

She shakes her head as she tries to throw the sheets off her. I grab her arm. "Ray, calm down. Calm down." Her legs kick out as her back presses against the cushions. She pants, her breathing sharp, panicked, and then I scoot closer to hold her tightly as she sobs.

Afternoon

Before I left the hospital, I asked to see Lorraine's doctor. The secretary said he'd be available on Sunday, so I scheduled an appointment; I need to know more about my sister's condition, about her health.

Now, at the police station, I ask Aliya to take a step back from Lorraine—all this has taken a toll on her health. She reassures me that they'll approach her in a gentler manner, but they can't back off entirely. Then I remember the photo of Logan with the petite blond girl on Facebook and ask her if he has a girlfriend.

"Yes," Aliya says, "but Lorraine said they've been going through a rough patch. Her name's Carmen Roth."

"Have you spoken to her yet?"

"Not yet. They want a lawyer first." She's busy filing papers, and then she pauses. "The girl won't talk to us."

"Well, that's odd. Don't you think?"

"Yes, but you know how it goes with the filthy rich."

I don't—I have no idea—but I nod anyway. I want to pry a bit more, but sometimes silence grabs the information tucked within someone and pulls it right out, so I reason that the less I ask, the more they'll give. But Aliya is quiet as she stumbles around her office, stepping high over piles of paper and boxes. After a few more minutes of conversation, I thank her, shake her hand, and leave.

In the hallway, I see him.

"Wayne!" I say, but he ignores me as he strides toward the door. I grab his arm. "Please, I need to speak to you." He throws my hand off.

"What is it?" he snarls, his face twisted in an ugly grimace.

"Sorry," I say, my palm up. "I'm Lorraine's sister. I just want to ask you something."

"My lawyer advised me to keep my mouth shut."

"One question…one." He stares at me. "When did you see Lexy last?" He says nothing. "Did she tell you she was pregnant?"

"That's two questions. I told the detectives what they need to know. And here's some information for you: Lexy is freaking crazy…unstable. Leave me out of this!" He eyes me for a second before he reaches for the door handle and storms out.

I watch him as he gets into an old Buick Century, the paint a faded green, scraped at the side. He drives off faster than I think the car can manage, then skids to a stop at a red light, still in sight. I avert my eyes as I make my way to Lorraine's car: a typical soccer-mom van. A car I thought I'd never have to drive.

Inside, I search for Carmen's name on Facebook. *Carmen Roth.* I Google her and easily find her address. *So much for keeping things under wraps,* I think.

When I arrive at the Roths' house, I stare at the beautiful oak tree that dominates the front yard, stealing the bit of sun that would have beamed through their casement windows if it weren't there. The shadow it casts darkens the white paint to a light gray, almost blending the house in with the sky.

I knock on the door, but no one answers. I stand there for a minute or two before I try again. This time, a voice emerges from within the house. *I didn't hear any movement. Has someone been watching me all this time?* I take a step back, my neck curving down as I stare at the bottom of the door. *Is Carmen sitting against it?*

"Hello?" I say.

"Who's there?" Her tone slices through the wood.

"Ella. I'm Lorraine's sister, Logan's aunt." There's silence for a few seconds, and then I hear some shuffling inside. "Carmen?"

The handle moves down after the lock turns with a satisfying click. A face appears, but it's not who I expected. She opens the door slightly, leaving half her body hidden.

"Leave my daughter alone," the woman says. "I'm terribly sorry for what happened to your family, but keep *mine* out of this."

She barely finishes her sentence when the door clicks back closed. My glare burns through the wood. I'd be surprised if she doesn't feel it. *Self-righteous bitch.* I cup my hands around my mouth. "Never come knocking on my door if your precious daughter ever goes missing!" I scream. "And I hope no one would *want* to help you!"

I storm back to the car, trampling all over her little garden. If this woman doesn't have time to help a family in need, then I don't have time to walk around her fucking roses.

On my way home, I fight the rage boiling inside me. *That woman isn't much different than I am,* I think, as I pull into the driveway. *That's exactly how you treat strangers,* a voice says as I stride into the house. I try not to think about it as I pull the copies of Lexy's poems out of my handbag. I slam them onto the table, determined to unravel them.

The second poem's heading reads, "You don't need to be loyal to your sufferings, unless you choose to."

Impeded my progress, troubled my thoughts,
disappeared after (one) too many whores.
Distorted my judgment, wrecked my heart,
I followed you for a brand new start.
I missed your touch; I missed you too much.
I tracked you down and realized we were never apart.

A name is written underneath the poem: "Brent." I stare at it. Perhaps it's the guy who went to Deception Bridge with her. Next to the poem, in the margins, she wrote:

I knew that I could find my way back.
I hear your heart pounding; you are in the darkness too.
So I'll stay in the darkness with you.

This girl is troubled, I think as I turn a page. There's a third poem with a picture of a snarling wolf. It reads:

When the apple doesn't fall far from the tree, why only have one apple?
Take it all.

Danielle Esplin

These badgers dug the same hole, deeper, and deeper, and deeper. Now take it.

With a sigh, I throw the papers back on the table. Today has given me more questions than answers. It's been five days and six nights since Logan and Lexy went missing. We found the car. That's it. We have the car and dozens of unanswered questions.

Lexy

Tuesday, February 17, 2015
Evening - 4 Months Before Disappearance

Eager revellers swarm into Claret as if there's been a reverse evacuation. Some make their way to the dance floor, where bodies move to the beat as their hands pound the air. Others tread in my direction, where the lights reflect in the mirror behind the bartenders, dancing across the walls and illuminating blue swirls of smoke.

I order another gin and tonic before the inebriated blonde behind me can take my spot. Drink in hand, I shove my way out of the horde and up the stairs to lean against the railing. I find myself doing it again, scanning the dance floor, searching for him. He might not be here, but the day he misses an opportunity to party will be the day Jocelyn Wildenstein is considered the paragon of beauty. My eyes sweep across dozens of faces, but I recognise none of them. I clutch my arm, and my chest flutters. I'm not sure I'm ready for this, and I don't know what I'll do if I see him.

"We Found Love" by Calvin Harris and Rihanna blasts through the club. I bite my lower lip until it hurts. One moment I love this song; the other moment I hate it.

The song brings back memories. When I danced with Roy, when I had tunnel vision, fixating on him, when nothing mattered but us. I forgot about my homework that was due the next day, about all my worries, about everything and everyone else. We became so reckless that I once flattened his back on the bar at the nightclub and unbuttoned his shirt. It took me a few seconds to realise we were encircled by students gaping at us. He whispered into my ear, "Jesus, just marry me," and we stumbled out of the club, confessing our love with hazy eyes, hanging on to each other as we tried to find our balance. The next day, we skipped class and slept in, cuddling between McDonald's wrappers. We'd jokingly harmonise "The Circle of Life" in the shower as we scrubbed the pungent scent of smoke off our bodies. Some nights we'd go to the library in an attempt to study, just to judge people walking by and get ab spasms from laughing. When we were together, nothing else mattered but us, or so I thought.

Now, every neuron inside me is ablaze with adrenaline. I lift the glass to my lips, but there's not a drop left. I head downstairs, pressing against torsos, squeezing my way back to the bar. I pause halfway, facing a group of people sitting around a table. I can't move. It's as though something has hit me right in my chest, and I gasp for air.

There he is, staring at me, ignoring the girl I recognise from the picture I saw yesterday, Maria Ivanova, who's telling him something with her hand on his thigh. My eyes move from her to Roy's, whose jaw muscles twitch as he clenches his teeth.

Instantly I feel connected to him. It feels like I saw him yesterday, like we still know every inch of each other. Despite his angry expression, he looks good, even better than before. He's gained muscle weight, and his light-brown hair is cut short, accentuating his jawline and arcane eyes.

He gets to his feet, throwing the girl's hand off him. I take a step back as he elbows people out of the way, coming at me like a nor'easter. I steady myself against a wall, holding his wicked glare.

I want to run, but this is exactly what I came for. My head shifts from left to right, looking for a way out, but before I can move, his hands come flying at me. The wall shudders behind me as they smack down beside my ears. His face hovers over mine. The familiar scent of his cologne hits me, a mixture of olive blossom, star anise, and leather. I stare at his chest.

"What the fuck are you doing here?" he screams, slamming his hand with every word. I swallow hard. "What are you doing here?"

My eyes slowly move to his shoulders. He bends his upper body until his hazel eyes meet mine. I open my mouth to say something, but nothing comes.

I tilt my head forward so my forehead touches his. "I…I'm sorry," I say.

Roy shoves himself away from the wall and taps my shoulder, indicating that I should follow him. He moves through clusters of people, breaking up conversations, pushing his way to a quieter place. I try to keep up, but he's not waiting for me. A girl screams at me from behind, her top stained with red wine, swearing at me to apologise for bumping into her, but I keep moving forward.

Roy's shoulders stick out from the crowd, twisting left and right as he makes his way out.

Once we're outside, he presses a palm against his head. "How long have you been in town?" he asks.

"A few months," I say, and he looks away, staring into the air.

"Why?"

"I got a job here in Sea—"

"Bullshit." He shakes his head, wiping his face with his hand as he paces back and forth.

"You don't own Seattle, Roy."

"You followed me all the way from London?"

"Don't flatter yourself. Jesus."

"Go back home, Lexy," he says, his hands cutting the air. "Just fuck off, would ya?"

I shove my hands against his chest. "Fuck you!"

"You did, and it didn't turn out so well, did it?"

My hand strikes his cheek. He gives me a blank stare. I've never hit him before, but I've been waiting for this day for eighteen months.

He grasps my face, forcing his fingers into my cheeks, and shoves me against the wall. We hold each other's glare, and then he moves in, his mouth pressing against mine. First softly, then with intense passion. His hands pin my arms above my head. My forehead puckers, and I kiss him back.

Lorraine

Friday, February 20 2015
Evening - 4 Months Before Disappearance

When I woke up after my surgery, anxiety flooded me. The nurse took my blood pressure while I was still hooked up to IV drips and monitors. All I wanted to know was: *Is it out? Did he manage to take it out? Will I live?* I was so sure my neurosurgeon had managed to remove more than he said he could. But it was only the pain medication numbing all sensation, numbing the pressure of the tumor in my temporal lobe, which he hadn't even touched.

The doctor finally came into sight and said he was sorry. He could remove only a fraction of the tumor in my occipital lobe, and there's still a mass of cancer embed in my temporal lobe. "There's good news, though," he said, but my expression didn't change; I was motionless, depressed. "We removed the entire tumor in your frontal lobe." I nodded and thought, *Hopefully radiation will work.*

I also received confirmation that it's secondary brain cancer, which means that the cancer has spread from the primary site to my brain. Before I left, the doctor filled my hands with pain medication, ointments, and syringes. I was petrified when he told me I have to stick a needle into my stomach every day.

"To thin your blood," he said, "to avoid blood clots…you know, strokes." And here I thought it couldn't get any worse.

I'm relieved to be home, to have Sam in my arms again. It was extremely hard to leave him with someone I've only known for four and a half months, but I'm grateful to have Lexy in my life. I have no complaints about her, but I can't help wonder if this is too good to be true. I've read a lot of horror stories about au pairs online. If it's not the au pair, then there's something wrong with the host parents. I guess it's what mothers do when it comes to their children. We want what's best for them. We'll always worry about our kids, so we get paranoid and dig deeper just to find nothing. I guess some mothers are just unlucky—they get a bad match, an au pair who came for the booze and nightlife, someone irresponsible. But so far, I'm really happy with Lexy.

She's cooking dinner right now, although I told her to take the night off. She's been working for eight days straight. I thought about hiring a second nanny, but I can't afford it. It makes me feel like a burden; I'm making the poor girl work overtime, without compensating her for it, and when she's not home, Logan feels like he has to hang around. It's as if everyone got cancer the day I was diagnosed, except I'm their tumor.

"I thought about bringing your journal to the hospital, Mom." Logan is doing his homework at the dinner table with Carmen so they can relax for the rest of the weekend.

"Thank you, my angel. That would've been very thoughtful of you, but I slept most of the time," I say, trudging toward the kitchen. "I'm still extreme…ly…" My mouth hangs open to finish my sentence, but I can't speak. I'm frozen in front of the mirror in the hallway.

A woman I barely recognize stares back at me. A three-dimensional line, bordered by thin strips of hair, runs like a train track across her head.

"Oh, my God," I say, my hand pressed against my mouth. "I look awful." It's like someone attacked my head with a heavy-duty stapler.

"You don't need hair to be gorgeous," Carmen says, and I rush past the mirror. I was aware that I'd have a scar, but I didn't imagine it would be this horrendous.

They gaze at me as I take a seat at the dinner table, almost as though they're reevaluating how repulsive my wounds are. I cringe at the thought of sitting here with crispy flakes of dried blood tangled in my hair. My wounds feel tight and swollen. I'm disgusted by myself, and my appetite vanishes.

"Food's ready," Lexy says, carrying a pan of lasagna to the table.

"Lorraine, you were saying?" Carmen leans in, her long blond braid hanging down her shoulder.

My lips press together, and I shake my head. "Sorry, what?"

"You said something…and I don't think you finished your sentence," she says.

Carmen lets it sink in for a few seconds before Logan interjects. "You said you wanted to do something, and then you went silent."

I chuckle. "Gosh, I'm barely out of the hospital, and you kids are already making fun of me."

Logan and Carmen exchange glances. "No…seriously, Mom, we're not joking."

I turn to Lexy. "Oh…ha…no," she says, holding her palms up. "Keep me out of this one."

I lean back, my arms resting on the table, "Well, it must be all these meds then," I say, and shrug.

"Anyway, let's eat," Lexy says, and my hand closes into a fist.

Saturday, February 21, 2015
Evening

I tilt my head sideways, holding up a hand mirror to get a clear view of my scars. I wince at the feeling of stitches pricking my fingers as I dab bacitracin ointment on my incisions to prevent an infection. As I wipe my hands on a towel, a text message comes through from Craig:

> Hi. I'm wondering if you'll be OK tonight. Will you be alone at the house?

My pulse slows to an unsettling degree, and my posture stiffens. I read it again and again. For the first time, it's not about Logan but about me. I stare at the screen for a moment before I write him back. I revise my message over and over, and then I delete it. I shouldn't reply. He can wonder about it, about me.

Determined to distract myself, I slog downstairs. "Did you get her a present at least?" Carmen asks Logan.

"No, I don't do presents," he says. "You know that."

Today's Martha's birthday, and she invited them over tonight. Some of my old friends will be there, or at least I thought they were my friends, especially Dorlean.

It became clear she was talking behind my back not long after my divorce. Craig refused to let me buy a new car during the last few years of our marriage, so I was quite upset when Martha picked Logan up in a brand-new Audi last year. I called Dorlean, and the first thing she said was: "No, she worked for it,

Ray. She didn't get it on a silver platter. She earned it." *Worked for it? She's a twenty-eight-year-old college student.* We never spoke again, and I can say the same of most of the others. It didn't take them long to fall under Martha's two-faced spell.

I hear a car pull up into the driveway. "Ready to go?" I ask, and Carmen jumps, bringing her hand to her chest.

"Oh…wow," she says. "Didn't see you there."

"Yeah, we're good to go," Logan says, pulling his beanie flat against his head.

"Where's Lexy?" I ask.

"She left about an hour ago," Carmen says, as they gather all their things—a birthday card, their phones, Logan's wallet, and a jacket.

Logan cracks his neck before he swings the door wide open, a crisp breeze swirling in. They head outside, and I hear car doors slam. *Craig's car? Martha's?* I shudder at the thought that I didn't ask who was picking them up. I hurry to the window and see Craig's BMW drive off. I sigh in relief, watching them go.

Whenever I ask Logan questions about the time he spends with his father, he gets annoyed. He thinks I'm trying to pry into their affairs. In the beginning, it was hard not to ask questions. *Oh, she bought you dinner. That's nice. When was this?* But now I feel like I'm pushing his buttons whenever I ask him about Craig. Lately, I really just want to make conversation with my son, but when I talk to him, it often feels as if we're a couple of exposed wires about to connect and explode.

I turn and step into my trainers. The doctor ordered me to take regular walks to get my blood flowing, whether I want to or not. What I really want to do is climb into bed and sleep my headache off. I'm exhausted because I barely slept the last few nights. I constantly hear my neurosurgeon's voice: *Remember, no pressure on the wounds.*

I strap Sam into his stroller and lock the door behind me. A few miles into my hike, a vibration in my pocket brings me to a halt. It's another text from Craig.

Ray…please don't ignore me.

I can't remember the last time he called me that. I want to hurl my phone onto the asphalt and stomp on it. *Damn you,* I think. *Why now? Because I'm some goddamn charity case?*

I stand there, motionless, troubled. The neurosurgeon said I need to walk at least ten minutes, three times a day. Then twenty minutes, then thirty. I want to move forward, but I can't, so this will have to do for now. I turn around and stride back home.

After I struggle up the steps with the stroller, I dash through the front door and run to the toilet and vomit. It feels as if my eyes are about to shoot out from my skull. It feels like I'm dying.

Ella

Friday, July 3, 2015
Morning - 1 Week After Disappearance

I lean forward to apply every ounce of my weight on the tube, but nothing comes out. No way in hell am I leaving this house without brushing my teeth, and there's no time for shopping, because Craig and Martha are expecting me at their place in twenty minutes. New evidence has surfaced, and Detective Baldwin is joining us.

I rummage through curlers and brushes in Lorraine's drawers, but there's no toothpaste or mouthwash. I sigh; lately it seems I can't find anything I'm searching for.

I trudge down the hall toward Logan's room. As the door creaks open, the musty air crawls down my throat. I don't know why I've avoided coming in here since I arrived. I guess part of me was in denial—almost as though I was worried he'd come back and catch me invading his space.

To my right is his bathroom, where his grooming clay has been left open on the counter. Blotches of toothpaste stain the sink, and his razor rests on the side of the acrylic curve, facing downward. I rifle through his cabinets and finally find an unopened Colgate box. I quickly brush my teeth and glance at my watch; it's 11:38 a.m.

As I straighten my back, I spot a plastic bag behind an organizer tray, stashed in the corner of the cabinet on the top shelf. I roll my feet onto my toes to reach it.

Inside is a glass bottle and a syringe. *Steroids? For his football games?* No wonder he looks like a college student. *This is why I don't have kids*, I think, *because of shit like this, the things they do behind your back*. I clench my teeth, hoping this didn't get him in trouble. Then I think of Lorraine, I assume she doesn't know. She shouldn't learn about the steroids, not now. Hell, maybe it would be better if she never found out.

Afternoon

Eric sits in a chair across from me, with Martha and Craig sitting to my right on the sofa. My forehead is covered in a sheen of sweat—I had to rush over here after dropping Sam off at the daycare center.

"We went through footage from more than thirty surveillance cameras at nearby gas stations, hoping we'd find something." Eric pauses, his eyes scanning our faces. "One of them has Lexy and Logan on tape."

I straighten my back, and my stomach turns.

"Do you have the footage here?" Martha asks, leaning forward.

"Yes, I want to know if any of you can pick up on anything suspicious. We don't know Logan and Lexy like you do…or their body language, their mannerisms. We need confirmation too."

"So it might not be them," Craig scoffs.

"We can plug it into the TV," Martha says, as Eric waves a flash drive in the air.

"Which gas station is this?" I ask.

"At the 7-Eleven on 148th Avenue Northeast," Eric says, "About a fifteen-minute drive from Lorraine's house." He helps himself with the TV, forcing the stick into the side. A box pops up on the screen. One file is marked, "Wifey" and another one, "Kiddies." I smile—I didn't take him as a family man—and then, as I notice his discomfort, I pretend I didn't see them. With reddened cheeks, he hastily selects the third icon, "Surveillance Vid."

An image appears from inside the convenience store. In the lower-right corner of the video, a time stamp appears: 5:15 p.m. In the upper left, the tires of a nondescript car are visible. The quality of the video is poor, grainy.

Logan enters the store, roaming up and down the aisles. He's wearing an orange shirt, blue jeans, and black sneakers. Lexy comes into the shop a few seconds later. She's dressed in black leggings with a blue blouse and black boots. She says something to Logan before she leaves the frame. As she walks outside, her upper body moves out of view, but her legs are still visible at the top of the screen. Logan takes some candy and then something from the fridge, perhaps a sandwich. He strides over to the cashier but stops midway to grab a bottle of water. My eyes glide back to Lexy. She hasn't moved. Logan pays and leaves the store. Another minute passes, and Lexy walks out of view.

Eric presses the remote to stop the video. Martha shifts her weight on the couch. "My son appears normal," Craig says.

"So it is Logan?" Eric asks."Yes."

"Yes."

"And the girl?"

"Yes, that's Lexy," Martha says.

I stare at my hands. What if that was the last image I'll ever see of my nephew? This damn video will haunt me. *What happened after they left?*

"We believe they left the house around five p.m.," Eric says.

"And?" I ask.

"Well, now we also know what clothes they were wearing," he adds.

"And that's it?" I let out a wry chuckle. "Jesus Christ." I drop my head into my hands, giving a barely audible sigh.

"Well, thank you, Detective," Craig says, his face blank. He shakes Eric's hand, and they get to their feet.

"That's not all," Eric says, turning to us. "Carmen came forward with a team of lawyers." He falls silent, glancing at each of us. "She seems to be the last person who saw Logan."

"What a fucking brat," I say. "She took a *week* to tell you this?"

Craig holds his palm up, silencing me, eager to hear more. Eric continues, "She said he came over around five twenty p.m. the night he went missing, and they had a fight. He apparently ended their relationship. He left thirty to forty minutes later, and she stayed in her room, crying."

"Left with who?" I ask.

"No one knows."

"It's strange that she didn't show up at the search on Monday," Martha says.

"Yeah…that *is* odd," I add. We stand in a half circle, staring at each other, all of us baffled. "Who dropped him off at her house?"

"She said when she opened the door, he was alone, waiting for her."

"Probably Lexy then," Martha says, blinking fast, as though she's trying to unravel her thoughts.

"Well, we're bringing Carmen in again for questioning tomorrow," Eric says, "but for now, keep this to yourselves. If this comes out, it might jeopardize the case." He turns to me. "And…uh…we sent the poems to the newspapers. Not sure if you saw them."

"No. Haven't been to a store in days."

"We bought today's paper," Craig says, as he walks to the kitchen in a way that would enervate even an insomnia-prone adrenaline junkie. He returns with *The Seattle Times* and hands it to me.

The poems are published in a box on the front page. It looks more like an advertisement than anything else. "Anonymous?" My eyes rest on Eric.

"Yes…for now."

I turn to Craig. "Why do we want to play it safe?" I ask. "Lives depend on this."

"If we say Lexy wrote these poems, it might expose her personal life," he says. "We just said they were related to a missing-persons case and offered a thousand-dollar reward for the best interpretation. Hopefully it'll motivate some poetry-obsessed individuals to analyze them."

I stare at the newspaper for a minute, and then I hold it out to Martha. "What do you think?"

She shrugs, her eyes dancing around as though she's embarrassed. "My guess is as good as yours."

Before anyone can say anything else, Eric cuts the conversation short. "I need to go," he says, glancing at his watch. "I have a case to attend to." He nods in my direction then lumbers toward the front door. "I'll call as soon as we make any progress," he adds, and Martha touches his shoulder to walk him out.

Evening

If I turn right, I'll end up at Lorraine's house. If I turn left, I'll be heading toward the 7-Eleven on 148th Avenue Northeast. I just picked up Sam, and I'm starving. I need to know what Lexy did outside the convenience store, why she didn't move for four long minutes, and while I'm at it, I'll buy myself a sandwich.

I park the car and enter the store. My neck extends as I turn from left to right, searching for the cameras. The cashier lowers his eyebrows. "How can I help you?" he asks in a foreign accent, one I can't place.

"Where are the cameras?" I ask, and his frown deepens, stressing the jagged scar on his forehead. "My nephew went missing last week and—"

"Oh, yeah," he says, seemingly relieved. "The one with the nanny?"

"Did you see them?"

"No, but it's all over the news."

"Oh, yeah…right." I sigh. "Listen, I just want to have a look at your cameras. The one from this corner," I say, pointing to my right. He gestures toward it, nodding in approval.

I stand on my tiptoes, trying to direct my eyes in the same angle the camera's facing. "You need a chair?" he asks, and before I can reply, he slides one across the tile floor, sending an ear-splitting screech through the store. I climb onto the woven textile seat, almost losing my balance. My eyes scan the window, and they stop where Lexy stood. I bend my back, and then I see it.

A *pay phone.* She was talking on the phone. My mind races. She might have called her mother or a friend, but why didn't she use her cell phone? Why did she use an *untraceable* device? And *who* did she speak to?

Lexy

Saturday, February 21, 2015
Evening - 4 Months Before Disappearance

My stomach hurts from laughing all night. Craig's friends are hilarious. We celebrated Martha's twenty-eighth birthday. I had no idea she's only six years older than me, which makes Craig almost twelve years her senior. I won't be surprised if there's another mini Davis one day.

Logan decided to spend the night at his dad's house. Craig invited me and Carmen to stay over too, but I politely declined because someone needs to be home with Lorraine.

I thought she'd be asleep by now, but the beige curtains in the front windows are illuminated. I enter the house and find Lorraine at the kitchen table with her face buried in her hands.

"Are you okay?" I ask, taking a step toward her.

She lifts her head without saying a word, and it's as though someone's pulling my heart down into my stomach. I stare at Lorraine for a second before grabbing some paper napkins and handing them to her.

"What happened?" I ask, sliding a chair out from the table.

She wipes away the tears. "Oh, honey. You're so young and beautiful." As she reaches out to my face, it feels as if she's entangling me in a world of despair. "Please make every second worth it." Her forehead scrunches. "Just, you know, live life."

I don't know what to say, so I stand and offer her a cup of tea.

"I rushed into so many things," Lorraine says, sniffling. "You know, after college you land a job, get married, and have kids. All that crap."

"Do you regret any of that?" I ask.

"Some I do…some I don't."

As I make my way around the counter, I almost step on a phone with its battery a few feet away. I pick up the parts and place them on the counter, wondering what happened. I glance at Lorraine and realise she's not talking to me anymore but to herself, almost as though I'm not here.

"All I'm saying is…even though you do all the right things, it doesn't mean anything will turn out right."

"You mean, like with Craig?" I ask, and I immediately regret it. She glares at me, and I hastily turn my back to her as I flip the lever of the kettle.

"Exactly, yes," she says, the chair creaking as she shifts her weight. "Did I tell you that he hit me?"

I drop the tea bag into the cup and pause, staring at the maple-colored tile wall in front of me. "He did what?"

"He was everything I wanted. Then, a few months before he filed for divorce, he abused me," she says, but for some reason it doesn't ring true.

"Like…physically assaulted you?" I ask, turning to face her.

"Do I need to spell it out?" she says, and her hazel eyes turn dark, smouldering with enmity and aversion. I've never seen her like this before.

"No…I didn't know that," I say, shocked.

"Well, now you do."

Sunday, February 22, 2015
Afternoon

Have you ever loved someone so much that even when they chip pieces away from you, you still try to give them what's left? I know I have…I know I do.

Wayne invited me to his place, but I don't want to see him, not after what happened with Roy. Tuesday night, I left Claret and went to Roy's apartment. He told me how much he missed me and said he never wanted to lose me again. "I've been thinking about you every night, wondering where you were," he said.

But after we slept together that night, out of nowhere he said it was a mistake. I stared at the ceiling when he once again said we shouldn't have had sex. He was throwing me away like a pair of worn-out shoes. He then told me his brother would be home soon and I needed to go. So I did the shameful got-laid parade out of there. I haven't heard from him since.

On top of that, after what happened yesterday, I've been avoiding Lorraine all morning. I've been timing every movement in an attempt to sidestep her. I eventually called Logan and told him to come home, to keep an eye on his mum, and then I accepted Wayne's invitation. Because I don't feel like spending another day in this house, even more than I don't feel like seeing Wayne.

Evening

"How was your week?" Wayne asks, walking toward me.

"Okay. How about yours?" My eyes are fixed on the glass of Cabernet Sauvignon in my hands.

"Hmm. It was all right." He falls onto the couch then places a hand on my leg.

"Why did you go all silent on me the last few days?"

"I was busy," he says, "working."

"The entire time?"

"Most of the time."

My eyes narrow, examining his face. I'm tired of the same shit over and over, so I decide to let it go. "Well, I hope to hear more from you this week."

He leans in, and our lips touch. "Promise."

My phone vibrates. There's a message from Roy, but I saved his number as "Vicky."

"Who's that?" Wayne asks.

"A friend. She's an au pair too. She lives in Redmond. Met her a few weeks ago at the park."

"Good to see you're making friends," he says, smiling the way he does whenever he teases me.

I've had a hard time making friends since I arrived in Seattle. I'm too busy with work, and whenever I bond with another au pair, it's useless, because their work year always ends at a different time than mine does. The girls I've met all went home within the first three months. It's a waste of time.

With a smirk, I hand Wayne my empty glass. He eyes me for a while then heads to the kitchen to pour me another drink. I read the message:

> I'm sorry for how things turned out. I'm sorry for taking advantage of you on Tuesday. I want to make it up to you. Dinner at my place next weekend?

"Why are you smiling at your phone?" Wayne asks, returning to the sofa.

My heart pounds in my chest. "Ha, nothing interesting. We're just discussing you," I say, managing a wink.

"Nothing interesting." He chuckles. "Well, if she knows you like I do, she'd say we make a perfect match."

"Why? Because we complete each other?" I roll my eyes, laughing.

"No, because you're the least interesting person I know."

My mouth falls open, and then I smile. "Really?"

"Well, we've been together for…what? How long?"

"Wait, are we together?" I smirk. "You never asked me out."

"Okay, well, we met…uh…three months ago, and all I really know about you is that you're from London, which I could tell from the get-go. So the only thing you've actually told me is about Lorraine and Martha and all that shit."

"Don't lie. I told you about my mother," I say.

"What? That you have one?" He laughs. "No, seriously, Lexy, you never speak about yourself. Why?"

I shrug then take a sip of my wine. "I don't know. I didn't notice."

"Okay," he begins, forking his fingers through his hair. "Then tonight will be the night. Tell me something about yourself, anything."

"What do you want to know?"

"Well…uh…" His eyes shift from left to right, as if he's searching for something. "What's your…biggest fear?"

I turn my head away, my eyes darting around. "Well, I think my biggest fear is that if I die, my mother would try to sell my shoes back in London for what I told her they cost."

He laughs and shakes his head. "See, you're doing it again."

"Okay, okay. I don't know." I don't want to tell him what I'm actually afraid of. People prey on what they know. They always do, and I don't trust anyone.

"Okay, fine." He flicks his hand in the air. "Be the most boring girl I know."

"So why are you with me then?" This time I'm not smiling.

"For your tits and lack of an ass." He smiles, but I don't reciprocate.

"No, really," I say with a probing gaze.

"Well, it's the way you speak, Lexy. The way you carry yourself. Your mannerisms. I know there's a lot more to you—you're just too afraid to share it with others."

"Ha." I force a smile. "Keep telling yourself that."

"I will," he says, and kisses my forehead.

Lorraine

Sunday, February 22, 2015
Morning - 4 Months Before Disappearance

I made a complete fool out of myself yesterday. I never told anyone about the night Craig hit me, not even Ella. I have no idea why I felt the need to blurt it out. Of course I didn't tell Lexy that I'd provoked him.

I grab my phone from the nightstand; there's a voice mail from Craig, but all I can hear is people laughing in the background, a celebration. What the hell does he want? I take off my jacket as a wave of heat flashes through me, and then I send him a text:

> What is it?

I draw in slow, steady breaths in an attempt to calm myself down. In the bathroom, I dab ointment onto my scar. I need to wait a few more days before I'm allowed to wash my hair, which feels greasy. I cautiously massage my scalp to unstick my skin from my wound, but I'm distracted by the chime of an incoming message. I wash my hands and hurry to my bed. He replied:

> Hi. Lexy borrowed my phone because hers died. She called to make sure you're okay. She wanted to check in with you. Sorry about that.

I open my phone log. The call came in before she got home, which was around 11:45 p.m., right after I tried to text Craig back. I deleted the same message several times, and then I tried to type him an e-mail on my laptop. When I read it aloud, I realized I'd used the wrong words in the wrong places. I lost it. I hurled my Samsung against the wall and threw my laptop off the table. Then I gaped at the devices on the floor, shocked by my reaction.

Evening

"Thanks for coming with me on my walk," I say, placing my hand on Logan's shoulder.

"Anytime." He gives me a faint smile. "Besides, I could use some fresh air after yesterday."

"Why?" I ask. "Did something happen?"

"No, nothing happened. Relax, Mom." He presses his lips into a smile. "Dad's friends smoked inside the house, that's all."

"Oh," I say, my eyes fixed on the footpath ahead. "He let them do that?"

"Yeah…it's strange. Never thought that day would come."

It *is* strange. Craig hates the scent of smoke sticking to his clothes, not to mention his furniture.

"Well, did you have a good night at least?" I ask, and Logan sighs.

"Mom, we're not going there. I asked you to stop."

"I'm just asking if you enjoyed your evening." My blood starts to boil. "Jesus, am I not allowed to ask my son how his night was?"

"I'm not doing this," he says, his palms up. "Sorry, Mom. I can't do this." I bring myself to a halt as he turns around and heads back home.

It starts to drizzle as I turn the stroller to follow him. He walks fast, striding up the hill. I try to keep up, shooting my legs out from beneath me.

Back at home, I struggle up the steps, curving my back to hoist the stroller from the ground. Logan turns to help me. "I'm sorry," I say, as he straightens his back. I look up at my son – my tall, big boy. "I don't know what go into me. I know you hate it when I do that."

He says nothing; instead he bends down to hug me, and his body softens into my arms. "I love you, Mom," he says into my neck. I realize my cheeks are wet…and it's not from the rain. "You need to let go. Dad has moved on. It's time for you to do the same."

Tuesday, February 24, 2015
Morning

I'm online, researching cognitive behavioral therapy. Lately the smallest things set me off, which is unusual for me. I've never had a temper—Ella had one for me, an extra one. At first I felt positive about possibly undergoing this type of psychotherapy, but then I read a quote: "The happiness of your life depends on the quality of your thoughts." Any hope I had was snatched away by that sentence, because I don't know if my brain tumors are doing the thinking or if it's just me. How many times will I say something and wonder afterward what the hell I just said? I don't recognize myself anymore.

Who have I become?

Ella

Saturday, July 4, 2015
Morning - 8 Days After Disappearance

Diapers. Diapers. Diapers. God, they're expensive. Cloth diapers, pocket, prefold, flat, two-in-one, bikini fold, safari fold, burrito fold…what the fuck? I just want pizza.

I grab the nearest package and throw it into the shopping cart. Sam smiles at me, and I find myself smiling back. Suddenly I feel silly, or perhaps surprised, for feeling something I haven't felt before. Something deep and warm. I shake the thought off then think about how much I hate it when he wakes me up at night.

Lately, he's leopard-crawling through the living room. I can't keep up anymore. I can't enjoy a cup of coffee in the morning without following him step by step like a fly hovering over a turd, but let's not get all broody now.

The store is filled with last-minute shoppers getting ready to celebrate the Fourth of July. As I walk up to the cashier, my eyes catch sight of *The Seattle Times*. The headline, in big bold letters, reads, "Incoming Poem Interpretations Might Lead to Missing Nanny and 16-Year-Old." Well, that didn't take long. *So much for anonymity.*

"Anything else?" the woman asks.

"Hold on a sec." I grab the newspaper. "There we go," I say, and the cash register beeps as she sweeps the paper across the laser.

Afternoon

A picture of Lexy and Logan covers half the front page of *The Seattle Times*. There's a short article with quotes and comments made by eager poem enthusiasts. Tweets, hashtags and Facebook statuses are neatly aligned in columns beneath the article.

"It's obvious," one Tweet says. "In the second poem she's talking about a guy named Brent who cheated on her and left her."

"Something happened to the poet that turned her life upside down," says Carin from the University of Washington. "In the first poem, she says 'pearly gates to our divine abode,' which changes to 'locked gates to my divine abode.' It also signifies that she's alone after what happened to her."

"What did the boy's father do? She said the apple doesn't fall far from the tree. He probably has something to do with their disappearance." *Craig?*

"She's a murderer," someone wrote. "If you consider all the poems at once, it becomes clear that she probably killed a prostitute." I laugh at how ridiculous this sounds. Whatever the detectives are trying to do isn't working. You can make anything out of a stupid poem. Even so, the next paragraph might be of help.

"The first poem seems to express death and sadness in a relationship in which the man and the woman were in love but something changed drastically," Michelle Fambrough, a psychologist in Bellevue, Washington, wrote. "My interpretation is that possibly the man decides to kill his lover. Or kill himself because he's heartbroken after losing the love of his life. The scene is very dark, but I wonder if somehow he finds peace, knowing he no longer has to suffer."

Next she shares her opinion about the second poem: "The title seems to mean you don't have to keep allowing the same pain in your life—as in relationships, where you accept the suffering in order to stay with someone. Because you love them, you're willing to go through it over and over. Even though you're miserable. The poem, I think, is written by Brent, whose name appears at the bottom of the poem. He's expressing the pain he feels after a bad breakup and how the breakup affected him. He could be talking about what he did to cause the breakup by sleeping around. Afterward, he realizes he made bad decisions, and he regrets what he did. Now the pain and guilt weigh heavily on him. He thinks he can make her understand how hurt he is, and they can start over. They find each other and realize nothing will ever change. They're both in too much pain to be together again."

The newspaper also posted Michelle's interpretation on the third poem: "I think the picture of the wolf depicts someone on the prowl, always looking for more. Greedy and never satisfied. The poem seems to say they aren't happy with only a little—they want it all. Even to the point of taking what doesn't belong to them, without remorse or guilt or shame. And the more they get, the more they want. A little is never enough. The more dissatisfied they are, the more their need increases to just take it all. They keep trying to satisfy their hunger but never will. So they'll always be on the prowl to take whatever they want. As much as they want."

I feel like jumping out of my seat and slow clapping. Hopefully this psychologist is right. If so, we can track down Brent, whoever the hell he is, and get to the bottom of this. Perhaps he's the guy who took Lexy to Deception Pass Bridge.

My phone rings, and an unknown number flickers on the screen.

"Hi," I say. There's silence. "Hello?" Someone clears their throat on the other end. "Can you hear me?" I ask.

"Hi," a woman says.

"Who's this?"

"It's me. Don't tell Craig I called."

"Who?"

"Martha."

"Oh, what is it?"

"They received the results…from Lexy's car." She sniffs, and my mouth turns sour.

"Did they disclose anything to you?"

"They found Logan's DNA in the car."

There's a pause. "And?"

"With Craig's."

Another pause. "There must be some explanation for that," I say, ignoring the chills slithering down my spine.

"They found Logan's blood on the backseat of the car." My face goes slack. I stop breathing. "It doesn't look good, Ella. I'm scared."

A few seconds of silence pass. "All right. Don't say anything to Craig. I'll take care of it," I say, and I hear her gasping for air, sobbing. "Come on…I've known him for many years. He's not part of this, okay?"

"Hope not," she replies, then suddenly says, "I need to go. He just pulled into the driveway."

The phone goes dead.

Danielle Esplin

Evening

I turn down the radio. It's everywhere. The news crews have jumped back onto the story, making ridiculous assumptions, driving my nerves through the roof. I don't want Lorraine to hear these new developments from anyone other than me. I need to tell her as soon as possible.

I called the day-care center, told them I'd be late, then offered some extra money to the woman on the other end of the line. She reminded me that it's the Fourth of July, so I doubled the amount.

I swing the car into a parking spot and run up to the front desk at Westbridge Hospital.

"I need to see my sister," I say.

"And she is…?" the receptionist asks in a flat tone. Her hands seem heavy as she turns the pages of a document.

"Lorraine…Lorraine Davis." She widens her eyes, glancing at the nurse sitting next to her. "One second, please," she says, and disappears around the corner.

I turn to the nurse, whose fingers are curled up as though they're mimicking a spider's legs, dancing across the keyboard. "What's going on?" I ask.

"Please take a seat, ma'am," she insists.

"What the hell's going on?" My stomach tightens. "Can I go?"

"Go where?" She stops typing, eyeing me.

"To my sister's room."

"Ma'am, you need to sit down," she says.

I turn around and stare at my feet. Strangers glare at me from their seats. The tension thickens in the air. My mouth dries. *What's going on? What aren't they telling me?* I take two steps toward the metal bench, fretting, and then I take off. The nurse screams for me to come back. Her chair darts across the floor as she jumps to her feet to inform security. I run to Lorraine's room, jostling through the hallway. My feet strike the floor to the rhythm of my heart, which beats against my chest. The farther I run, the quieter it gets, and the antiseptic smell grows stronger.

Panting, I stumble over the threshold of the door. No one's here. I turn around and peer down the hallway. "Where's my sister?" I bawl, swinging my head from side to side. "Where is she!" I yell, sending shrieks down the bare walls of the hospital.

"*Where is she?*"

Lexy

Saturday, February 28, 2015

Evening - 4 Months Before Disappearance

I decided to take Roy up on his offer, so here I am sitting at his small dinner table with a feast before me. His brother, Dean, whom I haven't seen in years, is out of town.

For the first time, I'm getting a good look at their place. It's a well-appointed apartment with large windows, welcoming the little sun Seattle offers. Spacious, bigger than I remember.

I quickly look down at my hands, which are resting on my lap, before he can see I'm impressed that this frat boy somehow turned into a successful man. Or he's just crashing on his brother's high-end Bugatti sofa. Could he have changed from the boy who always had to do the most shocking things to impress his friends? Is he more responsible now? Did his priorities change? For some reason, I doubt they did—well, maybe a little; I can't tell.

"Whiskey?" he asks, bobbing the bottle in the air.

"No, thanks."

"You just said no to whiskey?"

"I know what I said." I look up at him, and he turns away.

"Since when?"

"A while ago. Grew tired of it."

"Hmm. What would you like then?"

"Water." I don't want to get drunk around him. Not anymore.

"Water it is," he says, then holds a glass underneath the tap. I stare at my handbag, wondering if I should call Wayne and leave, but he thinks I'm at Vicky's place—well, at her host family's house. I told him we were going to the movies and I'd be switching my phone off. I made a mental note to turn it back on within the next three hours.

"So we didn't get to speak much last time," Roy says, and he pauses to cast me a smirk. "How are you doing?"

"I'm good," I say, as he sits across from me at the table. "I kind of like my new job. Sometimes I get a bit overwhelmed, but I've always liked a challenge."

"Yeah, I remember," he says, and our eyes meet. He gazes at me until I break eye contact.

"Anyway…how long have you been here?" I ask, faster than intended.

His nostrils flare as he chuckles. "Oh, come on…you know how long I've been here."

I bite down on my smile, and he grinds some pepper on his steak. I remain silent, my foot tapping the air beneath the table.

"So…" he says. "Are you seeing anyone?"

My eyes scan his face, moving in a triangle along his perfect features, his slightly protruded jaw, and deep-green eyes. "Yeah, I am."

He holds my gaze. "So why are you here then?"

My body suddenly tenses; I'm confused by his intentions. "Just curious, you know, how your cooking is." I poke the steak with my fork. "Since you've never made me dinner in the two years we…kind of dated." I smirk.

"Is it better than your boyfriend's cooking?"

"No," I say with a firm tone, and he takes a sip of his whiskey, wagging his eyebrows as he disregards my opinion. "Listen," I tell him, "I just want to say I totally agree with you. What happened last week was a mistake. We shouldn't have done it. I mean…I should never have left Claret with you. I was drunk." I search his face for any hints of regret, but I can't pounce.

"Yeah, me too. Had way too much."

"Good. I'm glad we can agree on something," I say, and he laughs.

"So…we're good?"

"Yeah…I think so," I say, but I know it's a lie, and he knows that too.

Lorraine

Monday, March 16, 2015

Morning - 3 ½ Months Before Disappearance

My heart hammers in my throat. My chest heaves rapidly, and I'm panting. I'm not sure if it's nostalgia or trepidation, but the very thought of it makes me quiver. I've been dreaming the same dream since Craig messaged me three weeks ago.

Every time my phone vibrates, my soul flutters. I'm like a teenager on a first date again, when the little things took my breath away.

In my dream, I relive the day I realized my marriage was over, beyond repair. It's like my mind is trying to remind me that Craig isn't good for me, in an attempt to keep me from running to him.

One Saturday morning, I woke up to an empty bed. Craig was nowhere to be seen. A short while later, I dropped Logan off at a friend's house. When I came home, Craig still hadn't returned. He said he'd be back the night before. He met up with an old college friend who recently moved to Seattle. I became worried and called him, but it went straight to voice mail. Craig returned home two hours later, dressed in the clothes he'd left in.

"Where were you?" I asked him.

"Out with Dave. I told you."

"You also told me you'd be back before midnight." I stood in the kitchen, staring at him as he placed his keys on the table. "So did something happen?" I asked, waiting for a reasonable explanation.

"No, just had a good night out," he said. "I crashed at Dave's place. Sorry for not coming back earlier." He paused as he raised his head to look at me for the first time. "You're all dressed up," he said, gimlet eyed. "Where are you going?"

"To a party," I said, and a dagger twisted in my heart.

"Whose?"

"It's my birthday, Craig." I tried to force a smile, but I couldn't. Instead, I grimaced, my lip trembling. He didn't even look me in the eye. He dropped his head, staring at his chukka boots.

"I'm joking," he said, his hands up. I knew he was lying, and he'd forgotten about my birthday, because he was supposed to drive me to my party, the one I'd organized for myself. He rubbed a hand over his dark stubble and expelled a sharp breath. I stormed out to the car. He didn't even try to follow me. He just stood there, watching me leave.

At the party, my face flushed a cerise red when our friends asked where Craig was. I kept making excuses. "Oh, he had a crisis at work," I lied. "He'll be here soon." They suspiciously nodded then changed the subject. He showed up at the last minute, glancing at me from time to time.

The entire night I felt like crying. I wanted to scream. I wanted him to see the pain he caused me, to *see* me. After too many beers, we left the party, and he apologized at home. As he held me tightly, I broke down in tears. I felt invisible, worthless, like a ghost sharing his bed.

The next morning, I snatched his phone as he took a shower. I scanned through his messages as fast as I could. There were a few business-related texts, and then I paused when I saw an unknown number. At first I thought it might be work related. The message read: "Meeting at Thornton Office 3 at 4 p.m." As I scrolled through the thread, I knew that it was over between us, that I'd never trust him again.

I gaped as I read the messages:

> I told him. Have you told her?

Craig replied:

> No, not yet. I will, soon. Are you okay? I can't wait to be with you. Like I said, I had no idea what love was until I met you. Just remember, all this will be worth it, I promise.

At first I couldn't feel the hurt that would soon haunt me, but my world came to a stop. *Why am I not good enough for him?* I thought. *What could I have done differently?* My hands went slack, dropping his phone to the floor. The surge of the shower water ebbed, and the curtain rattled on the metal tube as he drew it aside. His footsteps closed in on me, and I remained silent. My heart shattered as he went on with his day, pretending as though he'd done nothing wrong.

My dream always ends there. Mostly I wake up with a heaviness in my chest; sometimes my cheeks are wet. I haven't seen Craig since I told him about my cancer four months ago. I've been trying my best to avoid him because I can't face another day with him in sight.

Wednesday, March 18, 2015
Afternoon

The drizzle of rain taps on the window, waking me up. I glance at the clock—I've been sleeping for three hours. The fatigue is getting worse by the day. I had my first radiation treatment yesterday, which lasted ten minutes. "You won't smell, feel, or see it," the oncologist said. He made me sign a form that confirmed that I'd received information about treatment options and that I was consenting to undergo radiation therapy. This basically tells them, "Yes, I understand there's no guarantee that the treatment will work." Well, at least I'm not nauseous yet.

I take my journal from the nightstand. I want to write, but I know it'll only upset me. The oncologist warned me about aphasia, a language disorder that might affect my ability to communicate, due to the tumor in my occipital lobe. He said I can try to prevent it by reading, but he can't guarantee anything.

As I flick through the pages of my journal, my face breaks into a smile. I'm glad I documented parts of my life. I'm at a point in life where things like this matter, since it seems I don't have much time left to regret the decisions I've made. Lately I've been evaluating everything as if it's my last day on earth. *See, you made a good decision when you donated a thousand dollars to the Seattle Children's Home instead of buying Logan more toys.* And: *Now you can appreciate not taking a second job. You filled that time with precious memories of your son, time you never thought would run out this fast.*

I don't have many regrets, except for Craig. I don't regret marrying him at all, but I regret not trying hard enough. I did the "normal wife" thing. A year into my divorce, I sat down and thought about our time together. I realized I didn't do enough. Yes, I cooked him dinner, cleaned the house, spent nights waiting for him when he worked late, but I did nothing *extra*. It became a boring routine. If only I'd spiced things up. Yes, he didn't really try either, and I don't blame myself for our divorce, but I certainly played my part in it.

I decide not to read my journal, and place it back on the nightstand. My phone's screen illuminates. I grab it and feel foolish for being disappointed. The message is from Robert, not Craig.

He wants to drop off some clothes for Sam. It's about time he spent some money on his son—that's *if* he didn't get the clothes from friends or family. Something tells me he didn't buy them, but I guess that's the least of my worries.

Ella

Saturday, July 4, 2015
Evening - 8 Days After Disappearance

The security guard dashes around the corner.

"Ma'am, if you fail to return to the waiting area, I'll have to call the police." His flawless dark skin contrasts with the white wall; his eyes and teeth appear almost luminous.

He squeezes my upper arm as he leads me back to the reception area. "I need to see my sister," I say, as we scuffle down the hallway. "Can someone please tell me where she is?" I don't recognize my voice; it's trembling.

"Oh, wow. You really do air about me," a voice behind me says, and I swing around. *Care—it's care.* Lorraine laughs, her eyes creasing as she watches me from her wheelchair.

I swallow the knot in my throat and manage a smile. "I was just petrified that I'll be stuck with Sam for the rest of my life," I say and wink. The guard lets go of my arm but still keeps his eyes on me.

"I'm coming home," she says, gesturing for me to follow her to the corner of the reception area, away from all the bustle. "You need to come to terms with this…with my illness."

"Don't say that." There's silence. I hold her gaze. We're not joking anymore. After all these months, it's starting to set in. "Why are you coming home?" I ask.

Lorraine doesn't reply; instead, she gives me a sad smile, and I stand here as reality stares me in the eyes. I feel powerless, hopeless…broken.

Sunday, July 5, 2015
Morning

I've been waiting for more than forty minutes. I've scrolled through the same magazine twice, checked my Facebook news feed, judged everyone around me, and gone to the bathroom. As I prepare to leave, the oncologist's door opens.

"Miss Jensen," Dr. Rowe says, his shoes curving down the threshold, his silver hair neatly styled in a backward wave. "Sorry for the wait."

I walk up to him, and I realize how short he is. "Yeah, I have things to do."

"Well, then, let's get started," he says, shambling to his desk. His chair rolls over the carpet, and he sits down in front of his computer. "How can I help you today?"

"I came to ask about my sister, Lorraine Davis."

He slants his chair back, leaving some space between his tiny bulging stomach and the table.

"I have written consent," I say, realizing he's resisting my request. A few days ago, I asked Lorraine to write a letter stating that he can disclose any medical information to me, just in case.

"You're reading my mind," he says, as I slide the piece of paper toward him. "Just let me get her records…give me a minute."

I take out my notebook and pen to make notes. Dr. Rowe glances at it as he runs his fingers along some files stacked horizontally inside a cabinet.

"What do you want to know exactly?" he asks.

"About her overall health, her latest neurological test results."

"All right," he says, holding up a file. "Got it." He sits down in his chair, pushing his glasses up his nose. "I've been informed that she went home." He peers at me over the rim of his spectacles, "with a home-health aide, Tessa Sharpe."

"Yes."

"If you have any problems with her, let me know, and I'll replace her with someone else." I want to laugh, but then I realize he's not joking.

"So far we're doing well," I say. "She arrived early this morning…which is good." I hate it. I'm going to have to let her in at 7:00 a.m. every morning. I would have preferred that she'd come at 9:00 a.m., at the earliest.

"And she stays till five. Am I right?"

"Yes."

"Good. So how do you want me to put it?"

"What do you mean?" I ask. He arches his eyebrows toward the document in his hand. I shrug. "Just…say it."

"You sure?"

"Yes. I need to know…I need to understand."

"There's nothing we can do for your sister, Miss Jensen."

"I know that."

Dr. Rowe holds my stare for a few seconds before his eyes slowly glide back to the report. "Lorraine's latest neurological test was performed a few days ago. Her vision, language, and perception—her judgment skills—have severely diminished."

I take a deep breath. "So she's not a reliable witness?" I ask.

"No, reliable is exactly what she's not."

"Can this change her behavior? Make her do…dangerous things?"

He nods. "Yes, it most certainly can. If it already has…well, that's something I can't help you with," he says, clarifying that he knows Logan and Lexy are missing and that he's been watching the news. Perhaps Aliya or Eric already asked him these questions. Maybe that's why they're suspicious of Lorraine.

"Is it possible she might have seen things that aren't there?"

"Yes, with a tumor as large as hers in the occipital lobe, it's possible she's had hallucinations."

I shuffle in my chair, my hand unsteady as I write my notes. "Can I come back if I have more questions?"

"Of course. I believe we'll see more of each other."

"What's that supposed to mean?"

"Well…" He opens his mouth as though he wants to say something, but then he closes it just as fast.

"You think we'll have a court case." I sigh. "Jesus, my nephew might still be out there…alive."

"I hope that's the case," he says, fiddling with a pen on his desk. "Your sister is a strong woman." He clears his throat. "A couple of the nurses told me she's been studying hard to keep herself going…or at least she's trying."

"Studying?"

"I told her to exercise her brain. Anything that stimulates the brain will help, like reading, solving math problems, or playing sudoku."

"I haven't seen her do anything like that."

"Well," he says, "just make sure she continues with those exercises. They won't do her any harm."

"One more thing," I say before I get to my feet. "Lorraine said she heard Lexy and Logan drive off in the Honda CR-V. When I told her they located the car in Seahurst Park, she said the last time she checked, the car was still parked in the driveway. Does she have any memory loss?"

"That's possible, but you should consider that she's going through a traumatic event. This might be her way of coping."

"By making up stories?"

Dr. Rowe squints at the ceiling, his head bobbing slightly from side to side. "If you want to put it like that…sort of…yes. But it's highly likely that she's not aware of it."

I nod, realizing he has nothing more to offer. I move toward the door and pivot around on my heels. "Thanks, Dr. Rowe," I say belatedly.

"Call me whenever you need me," he replies, and I leave not knowing who or what to believe.

Afternoon

I bang my fist on the front door. Martha drove past me a few minutes ago, probably running some errands, so it's the perfect time to confront Craig.

On my way here, I worked myself up. Every day that passes makes it harder for me to believe that Logan is still alive. The blood evidence on the seat made me lose hope. I told Tessa that Lorraine's not allowed to watch TV or read the newspaper. At least not today. I don't know how to break the news to her; I don't know what to say.

Craig opens the door. "What the fuck, El? I was taking a nap." His hair is tousled, pointing in different directions.

I stride past him to the living room. "We need to talk."

He wipes a hand over his face. "What is it?"

"Your DNA was found in Lexy's car…and don't you lie to me about this."

"I know. I handled it."

"What?"

"With the detectives."

"What do you have to say for yourself, Craig?"

"It's quite obvious. I've driven her car."

"Why?"

"She works for me!"

"She works for Lorraine. My sister provided the car."

"And I paid Lexy for the hours at my house," he says. "You think I didn't spend a dime on Logan? I made sure Lexy got paid whenever Lorraine was struggling financially."

"Why would you do that?"

"Because it's the right thing to do."

"Since when do you give a flying fuck about doing the right thing?"

He clenches his teeth. "Listen, Sam is innocent, and so is Logan. I'll pay Lexy if it means my son will benefit from it. Not that you'd understand, you motherless fuck."

My face falls slack as my body goes numb. I take a step forward, and I can almost feel his skin against mine. "I'll find out what you did, *Craig*," I snarl.

"Well, good fucking luck. There's nothing to find."

"Is that so?" I ask, letting the question hang in the air as I glare at him. "We'll see."

"Yeah, we'll see," he says. "Now get out of my house."

Evening

"Any progress?" I ask. For the first time since I met her, Aliya is wearing a dash of makeup, covering the signs of fatigue, weakness. Her eyes move sluggishly across the room. For most people, the Fourth of July is fun—I guess not so much for the police.

"I told you we'd call," she says, falling into her ergonomic chair.

"But you didn't. I had to hear from Martha about Craig's DNA being in the car and that you found my nephew's blood on the backseat."

She sighs. "We're not intentionally withholding information from you, Miss Jensen. We can't inform everyone at once when we learn something new. You're not an immediate relative of Logan or Lexy. We aim to apprise *them* first."

"Did you tell Lorraine?" I ask, straightening myself in the chair.

"No, you asked us to take it slow with her."

I expel a sharp breath, my shoulders dropping with relief. "Thanks," I say. "I'll tell her tonight…or tomorrow."

Aliya starts to organize her desk, not looking me in the eye. "We got some information about Lexy's lawyer visit," she says.

I lean forward. "You talked to the lawyer?"

"Yes. All I can say is that he specializes in immigration law. The rest is confidential."

My eyebrows lower, creating a definite line between them. "An immigration lawyer? Why?"

"Perhaps she wanted to get married," she says, piling papers in her drawer.

"To whom? Wayne said she was 'freakin crazy' when I bumped into him the other day. Certainly not to him?"

"That's all I can tell you, Miss Jensen."

"Why did Wayne say that?"

Our eyes lock for a moment, and then she glances at the door, making sure no one's listening. "It's typical relationship shit," she says.

"Nothing serious?"

"Well, every ex-girlfriend is 'crazy' in their ex-boyfriend's opinion."

"True. Except this is a possible homicide case. So is—or was—Lexy dangerous? Was it serious?"

She flicks her hand in the air, slightly irritated. "She apparently made some serious threats."

"Toward whom?"

"Wayne."

"Only him?"

She stares at the door again. "No, toward others too, but that's enough for now."

"Yes, of course," I say, contemplating whether I should pry for more. But Aliya is a woman who'll give snippets of information until you push her too far. I stand up but then pause at the door. "Next time you call me," I say, pointing at her. She frowns, not seeming too pleased by my comment, and then I leave.

Lexy

Monday, March 23, 2015
Morning - 3 Months Before Disappearance

I stare at my cupped hand. I can throw the Zoloft into my mouth and be back at square one, or I can clench my fist, crumbling the pill into pieces.

I made so much progress—I was halfway off my antidepressants—but after I saw Roy, my psyche started to fall apart. Lately I've been tossing and turning in bed, wrestling with my duvet, frustrated at my inability to fall asleep. Not to mention how much I hate getting up in the morning as I drag my feet across the carpet.

Roy's pulling back. Again. He said it's not a good idea to see each other as much as we have been, which was four times after we had dinner at his place three weeks ago. We did nothing friends wouldn't have done. We didn't kiss or even hug when we said good-bye. It was strictly platonic. He wouldn't even touch me with a fucking jumbo breaker bar.

I avert my eyes from my hand and toss the entire pill onto my tongue. The bitterness seeps down my throat as I swallow a mouthful of water. I pinch my lips tightly to keep them from trembling, and then suddenly a wave of anger sheathes me.

Evening

Robert came over this afternoon; his beard is even longer than before. I asked Lorraine if I could get off work earlier. She couldn't really say no—she needs me, and she doesn't want to lose me—so I took a chance, and she said yes. I sent Wayne a text saying I'd be at Vicky's place. He replied and sarcastically asked if I was asking his permission to visit my friend. I realised how senseless it was to report to him. *Oh, I'm on my way to the grocery store.* Just because I'm on my way to another man. *Idiot.*

I made sure no one saw me and that he was alone. When he opened the door, I pressed myself against him.

"What the hell are you doing?" he asked, squinting. I didn't say a word; instead, I smirked. At first he resisted, but he gave in as my hands worked their way down his waist and into his pants. He looked desperate, hungry, deprived from sex. I was rejuvenated by my adrenaline, too excited to think straight. *No man will fucking resist me,* I thought.

I left with my head high, my lipstick smudged, my hair dishevelled. The night flew by, and now my eyes track down the crown moulding as I lie in bed. My senses scratch the back of my consciousness as I think about my day. I felt elated, but now I'm overwhelmed with guilt. I question my actions, why I'm doing what I do. Why I'm capable of cheating in the first place. I never thought I'd reach this point. I always swore to myself that I'd never cheat on my partner. I believed that—I honestly did. *I have to tell Wayne about Roy*, I think. I just don't know how and when. But then again, some things are better left unsaid.

I turn on my side, searching for my memo page on my phone. Whenever I don't write in my journal, I make some notes on my device. After I feel better, I delete them. It's therapeutic, and many online articles advise people to do this. To write my feelings and thoughts as straightforwardly on paper as I do on my phone would be risky. It's like carving the words into stone for everyone to see. Perhaps if I had a paper shredder, I'd consider that.

Lorraine

Friday, April 3, 2015
Afternoon - 2 ¾ Months Before Disappearance

"Uh-oh," the cashier says.

"What?" I ask.

"Your card was declined."

"Try it again," I insist. My hands rummage through my purse, searching for my other debit card, but I know that's also wiped out clean.

The slip prints. My heart quickens. Strangers peer at me from behind magazines while others glance over their shoulders. The cashier holds up the receipt. "Sorry," she says, staring at me. I manage to force a smile.

"Must be a mistake," I say, lowering my head, but I know it's not. I forgot to check my balance, and right here and now it's become official: I've run out of money. My skin tightens as my face flushes. I glance at the shopping cart filled with shopping bags before turning my head back to the young lady behind the register. "Now what?"

"You can just leave the cart here. We'll put everything back," she says, too loud for my liking. I stand there for a few more seconds as she waits for me to leave. The man behind me starts to unpack his shopping cart, inching to take my place in front of the cash register. I will myself to move, and with my chin tucked to my chest, I hurry outside, eyeing my fringed sandals.

I slam the car door behind me and take a deep breath. "Everything will be okay," I say, looking in the rearview mirror, but I know I'm not fooling anyone, including myself.

I turn my key and nervously gaze at the gas gauge. The indicator slides up forty-five degrees. That'll have to do for the rest of the month, and then I giggle as my eyes well up with tears, because I imagine Ella saying, "Or else your au pair will need to push your car around too."

Danielle Esplin

Evening

My phone rests on my palm as I contemplate what to do; there aren't many options left. My medical leave is maxed out for the year, and my boss said they'll have to let me go. I don't blame them, because it's been three months since I was supposed to return to work. I told them about my diagnosis, and they kept paying me, but this month I didn't get a notification stating that I'd received my monthly paycheck.

I think about the kids, about covering Logan's sports fees. I think about Robert, who's not contributing financially. The cost of being a single mother is awful, but the cost of being a single mother with cancer is even worse. Gas, childcare, formula, insurance, medical bills, clothes, and then the damn Internet that Logan can't live without. It's time for Craig and Robert to step up because I can't do this any longer, not on my own.

I phone Craig. The familiar chime of a call going through reverberates through the receiver.

"I need to talk to you," I say, once he answers.

"About what?" A muffled whisper in the background distracts me. Probably Martha. *Nosy bitch.* "What is it?"

"I need your help," I begin, "financially…with Logan. I can't keep up anymore."

There's a pause. "Sure. I mean…of course." The whispers grow imperceptible. "Sorry for not offering earlier. The treatments must be expensive." I hold the phone away from my face, looking at the receiver as though it's a foreign object, taken aback by his tone of concern.

I bring the phone back to my ear. "Yes…especially with Logan's football fees and school expenses."

Another pause. "Well," he says, suddenly retreating, "I'll have to discuss it with Martha first."

I suppress the need to snort. "Let me know then," I tell him, wondering why she has a say in this. Perhaps she *is* there with him, yapping away and telling him what to say before she throws one of her hissy fits.

We say our good-byes, and he hangs up. I call Robert, but he doesn't answer, so I leave him a voice mail. Not that I'm expecting anything to come from him, and I sure as hell don't have the means—or energy—to go to court over this.

Saturday, April 4, 2015
Evening

Craig got back to me this morning. He said he'll pay Lexy's salary since she does a lot for Logan. He also offered to pay for her gas whenever she needs to take Logan to school or football practice. Robert wired two hundred dollars into my account after he called me and said there's no guarantee he'll be able to help within the next few months, which made me laugh a little. At least it's *something*.

Now I'm standing in front of the mirror with my fingers curled through the openings of a pair of scissors—my hair looks hideous. The little curls I had left turned into a scraggly frizz. Without giving it a second thought, I grab a chunk, yank it down, and glide the scissors across my hair. The blades start to *snip snip snip*. I might as well stab myself in the heart with them; that's how much it hurts to see my dark curls drop into the white sink. A teardrop slides down my cheek, tingling my face. I saw this on TV before—people who lose their hair during radiation. I heard and read about it, but nothing could have prepared me for how it feels to cut off my hair.

I drop the scissors as I gaze at myself. My face appears rounder with my new hairstyle: a bob. I guess that's a good thing, since I've lost too much weight lately. Suddenly I feel a bit better, almost proud for getting the job done. As I fork my fingers through the remnants of hair, my phone chimes in my pocket. It's a text from Craig.

> Hi, Ray. I've been thinking about your request, and I immediately felt guilty for not offering to help earlier. I'm quite worried about you. This made me think…well, I miss you. Hope to hear from you soon.

My heart stops. My breathing too. *What?* A part of me wants to kill him for telling me this after all these years, after all the days I waited for him to crawl back to me or just acknowledge my existence. I delete the message, pounding my fingers against the screen, and just as I want to erase his number, I realize I need it for Logan's sake. I pace back and forth in the bathroom then bring myself to a halt, hovering over the sink. I raise my head, staring in the mirror, and then I catch myself wondering if Craig would like my new hairstyle.

Monday, April 6, 2015
Afternoon

I've been fighting the urge to reply to Craig's text. It's been two days since he said he misses me, and I just received another message from him.

> I understand that this might seem a bit strange. I want to speak to you in person. Do you want to meet up tonight at Marymoor Park around 7?

My forehead wrinkles as I rub the back of my neck. I delete the message, determined not to let him disturb me, but old memories manage to occupy my brain, reminiscences of the days when we'd go for Sunday-morning strolls at Marymoor Park. Another activity we used to enjoy as a family that ceased many years before our divorce. Craig always walked in front of me, and I'd stare at his back as a warm feeling filled me from within. I imagine him now, standing there among the trees as he stares at me with those blue-gray eyes, his back curved after all these years, wondering what he wants to tell me.

My eyes rest on my phone's screen for a few minutes, contemplating what I could lose if I agree to meet with him, and I figure nothing. *What can he possibly do to hurt me any more than he already has?* I think, and then I send him a message back, agreeing to see him tonight.

A loud thump grabs my attention, making me jerk my head up from my phone. Sam starts to bawl, his voice echoing down the hallway. I hurry out of the bathroom and into his room, where Lexy is bouncing him in her arms, twisting her torso from side to side as she kneels.

"What happened?" I ask, a little too desperately.

"He sat up. I turned to get his bottle, and he fell sideways. I'm sorry." Sam's face scrunches into a ball as he projects his wails into her ears. I straighten my arms out to take him. Wide-eyed, Lexy hands him over then leans back onto her palms, resting on the carpet.

I tilt Sam's head back, examining him. There's a red line across the side of his forehead. My eyes meet Lexy's, hers now piercing into me. "Leave," I demand, but she doesn't move.

"Bu—"

"Leave!" I repeat, and she scrambles to her feet, stumbling over the threshold as she exits the room.

Evening

I run my fingers through my hair and carefully pull at the strands in an attempt to cover my scars. I have more makeup on than usual, and I'm wearing clothes I thought I'd never fit into again. Many years ago, I put my jeans and favorite tops—the ones I'd grown too big for—in a box. I wanted to get rid of them, but then thought I'd keep them as a reference for days like this. Now I know I'm as thin as I was when I moved to Seattle, when Craig and I were madly in love. Perhaps even thinner, since I need a belt to tighten my size-six jeans around my hips.

I haven't seen Lexy since our fallout this afternoon. Her car isn't parked in the driveway. I guess I could have handled the situation better. I mean, I slammed Logan's fingers twice in the car door when he was a boy, and Craig spilled hot water on his foot; he still has a little scar from it. Okay, Logan *kicked* the cup out of Craig's hand, and I almost had a heart attack when the cup went flying.

I turn Sam's head to look at his face—there's no scar or bruises. It was only a little bump. Lexy is, after all, working overtime, which is my fault. I'll buy her a chocolate and some flowers to make it up to her.

I pull a sweater over Sam's head and place his tiny feet in his new shoes, the ones Robert brought over the other day. He smiles at me as I strap him into the car seat, and then I plant a kiss on his cheek.

The engine roars to life as I turn the key. I take a deep breath as I glance at myself in the rearview mirror. On my way to the park, thoughts swirl through my mind. *What's on his mind? What's so important? Why now?* My hands leave damp imprints on the wheel as I swing my car into a parking spot.

I bite my bottom lip as I look around. There's an elderly couple walking on the footpath ahead, with a Boston terrier not far behind them. Two teenagers are tossing a Frisbee across the field, while an old lady sits beneath a tree on a wooden bench, reading a book. Craig, however, is nowhere to be seen. *Did he say the east, south, or main entrance?* I want to text him, but I know better.

I wait and wait. Twenty minutes pass, then thirty, and before I know it, another twenty. I stare at my phone's screen—there's no text, voice mail, or apology. I glance at Sam, whose snoring the evening away, peacefully nestled among his blankets. My arms tingle as I try to keep my composure, as I try to keep my leg from jumping. I scratch the back of my head, then I grab a handful of thinned-out hair, clenching my fist. I catch myself almost making excuses for Craig. *Maybe he's stuck in traffic, maybe Martha won't let him leave*, but then I decide, *Fuck this.*

I put my car in gear and speed off. My skin tightens, and a feeling of vertigo overpowers me. The drive to Craig's feels like a few seconds, not the ten minutes it's supposed to. I grab Sam's car seat and head up the steps.

Without hesitation, I swing the door wide open, bashing the handle against the wall. A tremor shoots up my arm as Sam jolts awake. My eyes glide to the rear of the house, where Martha jumps up from the couch and takes a step back. They have people over, and there's my damn au pair too, drinking wine with *her*. And another traitor, Dorlean, sitting next to Carmen, motionless.

I walk toward the living area, and then I remember: it's Craig's fortieth birthday. He's sitting on the edge of the couch, clutching a beer. I glance at Sam, who's staring up at me, not making a sound. I place the car seat on the floor next to me. Everything in me tells me to back down, but instead I stride right up to Craig.

"Why the hell are you doing this to me?" I ask, pointing a finger in his face.

"Wha…what are you talking about?" He gets to his feet and forces a chuckle. "Let's talk somewhere else, okay?" He grabs my upper arm, but I pull away.

"No! I'm done playing your fucking game! It's time these people know who you really are." He freezes, bug-eyed, a suppressed grimace etched into his face.

Martha dashes around the couch and into the kitchen. "If you don't leave right now," she says, "I'm calling the police."

"That would be a pity," I say, staring at Craig, "because I think you'd love to hear what I have to say."

His eyebrows narrow. "Listen, Lorraine," he says, almost whispering. "You're losing it. You're completely delusional."

The phone receiver hovers in midair, tightly in Martha's grasp. She seems unsure what to do as she stares at me over the kitchen counter, always over the fucking counter.

"You're just denying it because *she's* here," I say, pointing at Martha, and then I turn to her. "Do you really think he wouldn't cheat on you?" She says nothing, and the house fills with an intense silence. "He texted me that he misses me, that he wants to see me." Her fingers tighten over the phone receiver, the tips turning a pale yellow. She slowly lowers her arm to the counter, breaking eye contact as she drops her head.

"Honey, that's not true," Craig says, his thumb and index finger curling around the bottle neck, his palms in the air.

"Lorraine, show me these messages," Martha says, ignoring him.

My eyes bounce around the room as my heart quickens. "Well…I deleted them."

Someone behind me chuckles, and the entire room fills with a snide buzz. "Jesus, Lorraine…you need help!" Craig roars, his voice almost breaking into an uncomfortable snicker.

"You have to believe me," I tell Martha, but she turns and leaves the kitchen, disappearing around the corner, away from the mockery.

Lexy

Monday, April 6, 2015
Evening - 2 ¾ Months Before Disappearance

She's standing there, in the middle of the living room, like a fool. Craig's body is stiff. He smiles at his friends, but his eyes don't correspond.

"Okay, Lorraine. You can leave now," he says, flicking his hand in the air like he's trying to get rid of a dog. Logan drops his head as though he wants to hide, also clutching a beer in his hand, but his mother doesn't seem to notice.

Lorraine doesn't move; instead her eyes jump from face to face, scanning the room. "Do you need a ride home?" I ask, and she jerks her head toward me.

"No," she hisses underneath her breath. Carmen gives me a forlorn look, her hand resting on Logan's back. Lorraine squints, and then she turns to grab Sam's car seat and storms out, slamming the door behind her, making my shoulders bounce.

Everyone awkwardly shuffles in their seats. Craig apologises to his friends, and then the discussion begins: how delusional you can get with a brain tumour.

"Not everything she does is a direct result of her brain tumour," I say, but I know Lorraine has changed. Over the last few weeks, her behaviour has become odd, unlike the woman I met last October.

I look at Craig from the corner of my eye. He's drinking faster, gulping down his beer. Suddenly everyone is Doctor-Know-It-All, jumping to conclusions, making assumptions. I want to believe Lorraine. Something tells me she's not lying on purpose. I really think she believes herself, but I don't think what she believes is the truth.

Ella

Monday July 6, 2015
Morning - 10 Days After Disappearance

My eyes flip open at 6:59 a.m. I drag myself out of bed and down the stairs.

There Tessa is, on the fucking dot.

"Good morning," I say, letting her in. She heads into the house like it's her own and places her bag on the kitchen table. "Lorraine's still asleep."

"I'll wake her up," she insists, flicking her scarlet hair over her shoulder. "She needs to take her medication." I scratch the back of my head, biting my lip as I watch her take out files and documents. "Don't worry. She's in good hands," she says, looking up at me, her eyes a cerulean blue.

"Tessa, Dr. Rowe told me she's been doing exercises for her brain. I've never seen her do any of that."

She pauses and clears her throat. "I think she feels embarrassed. She asked the nurses to take them out of her hospital room whenever people visited her."

"Take what out?"

"Her son's schoolbooks."

I swallow hard. "Like high-school work?"

"Yes." She leans forward, whispering. "Sometimes the nurses would leave her in her room for a few hours, and when they returned, she'd still be on the same page."

I clench my teeth.

"Apparently, she hasn't done the exercises in a long time, though. Guess she gave up."

"But she mentioned that Robert sent her a text the other day. How did she—"

"One of the nurses read them for her," she says. "Not that there were many," she continues, pursing her lips.

"What about the letter she wrote? The one stating Dr. Rowe could disclose medical information to me?"

"A nurse wrote that for her too." She frowns, and I feel ashamed for not noticing that it wasn't my sister's handwriting. I nod as she takes out two pills in a napkin. "Excuse me. I have to give these to Ms. Davis," she says, holding a fist in the air.

"Sure," I say, as Tessa walks past me and up the stairs, somehow having a built-in radar for where to go.

Afternoon

I'm meeting up with Wayne. I sent him a message on Facebook, and to my surprise, he replied. First he apologized for how he acted during our first encounter, saying he was in shock. Then he said he'd meet me inside Starbucks on Pike Street at 2:00 p.m.

Now I'm leaning forward, my arm stretched out to show him the photos of Lexy on Deception Pass Bridge.

"Hmm," he says, his lips pressed flat. "That's Roy."

"Who's that?'

"Her ex-boyfriend…or ex-ex-boyfriend."

"Who's Brent?"

"Who?"

"Brent."

"I don't know anyone named Brent." He cocks his head. "She slept with him too?"

"What? No. Not that I know of." I sigh. "Haven't you seen Lexy's poems in the newspaper?"

"I've been avoiding all types of media lately," he says. "Tired of reading about false accusations and assumptions. It's screwing with my head."

"Right. Well, maybe you should read the paper."

He tilts a white sachet of sugar into his latte. "Soy milk" is written on the side of his cup with a Sharpie. "So what's this all about? These poems, I mean."

"Lexy wrote the name 'Brent' beneath one of her poems," I say, "in her journal."

"Great. Wouldn't be surprised if she slept with him too." He falls back into the chair, his chest expanding as he inhales deeply. "She said she only slept with

Roy once." He snorts. "Pretty sure that was a lie."

"She told you about Roy?"

"Kind of…she had to after I asked her about Vicky."

"Vicky? Who's Vicky?"

"Lexy saved Roy's number in her phone as 'Vicky,' a friend she made up…I was so stupid." He rests his arm on the chair, bulging his chest out.

"What can you tell me about Carmen?" I ask him.

He raises an eyebrow. "Why? Is she in trouble?"

"No," I reply, waiting for him to say something, but he remains silent. I move my hand forward in a circle, as a way to encourage him, and the corners of his mouth pull up.

"She's Logan's girlfriend," he says. "Saw her maybe twice, not much. Why the concern?"

I hold his gaze, wondering if I should tell him, but instead I shrug. "I just figured she's a brat," I say, and he laughs.

"You're really different from your sister." He shakes his head, smiling. "Lorraine loves Carmen."

I shrug again, and then we both turn our heads to a child screaming at her mother in the corner of the shop. *Four years old? Maybe five*, I think. A tiny girl wearing a pink dress—almost like the color of her mother's face at the moment—with shiny silver shoes, stomps her feet on the floor. I get that twitchy feeling inside, the one I get when I'm annoyed, when babies scream through flights and when brats get spoiled after throwing tantrums.

I turn back to Wayne, and the urge to bring up the threats Lexy made against him deepens, but I can't do it. He'll know Aliya told me. So I keep asking questions, waiting for him to blurt it out himself.

"Did you know Lexy's pregnant?" I ask, and he swallows hard.

"No," he says, blinking fast. "It was quite a shock to hear it from the detectives."

"You think it's yours?"

"I don't know. I don't know what to think. Could be Roy's…or the Brent guy's. I try not to dwell on it."

"Do you want the baby to be yours?" I ask, and I realize I've gone too far. "Sorry…you don't have to answer that."

"Honestly"—he leans forward, resting on his elbows, fingers entwined—"no."

I say nothing; instead I just nod. The kid in the corner screams something I can't make out; her mother has turned her back to her.

"How would you feel if you knew the mother bearing your child is missing and potentially in danger?" Wayne asks.

"That's a valid point," I tell him, ashamed. I realize the conversation isn't veering toward the threats she made; perhaps it will next time, *if* we see each other again. "Listen, if you ever want to…you know, just let it out…talk about things, give me a call."

"Sure," he says, still shaken by my prying. "I mean, it seems like you know more than I do."

"I think the more we cooperate, the faster this case will get solved."

"You think it will get solved?" he asks, and I search for a hint of jest, but there's none.

"It has to, Wayne. I won't rest until I know what happened."

"Well, it's been a week and a half. I'm preparing for the worst."

I stare at the kid, who's now sitting on the floor, slamming a fist against her mother's legs, and before I can stop myself, I say, "Me too."

Evening

I peer into Lorraine's room to see if she's okay. Tessa waves good-bye to me before she heads downstairs and out the front door. The house fills with silence. I stare at Lorraine's bony hand resting on the blankets, her jaw a sharp line, destitute of fat. I wonder what she's dreaming, if she's happy there, if her world is a better place when she's asleep. Does she feel loved in her dreams? Does she dream of Logan? Or Sam? I tiptoe toward her bedside and kiss her forehead. "I'm here for you," I whisper, fighting my heartache, the pang of guilt for not coming sooner.

In the hallway, I pull the door toward me, leaving it ajar. Troubled, I lumber downstairs and into the living room.

My eyes rest on the remote control, readying myself for the evening news. I switch on the television and lower the volume. I can't remember the last time I watched anything else.

A banner flashes across the screen: "Breaking News." A woman sits in a studio, her black hair tied flat against her head. I move closer to the TV, hoping I heard her wrong, and then my throat tightens, my limbs going numb.

"The Redmond Police Department has announced a break in the case of a sixteen-year-old boy and his au pair, who have been missing since June twenty-sixth."

The scene switches from the studio to a gleaming yellow wheat field swaying in the breeze. My eyes shift to the corner of the screen, where officers are carrying a body bag.

"Investigators have confirmed that a body was found sixty miles southeast of Redmond, where the sixteen-year-old boy and au pair were last seen. Authorities are waiting for autopsy results before releasing the official identification of the victim."

I lift my hand to my mouth. I feel like screaming, but I'll wake Lorraine. I want to rush to Craig's house, but I can't leave my sister here alone. I can't even leave a note. I mean, what if she can't read it?

I grab the handset and dial Craig's number. It barely rings before he answers.

"El!" he wails.

"My God, Craig. What's going on?" The phone trembles against my ear.

"We just identified the body at the morgue. It's him. It's Logan," he says, and my hand goes slack, dropping the receiver to the floor.

Tuesday, July 7, 2015
Morning

I tossed around in bed all night. It felt cruel not to tell Lorraine, to wait for today. I asked Craig to come over. I can't do this by myself, and after all, Logan was *their* son. *Was.* God, that sounds strange. I didn't expect Martha to come too, but I guess that's the least of our worries.

Tessa tilts the kettle to pour us tea. She hasn't said much after I told her about Logan when she arrived this morning. She knows what needs to happen next: I need to tell my sister that her son is dead. Our eyes meet, and I give Tessa the nod. She walks upstairs to get Lorraine.

Martha sips at her tea, staring at nothing. Craig nervously paces the kitchen floor, his face growing pale. It still feels surreal; Logan's death hasn't sunk in yet. I'm aware that he's no longer alive, but it's like an out-of-body experience—just a nightmare—and he'll come home soon.

Lorraine walks step by step down the stairs with Tessa assisting her. She doesn't see us because she's staring at her feet, trying to focus. As she reaches the bottom, she finally looks up. Her face speaks a thousand words. She knows that the day Craig and Martha are in her kitchen, something must have happened, something seriously wrong.

Martha still stares at her cup. Craig's eyes meet Lorraine's, and my heart breaks.

"No," she says, slanting her body away from Tessa.

"I'm so sorry, Ray," I say.

"No, no, no." She belts each one louder, her hands shaking, and then her knees give out as she falls to the floor, screaming.

Craig walks over to her, slightly bending forward to see her face. With a softened gaze he kneels next to Lorraine, then he gently places his hand on her lower back. Martha still hasn't moved, while Tessa is frozen at the bottom of the steps. I turn my back on them, fighting back my tears as I stare out at the deck.

I swallow the painful lump in my throat as my sister's unrecognizable voice breaks as she screams. After a few seconds, I get myself together and turn back to face her. She's still on the floor, but now Craig is holding her tightly as her shoulders quiver in his arms.

Martha turns her head into their direction, her face blank.

"How?" Lorraine shrieks.

"We don't know," Craig says, "All we know is that he's…not with us anymore."

She looks at him for a second, and then she curls forward on his lap, sobbing.

I stare at them as Tessa presses a hand against her mouth, her neck curved downward. Martha averts her eyes, now gazing into her tea, and then my mind jumps to a practical and heuristic mode, blocking out my surroundings as I try to keep it together.

Lexy

Tuesday, April 7, 2015
Afternoon - 2 ¾ Months Before Disappearance

Last night, when I came home, Lorraine was already asleep. I dreaded coming back to work. I didn't want to see her, so this morning I tried to avoid her as best I could.

I was untangling some socks when she approached me, straightening her posture in the laundry-room doorway. "I want to apologise for yesterday," she said, looking down at me as I sat on my haunches in front of the washer.

"It's fine. I know how troubling an ex can be."

Her face lit up. "Oh, no. I'm referring to yesterday afternoon…you know, with Sam."

Taken aback, I paused, my hand dropping a sweater into the machine's drum. "Um…sure."

"I know you didn't intentionally try to hurt him," she said, swinging an arm out from behind her back, clutching a chocolate bar. "I truly feel bad about the way I acted," she continued, waiting for me to take it.

The chocolate hovered in the air for a few seconds too long before I willed myself to reach for it, trying to pretend that nothing had happened. She offered me a polite smile before she turned and left, her fingers pressed against the beige walls as she tried to keep her balance.

Lately Lorraine's like a switch, with her tumours grappling to flip her on and off, on and off. I read all about it. Friends and relatives saying, "It's not *them* speaking; it's their tumour." Loved ones trying to come to terms with the patient's odd behaviour, trying to understand and support them.

Now I'm sitting with Logan in his room, my back turned to the doorway. He's confiding in me about how his mother made him feel yesterday.

"She embarrassed me," he says, "but at the same time, I felt sorry for her. I mean…there's no way my dad told her he misses her."

"You really think that?" I ask, realising this situation has forced him to grow up faster than he has to.

"My dad never speaks about my mom. He doesn't care about her, and he has way too much pride to admit he's made a mistake…especially if it was about leaving her."

"Do you think she would've acted like this a year ago?"

"No. Never. I barely recognised her last night." He swings his long legs onto the bed.

"Your mom said something the other night. Tell me if you don't want to talk about this…"

He narrows his eyes. "What is it?"

"She said your dad hit her."

He gazes at me for a second, and then he breaks into a shameful chuckle. "Oh, wow, she's totally lost it, hasn't she?"

I can't imagine Craig beating Lorraine. I want to laugh at the thought of it, at how ridiculous it sounds, but then I feel terrible for not believing her. What if she's telling the truth? It's just hard to believe a word she says these days.

"My dad would never do that," he says, and then he falls abruptly silent.

"Well, it's common with this type of cancer to belie—"

"Hi, Mom," he says, staring an inch or two above my head. My torso swings around. My mouth opens. I want to say something, but nothing comes.

She's standing in the doorway, leaning against the casing, arms crossed. She expels a sharp breath as she snorts, curling her upper lip, and then she walks off.

Evening

I'm frozen outside Lorraine's bedroom. My chest expands as I take a deep breath. I need to release some of the tension that's been building up lately. It's starting to affect me and everyone else in her life.

I gently push the door open with a letter in my hand, one I'm about to give her. She sits on the edge of the bed, her shoulders curled forward.

Before I can speak, she says, "I hope you didn't come to apologise."

"That's exactly why I'm here."

"You shouldn't," she says. "Logan needs someone to talk to. You did the right thing."

I sigh. "We're worried about you, Lorraine. We didn't mean to speak behind your back…or hurt you."

"But you did," she says, looking up at me, her face shadowed. "But I think what really hurts me is that it's the truth…what Logan said."

"Which part?"

"That I'm different now."

"It's not your fault," I hear myself say, thinking about what I read online, that this must be extremely difficult for her.

"The thing is, yes, I'm a bit different now, but Craig did send me those messages."

"How sure are you?"

"Well…all of you think I'm crazy, and I don't know anymore. I'm starting to doubt myself," she says. "You know, sometimes when you're really hurt, it's hard not to let your pain dictate your actions. It can make you do things you never thought you would."

I say nothing, because I know she's right.

She turns her gaze to my letter. "And this?"

I sit down next to her on the edge of the mattress. "It's just…about earlier," I say, handing it over. "An apology note." She places the folded letter on her nightstand. "Why do you still love him?"

"I don't know," she says, shrugging. "I wish I could tell you. Don't you think I would've stopped if I could?"

"I guess we always want what we can't have," I say, then cringe at the cliché.

"No, I think it's more about loving someone who doesn't love you back," Lorraine says, and for a moment she makes sense.

"Kind of the same thing, don't you think?"

"I don't think so. There are lots of things I can't have that I don't want. But as soon as you love someone who doesn't even acknowledge your existence, or who doesn't reciprocate, it just makes you …"

"Go crazy?" I ask, and she bumps me with her elbow.

"Don't say that." She chuckles.

"What? Or it's just your brain tumour," I say, and I almost choke on my words.

"God, you're impolite," she replies, and then she laughs.

Wednesday, April 8, 2015
Morning

Logan plods down the stairs, gives me a polite smile, and grabs his schoolbag. "Want me to take you?" I ask, and he pinches an eye shut, shaking his head.

"Nah. I'll take the bus."

"Why the sudden interest lately?" I smirk. "Carmen on it?"

He smiles with his lips pressed flat, unwilling to answer my question. His expression slowly fades as he gazes at me, and I swear there's a hint of sadness, a cry for help. I walk up to him and extend my arms. Logan pulls me in, holding me tightly. He remains silent, his head on my shoulder. We stand like that for a few seconds, and then he steps back, giving me a slight smile, one that says, *Thank you.* He squares his shoulders in front of the door, readying himself for the morning cold. I watch him as he walks down the road, the energy in his steps drained. This boy has turned into a man…and not in a way he deserves.

Afternoon

I wash the dishes, mop the floor, change Sam's diaper, have a cup of coffee, then tuck Sam in for his nap. It's as though I'm the only one in this house, since Lorraine's hasn't been coming out of her room as much. Just as I fall back onto the couch to rest for a bit, footsteps, slower than usual, trudge down the stairs.

I peer to my right where Lorraine pours herself a glass of water, her pyjamas baggy. I wonder how she stands the cold that must be creeping up her legs. Sitting here, I contemplate whether I should follow through with my plan. Then I think of Logan, how the uncertainty must be gnawing at him, how it's affecting Craig, and ultimately me. *I need to know*, I think, even though it might seem like a selfish thing to do.

I walk into the kitchen, where she's sitting at the table. "What did you think of my letter?" I ask.

She looks up at me, her eyes circled with a chromium grey. "Oh…I completely forgot—I wanted to thank you," she says, and that's when it strikes me. The severity of it all. It's set in stone. I know now.

We hold each other's gaze. "Why would you thank me?" I ask, and I can feel her discomfort. She fakes a smile, uncertain what to do. "I wrote nasty things in there," I continue, and her neck slightly cranes as her eyes narrow. "You can't read anymore, can you?"

"How dare you test me?" she says, emphasising every word as spit sprays across the table.

"Well, there you have it." I slam my palms down, leaning forward. "There's your answer: Craig never texted you," I say, and she glares at me as though she wants to kill me.

"How dare you!" she repeats, her face flushed. "Get the hell out of my house!" she screams, as her lower lip trembles. "Get out!"

Evening

I left as fast I could. I drove Logan to Craig's, and now I'm watching Martha prepare dinner, trying to buy some time before heading back. Logan planted himself in front of the telly behind me, fiddling with a bag of chips, and Craig is out with some friends, drinking at a pub in the city.

"I don't know if this will make you feel any better, but none of us believes Craig sent her those messages."

The knife glides down as Martha cuts the meat into cubes. "I haven't spoken to him in days," she says.

"Lorraine can't read anymore," I say, but she doesn't seem fazed at all.

Martha positions a rectangular baking dish, covered with aluminium foil, in the oven. Then she turns back to me, throwing her hands in the air. "Shit!" She rubs her forehead, exhaling a long breath.

"What's wrong?"

"I forgot about my assignment."

"When's it due?" I ask, awaiting the "favour."

"Tomorrow morning." She leans forward against the counter, seeming to ruminate for a while. "Oh, sweetie, will you *please* help me out here?" I try to hide my annoyance, but before I can say anything, she says, "Will you *please* do this little favour for me?" She walks over to her bag, takes some books and papers out, then throws them onto the table. "I didn't have time to look at it much, so that'll have to do. Can you just write that draft over for me, please?"

Without waiting for an answer, Martha turns around and continues to cut the meat. She glances sideways, her head still. "How do you know Lorraine can't read anymore?" she asks.

"Well, I don't want to really get into it, but I realised she couldn't read a letter I gave her."

Martha shakes her head. "Well, that's unfortunate."

"Yeah, she's pretty mad at me. Is it okay if I stay here a little longer?"

"Of course, sweetie. Make yourself at home," she says, and she gives me a faint smile.

Ella

Wednesday, July 8, 2015
Morning - 12 Days After Disappearance

Yesterday we tried to make sense of this ordeal. Reporters were bothering us at the house at all hours, asking ridiculous questions. *How do you feel about Logan's death?* Seriously? *I'm absolutely on cloud nine—how delightful this has been. Can't wait for the next surprise!*

I send Wayne a text, letting him know I'm outside. I switch off the van's engine and stare out the window. The dilapidated apartment building is sprawled out in front of me. Wayne appears at the tiny secured entrance on the right then approaches me with a grin.

"Nice car," he says, flicking his head back, finding it amusing that I'm driving a soccer-mom van.

"Still better than yours," I say, and he mouths "ouch," then laughs. Wayne leads the way, but now all the jokes have ceased, and I follow him as silence stretches out between us.

As he opens the door to his apartment, an acrid disinfectant scent reaches my nose. His place is snug, comfortable, and spotless. The couch is perfectly parallel to the wall, his counter tops gleaming. He gestures for me to sit down on one of the barstools.

"Want a cocktail?" he asks, knowing what's coming isn't a blithe matter. I nod, and he pours me a hefty shot of vodka. He holds a bottle of cranberry juice in the air.

"Sure," I say.

"So…as you advised, I started watching the news," he says, his eyes narrowing. "I'm so sorry for your loss."

I drop my head slightly. "Do you think Lexy had something to do with this?" I ask, sitting down on the other side of the kitchen island.

"Are you asking me if I think she murdered Logan?"

"Yes."

He shakes his head. "No. She might be a bit unstable, but she's not a killer."

"Did you think she's a cheater?" I ask.

Wayne lowers his glass from his lips as he swallows. "No, but that's two very different things."

"My point is…I don't think you know her as well as you think you do."

"What would you know?" he says gruffly. "Have you even met her?"

"Yes, when Sam was born in October." The drink grows stronger with every gulp. "So if it wasn't her, who then? What do you think?"

Craig's name pops up in my mind, but I'm not ready to tell him that yet. I want to hear what he has to say.

"Could've been Roy," Wayne says.

I chuckle. "Oh, please. How lame of you to do that." My head starts to spin a little. "To…blame it on the paramour."

"You think I'd never heard of him before? Yeah, I didn't expect Lexy to cheat on me, but she mentioned Roy to me. I just thought he was in London."

"Wait," I say, finger in the air, swaying. "He's from London?"

"Yeah, and the next thing I know, he's fucking my girl." I erupt in uncomfortable laughter, the kind of laugh you give when everything is so fucked up that no other response will do it justice. "But seriously now. She told me about him, and he seemed to be a real dick," Wayne says, which makes me laugh even harder.

"I'm sorry, it's just…God…" I try to catch my breath. "Everyone has something to say about everyone. They either hate or love each other, nothing in between. No one can find any middle ground. I…I just need to drink," I say, holding my glass up.

"Wow, you're a lightweight," he says, taking the glass from me. "You can't do this now."

"Oh, come on. Just a little."

"I know it's hard, but you need to keep yourself together. You're the only sane one left in that family," Wayne says, and my smile vanishes, because I know he's right. But I always keep it together, all the time, for everyone.

I sigh. "Have you told the detectives?"

"What?"

"About the impression Lexy gave you of Roy."

"Yes, I have."

"When?"

"A few days ago," he says.

There's a pause. "It feels like the detectives are withholding information from me."

"Of course they are. They're trying to conduct a solid investigation."

"No, I don't mean like…those things. I think in general. I learned about Logan when you did…on the news."

His eyes widen. "Oh, wow." He gapes at me as I take my drink back from him.

"Something tells me there's more to this."

"Just be patient," he says, and I purse my lips.

"Well, I can't be," I tell him, and we hold each other's gaze as I swig the rest of the drink down my throat.

Evening

I bring my hand up to my temple and wince at the throbbing in my head. I curl my upper lip under my teeth, stretching my skin to relieve the tightness. For a moment I'm confused about where I am, and then I realize I'm on Wayne's couch, and he's nowhere to be seen.

In his bathroom, I cup my hands to drink some water and rinse my face. I check the time on my phone and sigh; it's 5:04 p.m. I'll be stuck in traffic on my way to Brighter Horizons, which means I'll be late—again—not to mention that Tessa will have to work overtime. I head back to the couch to grab my handbag but stop midway, almost swinging an arm at Wayne.

"Jesus!" I yell. "You scared me!"

He laughs. "How's your head feeling?"

"Like shit." He's barefoot, and my eyes slowly work their way up his body. He's in his boxers, and he's shirtless. Barrel-chested. Ripped. "We didn't—" I start to say, my eyes still on his chest, but he cuts me short.

"No…no, please." He chuckles. "Relax. You wouldn't stop drinking, so I didn't let you drive back home."

"Well, that's quite pathetic of me."

"Anyway, we only took a nap," he says, then falls silent for a moment. "In separate rooms."

I stare at his biceps twitching as he gestures an arm toward the living room. "Good," I say, tugging my clothes into place. "Not that I thought anything else," I declare, and he smirks. "I need to go. The employees at Sam's day care already despise me."

He nods then disappears into his room. When he comes out, he's clothed in jeans and a plain black shirt. Wayne glances at his watch before he helps me out.

Downstairs, the residential gate opens with a buzz. "Thanks for intoxicating me," I say, without turning to look at him, and I hear him laugh as he closes the door behind me.

Lexy

Monday, April 20, 2015
Morning - 2 ¼ Months Before Disappearance

I wake up full of him. We drove out to Sammamish and rented a room at the Woods Motel Inn. We spoke for hours. He listened, and I babbled all night long, and then, after a few drinks, we slept together.

"This is wrong in so many ways," I said, but I felt good.

Wayne texted me earlier, asking how my night was. He had to work night shift. I received his text while cuddling with so-called Vicky. I told him we were celebrating her birthday.

The other day he asked when he could meet her, and I had to come up with something fast. I actually made a plan for the three of us to meet then cancelled it at the last minute: "Vicky called and said she has to work tonight." He hasn't brought her up since.

It's still early. I have two hours before work starts, and Lorraine won't even notice I was gone.

Afternoon

Carmen took Lorraine to the hospital for her checkup scan. I'm no longer driving her back and forth to her doctor's visits. I never said I wouldn't; she just stopped asking me. Lorraine adores Carmen. It's obvious. Maybe because she sees something of herself in her. I mean, they're both quite naïve.

I e-mailed my area director and requested a rematch behind Lorraine's back to see what my options are. If I fully explain my situation, she'll cancel my contract and send me back to London, so I only said I'd like to rematch with a family living in Seattle. Since the letter drama, Lorraine has been treating *me* like cancer. She wants to get rid of me—I know she does—but she also knows no one else will work overtime like I do. Ever since I've hit the "send" button, I've been constantly checking my e-mail, dreading the area director's reply.

I bounce Sam on my hip. He giggles. "Ah, little man, I'll always remember you," I tell him, and I kiss his forehead. He grabs my hair and pulls it to his mouth, which hurts like hell, but I let him. He'll never remember my face or my name, and I wonder if he'll even remember Lorraine. He smiles at me, and my heart suddenly aches.

How old will he be when his mother leaves him behind?

Evening

I walk past a small park, too small to be marked on a map. Kids swarm around, running wild. Au pairs, or older sisters, run after them, playing tag. I watch them for a minute or two before I head back home. It's nice out for a change. There are no grey clouds in the sky threatening rain. At night it still gets cold, but in the day, Seattle transforms into a lush paradise.

I trudge up Lorraine's driveway as I take my phone out of my jacket to see how long I've been out, but it slips out of my hand and scatters across the asphalt. I run to pick up the pieces before turning them over on my palm. *Shit. Worst bloody timing ever.* I curse at the air as I stare at the cracks webbing through my screen. I'll have to buy myself a new one tomorrow, use the money I've stashed away in the box on my dresser.

The front door creaks open. My shoulders drop. *Fuck.* I don't want to look up. I don't want to see the expression on Lorraine's face.

"What happened?" she asks, her tone slicing through me.

"I dropped the phone you bought me."

There's silence. The coarse gravel rasps underneath my shoe as I drag my foot over the tar. I find my balance and raise my head. The door is still cracked open, but she's gone. I stand there for a while, looking around. The house across the street, the one with no signs of life, seems more inviting than the one I'm living in.

A cold breeze seeps underneath my shirt, making me shiver. As I make my way to the front door, Lorraine reappears, extending a phone and charger toward me. "Here," she says. "It's one of my old phones. This will have to do."

I take it from her. "Thanks," I say, and she turns to walk back into the house.

Ella

Thursday, July 9, 2015
Morning - 13 Days After Disappearance

He taps his fingers on the table one by one, running them down in a ripple effect. I take a deep breath. My skin prickles. I try to distract myself, but my eyes keep following Eric's hand.

Craig got held up in traffic on his way to the police station. Logan's autopsy results came back, and Eric wants to discuss them with us before the media outlets jump back on the craze.

"Can we please get this over with?" I ask, glancing at the clock. I've been waiting for more than twenty minutes. That doesn't sound like a long time, but it feels like forever when you're about to learn the cause of your nephew's death.

I wonder where Aliya is. I like her more than Eric; she kind of gets me, and she knows when and where to draw the line. We have a mutual understanding—a fortuitous status quo for an unfortunate case.

Finally Craig comes panting around the corner, droplets tracking down his temples from the layer of sweat across his forehead. He pulls a chair out from the table and plants himself next to me. The stench of him, almost like a conglomeration of rotten vegetables, makes me turn sideways so my back is slightly to him.

"Right," Eric finally says, opening a file. "Logan's clothes are still missing. We found him naked underneath some debris next to a wheat field. He suffered two bullet wounds. One went through his chest, and another went through his head—from the front—and exited through the back of his skull." He's pointing at his forehead, pressing a yellow fingertip against his skin.

"Which one was fatal?" I ask, slumping forward.

"The gun was fired no more than twenty inches from his face. The shot through the chest missed his heart by two inches. Evidently it was a fast, painless death."

My stomach turns. I don't feel any better knowing it happened quickly.

Craig clears his throat, he's clearly uncomfortable. "When did this happen?"

"According to the level of decay," Eric says, making Craig wince, "he's been dead since the night he disappeared…or perhaps the morning after. It's hard to tell because it's been more than thirty-six hours since he was murdered. We had to bring in a forensic entomologist, Dr. Evan Green."

Craig frowns. "What does that mean?"

Eric leans back into his chair., clenching his teeth, clearly hating this part of his job: informing the family. He swallows then starts to explain what they've been doing in order to bring us closure. "Entomology is the study of insects and their relationship to the environment, humans, and other organisms," he says. "In this case, we deal with necrophagous feeding insects that typically infest human remains, and we need to repeat the procedure before we can narrow down the time frame of death." He falls silent for a moment, but Craig's expression prompts him to continue. "Unfortunately this means blood spatter analysis could be affected. Roaches, fleas, and flies can produce tracking as they walk through splattered blood. Flies could possibly…" Eric's voice trails off, and Craig covers his face with a wide palm.

I know what Eric's about to say. That flies could feed on Logan's blood then pass partially digested blood in their feces, something known as flyspecks. And that these fecal droppings could be confusing, because they can be tested positive for human blood.

"We'll get to the bottom of this," Eric assures us. "Fortunately, Dr. Green is an expert in forensic entomology."

I catch Craig's eye as I imagine Logan being eaten by insects. Carrion beetles creeping through raw blood craters in his skin. How forensic teams toss freshly killed pigs in areas with the same conditions where they found Logan's body, to note the progress of infestation and decomposition, and ultimately narrow the possible time frame of death. "And you found his body on Monday?" I ask, repulsed.

"Yes," Eric says, crossing his arms, and a wave of nausea flows over me.

"So now what?" I ask, throwing my hands in the air. "Do you have the weapon? Anything?"

"We're searching for it as we speak."

"Where?"

"In Craig's house," he says, and we all fall silent.

"The fuck?" Craig says, suddenly livid. "Where's your search warrant?"

"We issued one earlier today. Aliya has it."

Craig shrugs. "Well…go ahead. There's nothing to find." I remain silent. His tone sounds the same as when I confronted him on Sunday: belligerent. It's almost disturbing.

"Why didn't you search Lorraine's house?" I ask.

"She didn't give us consent, and we don't have enough evidence to issue a search warrant," Eric says.

"She refused you access?" I ask.

"Yes. Like we said, it doesn't look good for you or Lorraine," he says, holding Craig's glare. "Tell me, how did Lorraine get Logan's schoolbooks in the hospital?"

Craig frowns. "I took them to her. She was—"

"So you were in her house," Eric says.

Craig squints. "What are you implying?"

"Nothing. I'm asking you a question. Did you have access to Lorraine Davis's house?"

"No. The books were at my place. She said she had to do brain exercises, so I took them to her." Eric makes a note, and Craig grows uncomfortable. "You should stop wasting your time with me. You have a delusional woman with three brain tumors who claimed to see things that don't fucking exist!"

"What are you talking about?" I ask.

"*Your* sister accused me of harassing her. She made a complete fool of herself at my house."

Eric holds his hand up. "We'll get to the bottom of this as soon as we obtain the phone records."

"What's going on?" I ask.

"She said I texted her that I want her back," Craig says, scoffing.

"When?" I ask.

"Three months ago."

"There must be an explanation for this," I say, which makes Eric snicker.

"There always is," he says, eyeing Craig.

Afternoon

After I leave the police station, I head over to the hospital to see Dr. Rowe. I need to exonerate Lorraine as a suspect, even if it's just for myself, at least for now. I don't think she had anything to do with Logan's death, but lately I find myself doubting that. On my way over there, I call Dr. Rowe and beg him to see me during his lunch break, since he says he's booked for the rest of the day. He agrees to answer my questions quickly, knowing they found Logan's body the other day.

"You said her latest neurological test was done a few days ago, right?" I ask him, once I'm seated in his office.

"Yes, that's correct," he says, standing to search for her file. "Why?"

I straighten my back against the chair. "The detectives think Lorraine might have had something to do with her son's death," I say, shaking my head, "which is ludicrous."

He sits down with her file in his hand, peering at it down his nose, his head tilted back. "It was the second of July."

"A week after Logan went missing," I say. "And before that? Give me all the results," I demand, my hand stretched out.

Dr. Rowe hesitates, his eyebrow raised. "What are you trying to do?"

I drop my arm to my lap. "Lorraine's latest neurological exam was performed *after* Logan went missing. When did you last assess her *before* her most recent test?"

He stares at me for a moment then flips through the file. "Two and a half weeks before the last test."

"And?" I lean forward.

"She…uh…her reasoning skills weren't as bad as they were on this last one, but her vision deteriorated a little between the two tests. There are some minor changes," he says.

"Three months ago…do you have any results from then?"

"Yes," he says, turning a page. "She…wow…she's deteriorated quite quickly since then. She had no problem reading headlines, but she struggled significantly with the body of articles. Her vision was good, but her perception skills were slightly affected."

I stare off into his office, my mind rambling. "She could read headlines but struggled with the body of articles," I repeat, gazing into the air. "In other words, she probably could read short text messages." Dr. Rowe nods. "You have to show this to the detectives."

"Why?"

"Because that means three months ago my sister didn't lie about her ex-husband harassing her."

Lexy

Tuesday, April 21, 2015
Morning - 2 ¼ Months Before Disappearance

Logan was complaining about Carmen last night. I knew this day would come. When I asked him if he wants to marry her in the future, his jaw dropped. I think he's realised he's wasting his time with her, and besides, he certainly doesn't want to be tied down when he goes to college.

I told him to keep me out of whatever's going on with him and Carmen, that I don't need Lorraine to be angry with me about this too. He texted Carmen and told her he wants some space. It didn't take her long to contact Lorraine. I thought I wouldn't hear the end of it.

Now I'm in my room. I don't want to go downstairs. This morning I realised I hate my job. I'm starting to think this isn't worth it and sticking around is a stupid idea. But if I leave now, I might not be allowed back into the United States for the next two years—that is, if I'm subject to section 212(e) of the Immigration and Nationality Act, but I'm not sure I am.

I take Lorraine's old flip phone from the nightstand. It's been plugged in for ten hours and still isn't fully charged. I slide my SIM card over the metal chips and switch the phone on. The Motorola chimes to life. The wallpaper appears: a photo of Logan when he was a little boy, smiling in his swim shorts, one tooth missing. His feet are caked with wet sand as he holds up a bright-blue plastic shovel. I stare at the picture for a while, thinking about how fast things can go wrong, wondering if that family on the beach ever thought they'd be broken someday. Did Craig and Lorraine know by then?

I place the phone back on my nightstand so it can charge a bit more, but I doubt it will, as it seems like the battery gave out after all these eventful years.

Afternoon

I put Sam in his high chair as I warm up his cereal. He smashes his palms on the tray, making me chuckle. Usually I'll give him a toy to keep him busy, but it always goes flying across the kitchen floor. As I fasten the bib around his neck, someone knocks on the door.

My eyes meet Logan's, who's doing his geometry homework at the table. I cock my head to the side, gesturing for him to get the door as Sam grabs for his cereal, pulling the bowl closer to him. I extend my neck to see who it is, and then I fake a smile as Carmen walks in.

Logan follows her, clearly not happy since he didn't invite her over. "Hi, Lexy," she says, her voice higher than ever.

I greet her back, biting on my smile as Logan rolls his eyes. Carmen slides a chair out next to his, leaning in to check his homework. I look away and stir Sam's cereal with a plastic spoon.

"This was due *yesterday,*" she says. Logan remains silent, wincing at the cereal protruding from Sam's mouth. "You need help?" she continues, and Logan smirks, pushing the paper toward her.

"Yeah, I'm struggling with this," he says. She starts to explain the work, but he waves her off. "No, no…I'm better at self-studying…but I'm behind. Mind giving me the answers?"

Carmen stares at him for a second before she slides the assignment in front of her. "Sure," she says, taking the pen.

Logan grins at me as she completes his homework, and I mouth the word "asshole," because I know he isn't struggling with geometry; he just doesn't want to talk to her.

Evening

I plunge into bed and bury my face in the cushions. I feel like writing, like jotting down my thoughts to let out all this frustration, hurt, and resentment. I raise my head and stare at my closet, where I keep my dairy. My eyes glide to the phone, and I think, *Flip phones probably have memo pages too?* Seeing that it's still only charged halfway, I decide to unplug the device. It'll have to do, I guess.

After typing on my notepad, I try to save my draft, but a notification pops up: insufficient storage. I open the gallery. Six hundred photos. I want to wipe the phone clean, reset the damn thing, but I can't delete Lorraine's photos without asking. I open her inbox, which also is full. There are hundreds of messages. My eye catches one from an unsaved number, one I'm dying to open, but it feels wrong to sneak around. I stare at the screen for a few seconds, but then curiosity gets the better of me. The buttons click as I press down on them, stiff from being overused, and the message opens:

> Sorry for reacting the way I did, but you scared me.

I open the next one and the next. Then there's a reply:

> You're a stupid fucking bitch. You made me do it.

The details on the message shows it was sent in 2011. I stare at the number, contemplating if I should call it. I mean, it's been years; the number might not even exist by now. My fingers hover over the green icon, and the urge to know boils from within. Quickly I open the phone's settings to hide my caller ID. Then I press my thumb down, and it starts to ring. I jerk my head back, making sure I'm not mistaken, but it becomes clear as it grows louder and louder: a phone ringing from inside the house. He picks up. I can't speak or move…and then the line goes dead.

Ella

Friday, July 10, 2015
Morning - 2 Weeks After Disappearancce

Tessa strolls through the front door with the newspaper in her hand. She probably decrypted every word in there, since she's watching the case closely—too close for my liking. She wants to know every last detail, but it does seem like she has Lorraine's best interests at heart.

"Have you seen today's paper?" she asks calmly, completely at ease.

"No, not yet," I say, flicking through a catalog Lorraine received in the mail.

I look at her as she takes off her raincoat, and for a moment I find myself intrigued. Her red hair is damp from the drizzle outside, clinging to her freckled cheeks. I've never seen her car. How does she get to work? Does she take the train? A bus? Or does her husband or sister drop her off? Since I arrived in Seattle, I've developed a propensity to question everything and everyone, and I've never been more desperate for answers.

"Anything…interesting?" I ask.

"Eh…same old," she says, wrinkling her nose. She drops the paper on the table in front of me then plods upstairs.

I grab *The Seattle Times.* The box with the poems is printed on the front page, but it's getting smaller and smaller by the day. I scan through the article, and then I pause, rereading a quote from a college student: "The couple—the woman in the dress and the man with the quiver on his back—in the sketch beneath the first poem, is at Seahurst Park." I stare at the sentence for a few seconds then scoff. Wayne's right—the media does fuck with your brain.

Loud thumping on the stairs makes me peek over the newspaper. It's Tessa, paused halfway on the staircase, her face pale and her eyes wide. My limbs go numb, and my breathing stops as everything comes to a standstill. She doesn't have to say a word…because I know.

My chair darts back, and I run past Tessa. It feels like I left my body behind and I'm watching myself from the table. I can see her. Ella. Running like it might make a difference. Out of her mind. Desperate. The tenacity seems hopeful, but it's not.

My heart beats to the rate of my feet striking the stairs. I rush into Lorraine's room and fall to my knees. My face scrunches, and my eyebrows narrow. I look at Sam, who's sitting in his rocker next to her bed. He gives me an innocent smile. An unbearable countenance of an orphaned baby, a baby who has no idea what's happening. I extend my arm to take Lorraine's hand into mine. Her chest doesn't move, and her arm feels heavy. I lean forward to hold her against me, and my mouth emits a sound, a scream, a guttural shriek. I rock her back and forth, trying to rid myself of the pain. But then my body ceases to obey, and I sob uncontrollably as I hold her, my diaphragm forced out of rhythm, causing an uneven breathing cadence.

Afternoon

A mortician just took Lorraine's body away. It felt so wrong when I ordered a "pickup" to remove my sister from her own house. I feel empty, lifeless. Tessa said her rehearsed lines of condolences and left for her next shift somewhere else.

I think about what Lorraine would have wanted while she was on her deathbed. She wanted her family by her side. Was that too much to ask for? Another tear rolls down my face. She also desperately wanted her husband back—everyone knows that. How could she let that ruin the last couple of years she had left? She just wanted *it* back. The love she gave, the hours she'd spent on him. The respect. She wanted to be appreciated, to experience reciprocated love. It became such a big fucking deal that she couldn't look past it. She even tried to indirectly reach out to him through me. She asked me if I thought he'd shed a tear when she was gone. It's not like I would ask him, so I didn't know what to say. I just stared at her and shrugged.

The house is disturbingly quiet. I couldn't look at Sam, so I dropped him off at the day-care center. I need to distract myself. I need to keep it together. But for the first time in my life, I can't.

Evening

There's a crisp knock on the front door, and I take my wineglass from the kitchen counter to go answer it. Even though things don't look good for Craig, I asked him to come over but told him that Martha wasn't welcome, not tonight.

He steps inside, steeling himself for the night. In the kitchen, he turns around, eyeing the half-empty bottle of wine. "Are you okay?" he asks, placing his palms on my shoulders.

I shake my head, biting my lip as I feel my psyche crumble. I fall back into a chair, lowering my head, wondering how the fuck all this happened. Less than a year ago, Lorraine was fine. Healthy. Almost full-term pregnant with Sam. She called once, complaining about Robert. If she'd had any idea what was waiting for her, she wouldn't have let those problems trouble her. Or would she?

I tuck my hands underneath my armpits as my knee starts to jump. "I should've come to Seattle earlier," I say, staring at the tiles, my vision blurring. "I was so fucking selfish."

Craig says nothing, and I can feel the burn in my eyes, that sting at the back of your optic nerves, the moment you can't control it anymore. A rough hand touches my shoulder. He never knew how to handle me, and I can feel his uncertainty—he's contemplating whether he should console me or give me space.

"You know…I thought if I stayed away, her illness wouldn't trouble me, and I honestly didn't think she was *that* sick."

"Sometimes avoidance is the best medicine," he says, and I shoot him a look.

"What would you know?" He remains silent, and then he slides the wine bottle across the kitchen table to pour me a drink. "Just for starters, Craig, I still don't fucking like you. But Lorraine loved you more than she loved herself, and that's the only reason you're here. Because she would have wanted this."

He nods as he tilts the bottle, the wine swirling into my glass, then in his. "Well…then let's not make it about ourselves."

I take a deep breath and nod, taking the drink from him. "Everything always steered toward *Craig, Craig, Craig* with Lorraine. I thought she was obsessed with you. I even suggested therapy, but I guess if you don't understand, you just won't get it. It was something she couldn't help. She tried so hard to forget about you." I fall silent as I watch him, his features hardening.

"No one will ever love you as much as Lorraine did."

Craig swallows, eyeing the surface of the table, clenching his teeth. "I kno—" he starts to say, but the words hitch in his throat. "I know that." We sit in silence, staring at each other. He tries to force the corners of his mouth upward, but instead his chin starts to tremble. His eyes jitter around, almost as though he wants to hide, and they redden as the skin scrunches up around them. A sound emits from his mouth, a growling screech as he starts to weep like a child. Two fingers press over his eyelids, as if he's trying to stop the tears from coming.

I stare at him, his torso jerking as he sobs, and I can't see a man who could kill, the murderer the police have accused him of being. He's distraught, and for a moment I feel a short pang of satisfaction, but then it's overpowered by a deep disappointment that my sister didn't have the chance to see that Craig still has a place for her in his heart. Perhaps men do love their ex-wives. Perhaps not as much as they did, but somewhere there's a soft spot for them, tucked deeply in a dusty corner, whether or not they want to admit it.

"I still don't get why you left her," I say. "You two were great together. Hell, even I could see that." I swallow three gulps of wine with a tight jaw, determined not to crack in front of Craig.

He takes in sharp gusts of air, a tremble in his voice. "I never even fucking apologized."

I swallow my pride. I also did Lorraine wrong; I should've been there for her. We're both guilty. "Why did you leave her?"

He stares at his hands, the skin around his eyes swollen and red. "She loved being home. Lorraine always wanted to stay in—watch a movie or play the piano. In the beginning, it was fine, because I was working all the time. But when things settled down, I found myself locked up in the house. So I went out with my friends more…and well, I guess I enjoyed it too much. I'm not blaming them for my infidelity. I just really like to live in the moment.

"On weekends I'd hike with friends, maybe enjoy a beer or two at a pub after, and when I'd come home, it was the same thing over and over. Dinner, shower, movie, sleep."

"Why didn't you take her out? Do something exciting?" I ask.

"I tried. But Lorraine kept saying no. Other than going to work, she rarely left the house." He flicks a finger in the air. "Grocery shopping." And then another one. "Or to Logan's games."

I bring the wineglass back to my mouth, and I realize it's empty. "But why did you treat her like she was invisible after the divorce?"

Craig falls silent, his eyes welling up with tears again. "Because you can't encourage that kind of behavior. I, at least, owed her that."

"You know she didn't see it like that."

"Well, I wish she could have," he says, rubbing a hand over his pepper-colored stubble. He waves his glass in the air, which also is empty. I stand up to grab another bottle from the fridge. "And besides," he continues, "Martha is extremely territorial. Of course, I love Martha, but some things will never be the same again."

I cut off the foil at the top of the bottle before I position the corkscrew in the cork. "Like what?"

He fiddles with his thumbs, glancing at me from the corner of his eye. "Let's not talk about Martha tonight," he says as I twist my hand, forcing the corkscrew down. I grab the levers, and the bottle opens with a satisfying pop.

"How about we speak about the good things? The good memories of Lorraine?"

He nods, still seeming a bit reluctant. "Where's Sam?" he asks, frowning.

"Sleeping in his rocker upstairs." There's silence, and I point toward the baby monitor. "I'm not *that* bad."

He gives me a sad smile. "I didn't mean it like that."

I take a seat opposite him, placing the full bottle of wine in front of me. "Lorraine said Sam's nothing like Logan was. Apparently he screamed your ears off day and night." I say, trying to steer the conversation away from *now*. The *present*. The awful fucking present.

He winces, his head lowered, looking at the floor. "Let's not speak about Logan."

I shrug. "Why not?"

"Because I don't want to discuss my son right now!" he explodes.

I narrow my eyes, sickened by his outburst. "Craig, I hope to God this is because you're too emotional right now...and not because you're on some fucking guilt trip."

He lets out a sharp breath. "You still don't believe me, do you? I told you, I had nothing to do with Logan's murder."

I study him, my eyes moving along his features. "Fine then. Let's not talk about Logan." I fill our glasses to the brim. "Let's talk about my sister. The best person I've known in my entire life." I hold up my drink. "To Lorraine," I say, and Craig clinks his glass against mine; some of the wine splashes onto the table, and then we swig our drinks down.

I watch him as he gets lost in his thoughts, talking about the old days. The days when they were a happy family, the days when no one ever would have imagined things would go this wrong. He babbles for a few minutes, and then he'll tear up again, and then he'll laugh, and then it's my turn. I talk about the days in the orphanage. When Lorraine always had a bunch of friends, and when I was the tomboy, the girl everyone loved to hate. We joke about how she always spoke to her coffee mug in the mornings as she ruminated over one thing or another. God, her paranoia! *Let's not forget that,* I think. I don't want to forget any of it. Because every bit of her personality made her who she was, and every bit of her will live on inside our hearts.

A few hours pass, and then Sam interrupts my sentence as I hear him crying over the baby monitor. Craig's smile disappears as reality strikes him. He stares at the monitor, and despair washes over his face. We're reminded that there's a baby boy upstairs without his mother. A baby who hasn't had the chance to know the woman we've been discussing all night.

I leave Craig by himself as I attend to Sam upstairs. As I cradle him in my arms, he immediately stops crying. It feels good to know he's starting to warm up to me. I take him down to the kitchen, where Craig is standing at the table, keys in his hands.

"I should go," he says, staring at Sam.

"Are you okay to drive?"

"Yeah," he says, his features hardening again. "It's not that far."

I grab a blanket to fold over Sam before I follow Craig to the foyer.

"Thanks for having me over," he says, nodding without looking at me. Once outside, he ambles across the driveway and stumbles into his car. Sam tightens his tiny arms around my neck, and I wave as Craig drives off into the night.

Back in the kitchen, I feed Sam, trying my best to maintain my composure. "Babies can sense emotions," Lorraine said once. *Happy thoughts. Happy thoughts.* I bring a plastic spoon to his mouth, and he swallows the last bit of formula.

After I burp him, I take him to his crib. It's almost midnight, and tomorrow I'll have to start Lorraine's funeral arrangements. I lay Sam down and tuck him in. Then I lean over to kiss him on his mouth. He has no idea his mother is gone. For some reason, that thought hurts me the most—the fact that he doesn't understand where she is or where she went. I give him his pacifier, and as soon as he latches on to it, his eyes roll back and he falls asleep.

I trudge down the hallway and into Lorraine's room. I close the door behind me as though someone might see me, and then I crawl into a fetal position in her bed, clutching the sheets to my chest. I think about Miss McBeth, Logan, and my sister.

And then I break down in uncontrollable sobs.

Saturday, July 11, 2015
Morning

I couldn't sleep. I can't eat, and I didn't feel like getting out of bed. Robert wants to take Sam, but I won't give him up without a fight. I need to get a lawyer. He's so goddamn selfish to even bring that up, after everything we've been through. I bet someone reminded him of his child. *Yo, bro, you know that kid you had at your place once? Yeah…his mom died.* Cunts.

I told a caregiver at the day-care center to be on the lookout and said no one can pick Sam up besides me. She compliantly nodded and patted me on the back, which I thought was a bit weird.

Now I'm at the law firm Lexy visited before she went missing. I brought some estate planning documents I got from Lorraine's place. My eyes feel heavy and my head thick. All I want to do is sleep, but thoughts of Lorraine keep me alert. Thoughts about Logan, what happened to him, why anyone would hurt him, where Lexy is, and then I worry about my job. Life goes on; the clock is ticking; and no one back at my work is waiting around for me, but I can't leave this mess like this. I feel obliged to solve this; I owe it to Lorraine.

"Ella Jensen?" A thirtyish man dressed in a gray suit scans the room. I hold a hand up, and he nods, welcoming me into his office. "Please, have a seat," he says, his voice coated with a husky, guttural tone, making me feel as though I'm in good hands. "How can I help you?"

I try to talk quickly, to avoid those extra few minutes that might lead to a double charge for the second hour. He nods at the right times, listening intently as I describe my situation with Robert and that I want custody of Sam. When I said that, it felt right. For the first time I could see myself taking care of a baby.

"Well, I'll retrieve the necessary documents as soon as possible, and I'll call you," he says, and then he tries to stretch it out.

"Okay, okay, okay," I say, nodding like a bobblehead. "Thank you, Mr...."

"Torkaz."

"You are..."

"Brothers." He smiles.

I flick my head back. "Sorry, I didn't get your first name," I say, wondering how clients differentiate between them on the phone. *Hi. I'd like to make an appointment with Torkaz One, but if he's not available, I'll speak to Torkaz Two.*

"Right, sorry. I'm Dean," he states. "My brother is Roy."

And then it hits me. The resemblance is unmistakable. If I didn't stare at the pictures on Lexy's camera as much, I might've thought *he* was kissing her. *Roy's a lawyer? How? He's from London?*

Everything inside me tells me not to do it, but I can't resist: "Do you know Lexy Wright? The au pair who went missing with the sixteen-year-old boy?"

He takes a deep breath as he leans back into his chair, eyeing the door. "Ms. Jensen, I've tried my best to stay out of it," he says, his hand stretched out, rifling through a pile of papers. "You're not working with the reporters, are you?" He gives me an atrocious smile.

"No. I'm Logan's aunt. Lexy worked for my sister."

He holds my stare. "I realized that. We've been doing a good job of keeping our firm out of the public eye during all this. Besides, my brother is only shadowing me and helping out before he takes his bar exam."

A thought goes through my head: *If you win this custody case, I won't,* but I'm not that low. Dean rubs his forehead. "I won't, but I need your help," I tell him. "My nephew is dead, and I need to speak to everyone involved."

"My brother wasn't *involved* with the death of your nephew."

"That's not what I meant. Anyone who knew...her." I wait for him to say something, but he doesn't. "Did you see her?"

"When?"

"Before she went missing."

"No, I thought she was in London, until I saw the news."

"So you know her from back then."

"No, not really," he says, glancing at the door. "Look, Ms. Jensen, I have work to do."

There's silence. "All right, but call me when you have a chance to talk," I say, and then it slips out: "You don't want me to take this to the papers, do you?"

His jaw juts out as he radiates a look of superiority. "Go ahead then. Tell them everything you know. It'll only take you five seconds."

He gives me a fake smile and swallows. We eye each other for a few seconds before a genuine smile appears on my face. He *will* call. I can tell. The pulse in his neck is too visible for him not to be scared shitless.

Evening

It happened. My boss left a voice mail for me. I don't know what to do or say.

"Hi, Ella. I'm calling to inform you that if you don't return to work within the next two days, we'll have to ask you to leave," he said. He apparently sent me an e-mail or two, which I honestly didn't see. "There's a place and time for everything," he continued, referring to my family matters as though they're insignificant.

I fiddle with my pen, rolling the barrel through my fingers. I've worked extremely hard to get where I am today, and now I'm throwing it all away. Work was all I knew when I came here, but suddenly it doesn't seem so important anymore, because for the first time in my life, I know what it's like to love someone as my own, to open myself up to it.

I stare at Sam, who somehow grows cuter by the day. And then I experience something odd: a deep warmth, a need to protect, an urge to provide. I snuggle him against me, and then I tuck him into his crib.

Downstairs in the kitchen, I switch on Lorraine's laptop and write my boss an e-mail telling him I understand. There are many opportunities out there, and someday I'll find a suitable job again. In the meantime, I can live off my savings. I click the "send" button as fast as I can, scared that I might hesitate, and then I sit here motionless, staring at my screen.

Determined to distract myself, I open up Google, type "Redmond," and hit the search button. I can't think of my sister all night. If I do, I'll lose my mind. A list of articles pops up regarding the case. I click on a map, and then I use the ruler on Google Earth and stretch it out sixty miles southeast from Redmond, around Cle Elum, where they found Logan's body. The map loads as I scroll across the surface, and then my heart drops, my body going numb. I zoom out a bit to make sure that I'm at the right place, that it's exactly where they found his body. I zoom back in, and the name pops up again in a bright white. The location is marked, "Brent."

I grab my phone to call Craig, but then I remember he's a suspect. I glance at my watch; it's too late to call Aliya or Eric.

Startled, I open Facebook. Lorraine's news feed loads; she never logged out. I check to see if Craig is on "chat," but they're not friends on Facebook. I want to tell him, but a part of me hesitates, especially after he lied about the text messages he sent Lorraine. As I contemplate what all this might mean, I pause. I squeeze my eyes shut and open them again to make sure I'm not dreaming. I press the "print screen" button repeatedly, because no one will believe me unless I can prove it. My body goes rigid.

I've just caught Lexy online.

Lexy

Wednesday, April 22, 2015
Morning - 2 Months Before Disappearance

I reread the messages three or four times. I checked the number twice, and I still can't believe it. Logan would never speak to his mother like that. Yes, he can be rotten sometimes, but those texts just weren't like him, at all.

Earlier this morning, when I made myself some coffee, I kept a close eye on him and Lorraine. *Did I miss something?* I tried to see if there's something I haven't picked up on, but I just can't see it. Their relationship seems normal, like always. Unless it's not normal, and I just thought it was. *Maybe he's behaving differently since I'm around?* If he is, I wouldn't be able to tell. I don't have a brother, and I don't know how it's supposed to be. But I have common sense, and it's telling me that something isn't right. I just need to figure out what it is.

"Lexy," Craig says, approaching me on his driveway, "are you joining us tomorrow?"

"Oh, I can't," I say, shaking my head. "I need to work."

"Take an early weekend," he replies, forcing a fold-up chair into the boot of his car. "Invite Wayne too. I'll call Lorraine."

"No, no," I say, faster than intended. "Please don't. I'll ask her myself." My eyes follow him as he moves across the cobblestones to pick up a bag. Martha, Craig, and Logan are leaving tomorrow for Olympic National Park, a two-and-a-half-hour drive northwest of Seattle. A house at the lake, no cell-phone reception, no screaming baby, just tranquility. According to my contract, I have two weeks of vacation that I can take. I'll try to push my luck with Lorraine.

Craig is still speaking, but I'm not listening. I nod at the right times as I think about the questions my area director asked me. Why I want to rematch and why I can't work things out with Lorraine. I want to tell her about my situation but not before she guarantees me a rematch in Seattle. Then I imagine her calling Lorraine and telling her what I'm up to. The thought sends shivers down my spine.

Craig's voice pulls me back to the present. "Well, if you don't want to ask her, I can ask Logan to persuade her."

I remain silent as Martha walks up to me. She gives me a tight hug. "You need a break, sweetie," she says, brushing a few strands of hair out of my face. She's right. They both are. I do need a break, but how do I get that into Lorraine's delusional head?

Afternoon

"You're...going with *her*?" she asks, pursing her lips.

"That's beside the point," I say, shaking my head. Lorraine's sitting on the couch next to me, staring at her hands.

"Right. Off you go," she says. "Go pack your bags." It's not the "have fun; see you later" version—it's the "fuck you" one.

"I just need a break," I say.

She gives me a coveting gaze. "It's not about that," she says, spitting the words out in disgust. "That was *our* place!"

I sigh. "I can't do this any longer, Lorraine. I don't know what to say anymore. I'm not trying to take anything away from you. I'm only asking for a few days off. I work days and nights to make you happy, and you treat me like...shit."

"You wouldn't understand," she says, emphasising every word.

"Then don't expect me to."

"I know you're not *trying* to take something away from me, but it still feels like it. That house...it was special. It was *our* space, and I can't even go there anymore. I'm not allowed. It's *theirs* now."

I look away, my knee jerking. "Well, I'm sorry. I'm sorry about everything, but I can't be a part of this. I can't be treated like I'm your child. I'm an adult, and I'm going, whether you like it or not. I'm allowed two weeks of vacation, and so far I've barely had a weekend for myself."

Lorraine says nothing, because she knows I'm right and that she's fucking up. She gets to her feet to leave, but then she pivots around on her heels. "You're right," she says, not looking me in the eye. "I can't expect you to bear my burdens. I'm sorry."

My frown softens. "It's okay," I say, but the tone of my voice portrays something different. "When I come back, I think we should talk."

She gives me a forlorn look, her eyes filled with concern. "About what?"

I clench my teeth. "My job. About us."

"Right," she says, staring at me, and then she forces a slight smile.

Thursday, April 23, 2015
Afternoon

The dock runs out underneath my feet toward the setting sun, surreptitiously sneaking away, sinking into the lake. The reflection wanes, and the circle contorts into a dispersed hue of red roses.

Many nights I watch the sun set. Many nights I watch the moon. They fascinate me. They're the only things I get to share with everyone: the stars, the moon, the universe. They're the same stars Roy looks at when he stares at the sky, the same moon he sees, no matter where in the world he is. The ocean fascinates me too. How it connects everything and everyone, but at the same time it divides us. It's a mystery, full of life and possibilities. It's just…phenomenal.

I turn around. Nestled between trees is the two-storey wooden house, the only one in sight, with bay windows hovering over a little green yard.

Wayne is still unpacking my car, which is parked next to Craig's BMW. Martha, Logan, and Craig look like a string of ants, following each other in and out of the house, carrying coolers and bags. No one calls out for me to help; no one snaps at me for just standing here. They let me breathe; they let me rest, for once.

Evening

"Seriously, Lexy?" Martha says, smiling. "Give me the darn dictionary," she says, her arm stretched toward Logan.

"*Anisole* is a real word," I say. "It's a colourless, water-insoluble liquid. Usually it's used in perfumery and organic synthesis, and as a vermi—"

"Okay, okay," Martha says, staring at the dictionary, "You're right. I'll give it to you." She writes my score down. "Logan, it's your turn."

He smirks and grabs seven tiles, aligning them horizontally, the letter *o* integrating with my word. "Cabotage," he reads.

"Do you even know what that means?" Craig asks.

Logan gives a mischievous smile. "To sabotage a cab?"

Craig laughs. "If only English were that simple," he says, eyeing Martha.

"It means to navigate…or to have the right to operate on sea," she says, scanning our faces. "Seems like we ran out of tiles," she adds, her neck extended. She taps the paper with her pen as she counts the score. "Ah!" she exclaims, her eyes gleaming. "We have a winner!" Everyone sighs in unison. "Me!" she declares with a grin.

"We'd hope so," Logan mutters, elbowing Craig, and the two of them chuckle.

"And…Wayne, you have the second-highest score," she continues, ignoring the persiflage. "Lexy, you're third. That leaves us with the two Davis men," she says, her eyes squinting as she laughs.

"I don't need to know fancy words. I have a secretary for that," Craig says, almost snorting into his coffee. "I just have to know how to persuade people, and I'm very good at that." He winks at Martha, and my eyes shoot at Logan, who awkwardly turns his head away.

"Right," I say, slamming my palms onto the table, which makes Wayne jolt in his seat. "Who wants to take a swim with me?"

"It's ten p.m.," Martha says, snickering. "Give me that glass of wine. You've had enough."

I snatch it away from her. "Nope, I'm on holiday. And I'm going to make the most of it."

"Fair enough. I'll go swim with you." Wayne places a hand on my back.

"There are leeches," Logan says, as he wipes the Scrabble tiles over the table and into a bag. "Big, fat leeches."

"No, there aren't. But it's cold outside, and the lake drops to below forty-five degrees at night," Craig says, then gulps down his last bit of coffee.

Wayne stands, eyeing me. "Nah, we don't care," he replies, and my face breaks into a smile.

"You ready?" I ask, and he squints, giving me a wolfish smile, and then we run up the spiral stairs and into our room.

I slip my shirt off as Wayne jumps on one leg, trying to pull his foot through his shorts. "What do I get if I beat you there?" I ask, tying my bikini strings behind my back.

"Frostbite," he says, already dashing through the doorway. I race after him. Down the stairs, through the kitchen, and out the back door. As we run to the lake, wind seeps up my bikini top, giving my skin the appearance of a freshly plucked goose. Both of us stop short, our toes curled into the sand. We look at each other, grinning, ready to do something foolish. Wayne takes the first step, his shoulders bouncing as his feet touch the water.

"Oh, Jesus, Lexy, are you sure you want to do this?"

I lower my head, jokingly turning around to walk back to the house. The water splashes behind me as Wayne runs after me.

He picks me up and swings me around, running back to the lake. I scream and laugh, kicking the air. He pounds his way through the water, and then he tosses me a few meters away. An electric shock bolts through my body as I'm immersed in the water. I come up to the surface then let my limbs hang loose as I float on my back.

Wayne grabs me by my hips and pulls me closer. "I love you," he says, and a shiver runs down my neck. His eyes intensify, and a slight pain prickles my throat. I want to say it back, but I can't. He looks down, almost as though he's searching for something on the lake bed.

"You too," I say, forcing it out, but I don't mean it, at least not in *that* way. He presses himself against me, kissing my lips. He's hard against my pubic bone, and I feel alive.

"Do you…want to go inside?" he asks, his eyes fixed on me.

Before I can answer, my eye catches something in the distance, just a few inches higher than his head. He waits for a reply, but instead I extend my neck to get a better view.

"Hey," he says, trying to draw my attention back to him, but I can't look away. Craig's standing at the window on the second floor, glaring at us, and before I can look back at Wayne, he jerks the curtains together.

Friday, April 24, 2015
Afternoon

I take in the unbridled flow of the lake's gentle ripples as Wayne steers a paddle into the water. The canoe drifts forward, away from the lake house.

"Are you just going to sit there, or are you going to help me?" Wayne asks with a wink.

"This is supposed to be romantic," I say, my paddle resting on my life jacket. I stare into the distance. The tall trees dance in the breeze, casting uneven shadows on the surface of the lake.

"Like in *The Notebook*?"

I frown, pouting. Then I gape at him. "You watched *The Notebook*?"

"Of course."

"But…with who?"

"Alone."

I laugh. "Did you cry?" He eyes me as he propels the canoe forward by pushing the paddle through the water, faster than before.

"Maybe."

I slap a palm on the lake's surface. "Knew it."

"Do you know how long it took them to train those swans to swim around the boat like they did in the movie?"

I tilt my head. "Did you research the movie too?"

He stops rowing, slightly narrowing his eyes. "It took them a month."

"Well, why don't you train some swans for me?" I say, my eyes sweeping across his biceps.

"I'll train some alligators for you." I softly kick his shin, and he slams a palm through the water, splashing water on me. "And then I'll feed them," he continues, and I jump forward, almost losing my balance. We laugh, and he cups his hands around my cheeks as I lean forward on my knees. The boat shakes as we try to keep our balance, and then he kisses me softly. "I adore you, Lexy."

I slowly sit back and scoot to the end of the canoe to my seat. I open my mouth to say something, but suddenly my entire body jerks upright at the sound of a gunshot. Wayne's head swings around.

"It came from the house," he says, already rowing back toward the shore.

"No. Stop." I shove my paddle into the water, making the front of the boat swing to the left. "Wayne, please, it's not safe."

"Someone could be hurt," he says.

My heart speeds up as my eyes shift to his, and then we both paddle to the shore as fast we can.

Wayne jumps out first, pounding his way through the water, and I pull the canoe onto the little landing of sand before following him. He runs past the back door, and as we make our way around the house, Logan comes into view.

My eyes trace down his arm toward his hand, which is holding a gun. I let out the breath I was holding as Logan shoots a soda can off a log. "You could've told us," I tell him, as he walks over to inspect his target.

"We do this every time we come here," he says, rotating the Pepsi in his hand. "Did I scare you?" He holds my stare as the handgun hangs loosely beside his hip.

I don't answer him as Wayne steps forward. "Can I try?" he asks, pointing at the pistol. Logan nods, and I decide to leave them to fool around.

Still shaken, I walk through the back door and into the kitchen. Martha comes around the corner, wrapping a bandage around her hand. I take a step forward, and then I see glass shattered across the tiles, along with blood spatter. "What happened?" I ask.

She smiles. "Oh, don't worry about me. I just picked up a glass while doing the dishes, and it broke in my hand."

"Where's Craig?"

"Upstairs. He's taking a shower."

I stare at the blood on the floor, unable to break my gaze, and I realise I'm scared…petrified.

Ella

Sunday, July 12, 2015
Morning - 16 Days After Disappearance

I came to the police station with my screenshot folded in my pocket like a child running to her mother: "Mommy! Mommy! Look what I've got!"

"Fuck," Aliya says, her hands on her hips.

"Yeah," I say, "that's what I said."

Eric glances at the ceiling, and then he sighs heavily. "Oh, for fuck's sake. How stupid of her."

My stomach flips. "Excuse me?"

"You can't tell anyone about this," he says, leaning forward on the table, his face hovering too close to mine.

"Please tell me this is a joke." My mouth hangs open in a slight spastic smile.

"It's complicated," Aliya interjects. "Did you tell anyone about this? Who's seen this besides us?" She's pointing at the screenshot.

"No one…and don't bullshit me now with 'oh, it must be someone else using her profile.'" I throw my hands in the air, and they smack the table loudly. "Do you mind telling me what's going on?"

There's silence. Eric nods at Aliya, indicating to go ahead. "She's on her way here from London," she says. "A cab driver came forward…and we found an e-mail. We're not entirely sure what her story is yet. But we need to keep this to ourselves…for her safety."

"For her safety? Are you fucking kidding me?" I jump to my feet, leaning forward on the table. "You have someone who wrote poems indicating the *location* where you found Logan's body—if you haven't figured that out yet—and you let her fly down here…in what? A fucking private jet?"

They both have their hands glued to their hips; Eric's head is lowered. "What are you talking about? What location?"

I snicker. "Brent! The word 'Brent' is marked on the map where you found Logan's body. If you had any fucking common sense, you would've *Googled* it, and you would've seen it."

Aliya frowns, directing her gaze to Eric. "If you won't cooperate, and you jeopardize this case, there will be serious consequences," he says, which makes me snort.

"Well, hopefully I'll get to fly around on your watch," I say, hurling the chair against the table, making Aliya flinch. "You're both fucking useless!" I scream, eyeing them, but they just stand there, motionless. Eric looks up and glares at me: a warning—a "try that again" look—and then I storm out of the office.

Once I'm in the car, I call Craig.

"I'm on my way over," I tell him, and surprisingly he replies with an "okay." "Make sure you're alone," I say, and he assures me that Martha isn't there.

When I arrive, he comes out to the driveway, dressed in tattered clothes. His eyes are fixed on me as I park the car; he looks exhausted.

I follow him inside, not saying a word. He gestures for me to sit, but I'm too restless.

"Want something to drink?" he asks.

I shake my head, resting a palm on top of an overstuffed chair. "Tell me, Craig, and don't bullshit me. Why's your DNA in Lexy's car?" I'm spoiling for a fight.

"I already told you," he says, turning his head to the side. He won't look me in the eye, and I'm growing impatient.

"I'm not buying it." I say. "Something feels off." He lets out a bitter laugh. "Why are the detectives moving in on you?"

"Because they found my DNA in Lexy's car," he says, clearly annoyed by my persistence.

"I'm trying to help you," I tell him, but then he loses his temper.

"You're trying to help me?" he repeats. "No one can fucking help me!" His face grows red as the veins swell on his forehead. I can feel his anger, frustration, and exasperation. I take a step back as the chair skids across the floor as he gets to his feet. "How in this fucking world are you trying to help me?" His index finger cuts the air. "All of you just want answers, so you're blaming me. You blame me for your sister's misery, your nephew's…" He pauses. "*My* son's disappearance. Blame me all the fuck you want!"

"His death," I correct him. "His death." He's out of breath and breaking into a sweat. "I'm only trying to get some answers. If you're not guilty, why not cooperate?"

Craig's glare grows stronger. "You have nothing on me," he says, his eyes narrowing.

I give it a few seconds, and then I say it: "Well…we'll see what Lexy has to say."

His face grows pale. "Get out," he says, but I don't move. "Get out!" he repeats, this time louder.

A knock on the door makes me jerk around. Two faint figures are moving behind it, blurred by the textured glass. Craig rushes past me to open the door.

It's Aliya and Eric. Perhaps they're here to break the news about Lexy to Craig. Or maybe they followed me because they're scared I might tell him what I just did. But I'm wrong.

Eric takes a step inside the house. "Craig Davis, you're under arrest for the murder of Logan Davis." He grabs Craig's arm, forcing him around. Aliya starts to read Craig his Miranda rights, just like I've heard cops do in the movies.

"No." I head over to the door. "This has to be a mistake," I hear myself say, and then I question why I'm defending him. Eric tightens the cuffs around Craig's wrists and directs him to the car.

"Aliya," I say, my hand touching her shoulder. I open my mouth, but nothing comes.

Her eyes move in a triangle. "I'm sorry," she says. "We found Lexy's spare car key at Craig's house up in the Olympic Peninsula."

A piercing pain shoots through my head, and my vision starts to blur. "That doesn't mean shit," I try to say, squinting, but I lose my balance, and the floor soars to my face.

Afternoon

I shove fries into my mouth and gulp down a glass of water. Doctor's orders: consume calories. I hope my health insurance won't bill me for that. If only I'd realized I'd barely eaten in the last few days.

I'm waiting for Martha at the police station. She was hysterical over the phone. I could barely make out a word she said. First she said Craig would never do such a thing, and then she remembered the DNA the police found in Lexy's car. After that, she didn't stop crying.

I have no idea why I'm here. I guess I'm trying to make Aliya uncomfortable with my presence. Perhaps she'll disclose something to me—at least that's what I'm hoping for.

High heels click-clack my way. Martha's eyes are red, swollen. I feel awful for thinking what I just did—that Lorraine died at the right time, that she's lucky not to experience this.

"Where is he?" she asks, rubbing the skin underneath her eyes, trying to blend her makeup back in.

"They took him to a cell. I haven't spoken to the detectives yet."

"What if he gets out?" she asks, gazing into the air, her body not facing me.

"On bail?"

"Yes," she says. "Can I come stay with you at Lorraine's?"

I frown at how crazy that sounds, and then I realize she might have a point. But taking in my sister's ex-husband's wife is just wrong. "Don't you have…friends around?"

Martha faces me and grabs my arm. "Please," she says, staring at me. "I don't know what to do. What do I say to him? How do I act around him? What if he snaps at me?"

I push her hand away. It's all too fresh for me. I don't see Craig as a murderer, but from the look on Martha's face, I'm starting to doubt my judgment.

"It's a stupid idea for you to stay with me. It's the first place Craig would come looking for you…and besides, what makes you so special?" I force the zipper of my top up and cross my arms, slightly turning my shoulder to her.

Martha stands there, motionless, and then she leans back against the wall and slides down to the floor. I turn to stare at her as she cries with her face buried in her hands. She glances at me, and my expression makes my thoughts quite evident.

I feel absolutely fucking nothing for her.

Lexy

Saturday, April 26, 2015
Afternoon - 2 Months Before Disappearance

My phone is resting on my palm, my eyes fixed on the signal. We've been driving for twenty minutes, and there's still no mobile network available. If I had to sum up this trip, I'd say it was interesting. Martha had her little ups and downs, as usual; Wayne couldn't leave me alone; Craig made sure he was the man of the house; and Logan was a show-off. But most important, I feel well rested for the first time in months.

My phone's screen lights up, and I open the e-mail as fast as I can. It's from my area director.

> I can't guarantee you a rematch with another family in Seattle. To do so, unfortunately, would violate our rules. If you really do not want to work for Ms. Davis any longer, please let me know so we can schedule an appointment to discuss the matter with her. Maybe we can solve the problems instead.

I sigh.

"What's wrong?" Wayne asks, keeping his eyes on Craig's BMW ahead.

"Nothing."

"You sure?"

I shrug. "Just don't feel like going back to work."

He doesn't reply. Instead he places his hand on my thigh and turns off at a strip mall.

"What are you doing?" I ask, as he swings the car into a parking spot.

"Come on," he says, opening his door. "We're not cutting your weekend short." He gestures for me to follow him. "Let's grab something to eat." I walk around my car, feeling an overwhelming wave of relief, and he holds an arm out to entwine his fingers with mine.

Evening

I'm sitting on the couch next to Lorraine. I regret saying that we had to talk when I get back, because now, after reading the area director's email, I need to say exactly what I don't want to.

"I'm sorry for my behaviour the last few weeks," I begin. "I know you're going through a really difficult time. You're my boss, and I need to respect you." I feel like a robot, programmed to spout bullshit.

She directs her gaze toward me, and I avert mine to my hands. "And I need to respect you," she says. "You're so good to me, Lexy. And so good with Sam and Logan. I know I've had a bad way of showing my appreciation lately, but I really appreciate everything you've been doing for the kids and me."

I wish I could look her in the eye, tell her I meant it, but I can't. "So," I say, glancing at my phone to check the time, knowing Logan will be home any moment, "we're cool?" I ask, trying to cut it short.

"We're…cool," she says, giving a barely audible chuckle. She reaches a hand out, rubbing my upper arm. I let her, even though every neuron inside me wants to resist. I glide my eyes up to hers, and I manage a smile.

Game fucking on.

Saturday, May 2, 2015
Evening

I'm officially living a self-deluded lie. This week I felt like a treacherous, disembodied, stone-cold bitch. I've even played fictitious versions of events in my mind to sustain myself over the past few days.

Carmen came around yesterday to take Lorraine to her last radiation treatment. She was annoyingly enthusiastic about it, but Lorraine didn't share her excitement. She was nervous and scared. "Last stretch," she said with a sad smile, and I knew what she meant, since I could see she's done. If only that stupid brat could stop jumping around, saying shit like, "Boy, am I glad you're done with this." And "You can do it! You're strong." Like people die from cancer because they're not strong. What a fucking idiot.

I've decided to get what I came for. What's the use of doing something I hate and not reaping the benefits of it? That's pathetic. Why would I slave away for hours for nothing? I came to Seattle for a reason.

But that'll have to wait for a few days, because now I'm in Logan's room, trying to get him to tell me why he sent those messages to his mum—for my own sanity and also to know whom I should be wary of.

I try to be unobtrusive about it, so I begin by saying, "How old were you when you got your first cell phone?"

Logan shrugs. "Not sure. Why?"

"Just wondering. I mean, these days kids get them at a ridiculously young age."

"Mmm," he says, thinning his lips. "No, I got mine after my thirteenth birthday. My mom didn't want me to get one."

I smile. "But if it was up to your dad—"

"Then I'd have had a phone when I was eight," he says in a breathless rush.

I regard him for a second. "I think I was about fourteen when my mum gave me a disgusting brick of a phone. Of course, back then I was thrilled, since it was the best out there."

"I remember those," he says. "My aunt had one." He smiles at his bedcovers. "My first one was a flip phone. My dad passed it on to me without my mom knowing," he says, and his face lights up with impish glee. "When she eventually walked in on me when I was in bed one night…" he says, and I erupt in laughter, my hand pressed against my mouth.

"No!" I say. "Shut up…That's enough."

"You asked," he says, grinning. "So anyway, she punished my dad and me by making us switch SIM cards. My dad hated it, and I had to take his business calls, and then, after a few seconds, I'd just pass the phone to him. My parents had some big fights because of that. He eventually got a new number, trying to get a clean slate, and I kept his old one."

I raise an eyebrow. "Your mum didn't play around, eh?" I say, still beaming with amusement. For a moment I thought that was all I needed, but then I realise I have to ask one more question. "So when did she catch you… you know… jerking off?" I need to know who had the phone, whether the dates align. *Who sent those texts?*

His cheeks pull up again, creating fine lines underneath his eyes. "Not long after my thirteenth birthday. I didn't have the phone for long before I snooped around online." He falls silent, and then he chuckles. "They got divorced not long after."

We both burst out laughing again.

"That's messed up," I say, poking him on the shoulder and suppressing my smile, but the moment is short-lived as a deep, sudden, intuitive leap of understanding strikes me. It's like a thick mist creeping over an ominously dark mountain. Maybe Lorraine isn't lying. Perhaps Craig isn't the man I thought he is. Perhaps he did send her those messages. Was he playing with her for his own malicious gratification?

Saturday, May 9, 2015
Afternoon

Every morning this week, I couldn't look at Craig. I felt terrible for laughing at the thought of him beating Lorraine; it had felt so improbable that it was almost comical. After what I've learned lately, I've concluded that her statements are more credible than I'd thought. I almost confronted him, but I didn't want to stir up another squall, so I just did my work with my robotic smile planted on my face.

After much thought, I've decided that I need to come clean with Wayne. I need to tell him the truth, what I've been doing behind his back. Losing another night's sleep over it isn't worth it.

On my way to his place, I was pretty determined to get it off my chest, but now, as I sit next to him on his couch, I'm wavering.

He lowers the volume of the telly and turns slightly toward me. "I've got something for you," he says, resting a hand on my leg.

My stomach clenches. "You shouldn't have," I say as politely as I can, forcing a smile.

"No. You'll love it," he says, double-tapping my leg. He climbs off the couch and disappears into his room. *If he could read my mind,* I think, *he'd be rightfully pissed.* A minute later he drops two sheets of paper onto my lap, eagerly waiting for me to respond.

Instead of jumping from the couch and embracing him, which I would've done with different circumstances, I pause. Two tickets. Two bloody tickets to Fall Out Boy's upcoming concert. A moment of silence passes.

"I…I thought you liked them," he says, stuttering.

I stare at the tickets for another second, swallowing, and then I turn to him.

"Sorry. I…I'm shocked. I didn't know they were coming to Seattle." I knew—of course I did. *Damage control,* I think, and with all my willpower, I jump to my feet to embrace him. "Thank you, Wayne."

His arms tighten around my waist, and he presses his lips against my forehead. I tuck my head underneath his chin, determined not to show my face, and all I can think is, *I am the Devil.*

Sunday, May 10, 2015
Afternoon

I texted Roy. I told him I'm about to break up with Wayne and I'd like to see him soon. Doing this makes me feel more compelled to go through with it. He didn't reply, but I got a notification that he read my message.

The battery icon flickers in the upper corner of my screen. I quickly look at Wayne, who's taking a nap on the couch, trying to catch up on the sleep he lost working night shift. I tiptoe out of the apartment and down to my car to fetch my charger. I close the door as I sit in the passenger seat, ruminating on what's about to happen. It's not like Roy is waiting for me with open arms, and if I do end things with Wayne, I might be back at square one. Not that I've made any progress really, but he was the perfect distraction. We do have some chemistry, Wayne and me, but that's not enough, is it?

Stepping out of my car, I take a deep breath, and then I stride back to his apartment, avoiding any further delay. I tiptoe inside, expecting him to be asleep on the couch, but he's not there. My eyes glide to the kitchen counter where I left my phone, and my heart skips a beat.

It's gone.

I stand frozen for a few seconds, and then I bolt to his room. My boots rest on the threshold as I come to a halt, and my body goes numb. He's sitting on the edge of his mattress, staring at my phone. It vibrates in his hand, which sends a shiver down my spine. I clear my throat, but he won't look up. The old phone clicks to life as he presses the keys, probably opening the message I sent to Roy.

"Wayne, I—"

"When were you planning on telling me?" he says, his head lowered. Silence fills the room, and my throat dries out. His head jerks up. "Are you a lesbian?"

I snort, and his frown deepens. I think fast, biting my inner cheek. Would that make him feel better? The "cockpit clashers"? No, that would just be another lie, another dead end.

"No," I say, my hand on the doorjamb. Suddenly I feel sick with apprehension, and I'm not sure if it's because of what Roy might have replied or how Wayne might react.

"Then why would you tell *Vicky* you miss being close to her and you can't wait to see her?" he says. "Do you mind explaining yourself?"

"It's Roy," I say, and I'm surprised at how easily it rolled off my tongue.

He drops the phone next to him on the bed. Before I can say anything, he clenches a fist through his hair, pulling at it as he rocks back and forth, his back curved forward, his elbows pressed against his knees. It's an unfathomably disturbing sight.

I take a step back, my hands brushing against the door beside me. He jumps to his feet and charges toward me but stops abruptly to swing back around. Now he's pacing the floor, wiping a palm over his mouth. "You cheated," he says. "You fucking cheated on me," he repeats, this time more assured.

"Yes," I say. I want to apologise, but words fail me.

"Leave," he says, glaring at me. "Please," he adds, his voice breaking. "Please…leave."

I want to walk up to him, give him a hug. I knew this day would come, but I didn't expect the sight of Wayne tearing up to break my heart.

I cringe at what I'm about to say, but it would be an inane idea to approach him. "I…I need my phone," I say, and he pauses, his hand still on his chin as he glares at me. My eyes drop to the floor as he scuffles through the covers before lumbering toward me. He swings an arm up from his side, holding my phone out. I politely take it from him. "Thanks," I say, but he disregards me by flicking a hand, and then he turns to walk into the bathroom, slamming the door behind him.

I guess that's my cue to leave.

Ella

Monday, July 13, 2015
Afternoon - 17 Days After Disappearance

Dean Torkaz called. He said Lorraine designated me as the beneficiary of her life insurance and her 401(k) account. "I know you're in the midst of grieving the loss of a loved one," he said, "but don't wait too long to do something about this. The IRS has deadlines and penalties concerning inherited retirement accounts."

My head spun when he said that, and then I thought about stashing most of the money away for Sam's college tuition, and if I run out of money, I'll use some of it for living expenses until I get a job. If that wasn't enough, he also told me Lorraine wanted me to be Sam's legal guardian. Nothing is set in stone. There will be a custody case, and I'm not sure if the idea of motherhood is exhilarating or petrifying. Part of me wants to bring Lorraine back from the dead, ask her what the hell she was thinking. The other part wants to hold Sam close, away from Robert, and have him live the best life possible. I forgot to ask Dean about Roy and Lexy, since I was too baffled to think straight. I never thought that my sister, or anyone for that matter, would choose *me* of all people to take care of her son.

I immediately called Robert, who backed off pretty fast. He won't be able to afford a court battle, so we decided to appoint Family Court Services to create a parenting order so we can establish day-to-day care.

I haven't heard a word from Martha since our get-together at the police station. I also have no intention of calling her—at least not today.

After I got off the phone with Robert, I received a call from Wayne. He invited me over, said he heard that Craig was arrested, and then he proceeded to justify a drink or two. I decided not to drop Sam off at Brighter Horizons; I don't know Robert well enough to know what he's capable of.

Now I'm sitting on the floor in front of Wayne's television, tickling Sam.

He gives me a belly laugh as his little body jiggles. He reaches for a toy and slams it on the rug, giving me a mischievous smile.

"I'm sorry about your sister," Wayne says, hunching over to pass me a glass of vodka and Sprite. "Is it okay if I come to her funeral?" he asks.

"Of course," I say. "It's scheduled for Saturday morning at eleven."

"I know. I saw the Facebook post."

I purse my lips. "The investigation held us up…I wanted to schedule it earlier." He says nothing, and suddenly I realize how heavy and lifeless my eyes feel. "Thanks for having me over. Martha's probably knocked my front door off by now."

He chuckles softly. "I kind of feel sorry for her," he says, and I immediately wave it off.

"I don't. You know her well?"

"Kind of, yeah. I saw her a lot more than I saw Lorraine."

"Don't compare them," I say with a heaviness in my stomach. "Just don't."

"Sorry. I didn't mean to." He tilts his head, trying to make eye contact. "It's funny. Lexy didn't like her either, at first."

"Well, guess she's not a likable person."

"*At first,*" he repeats. "Then they warmed up to each other."

"And what…? You and Martha were friends?"

He shrugs. "No, not really, but I did confide in her now and then." There's a pause. "Okay, once," he says, taking a sip from his drink.

"You actually trust her?"

He breaks eye contact as his eyes shift to Sam. "I learned my lesson," he says, chuckling. "But, uh, one night I was drinking, and I tried to get a hold of Lexy after we broke up. Her phone was off. First I called Lorraine's house. She said Lexy wasn't there, so then I called Craig's landline. Martha picked up and told me the same thing, so I realized she had to be with Roy."

"Or out shopping or all the other possible reasons for someone not to be home," I say, and I give him a compassionate smile.

"Well, at the time I didn't think like that. I kind of lost it. So I confided in Martha. She just happened to lend an ear…and she gave me some good advice."

"What did she say?"

He shrugs again. "I'd rather not talk about it now."

"Well," I tell him, "to each to his own."

He gazes into his glass then looks up at me. "So why did they arrest Craig?"

"They found the spare key to Lexy's car at his house up in the Olympic Peninsula."

He frowns. "That actually makes sense. We went there a few months ago. Maybe she dropped them or forgot them there."

"Maybe, but they also found his DNA in her car. Guess the detectives have reached a dead end, so now they're closing in on Craig."

"Geez," he says. "Now I'm scared they'll come after me."

I give him a perceptible blink as I cock my head back. "Why would they?" I ask, holding Sam's hands as he sits up.

"Well, you know, phone records. After Lexy told me about Roy, I didn't take it so well." He scratches the back of his head.

"And? What did you do?" My elbows drop, my arms hanging low. Sam's wrists rest on his tiny knees, his hands still clutched in mine. Our heads turn to Wayne, staring at him in silence.

"Well, I sent her a text. It just…won't look good." He takes a big gulp of his drink.

"What did you say to her?"

He shifts his weight from one arm to the other. "Something along the lines of 'You lying fucking spawn of Satan.'"

I sigh, shaking my head. "You're right. That does look fucking bad."

"Yeah, but come on, what would you have done?"

His question makes me laugh. "I've never really had a serious romantic relationship…so I don't know."

"Why's that?" he asks, his tone incredulous.

"Let's just say I had a fling now and then, but it became a distraction. I haven't met a man I thought was more important than my career." He nods with the corners of his lips curled down, considering my statement. I don't want to discuss the thing Lorraine always gave me shit about. She'd always say it was because of what happened to Miss McBeth, that I'd turned sour. And because all the other kids didn't like me, I started to avoid relationships. Lorraine cornered me back in college once—I was surprised to see her taking a stand against me—and said I need to see a therapist. I laughed it off and left for class.

"But anyway," I continue, "let's stay on topic. Did Lexy respond to your message?"

"Yes, which was even worse than what I wrote her."

I straighten my back. "And that was?"

"She told me I'd regret contacting her again, because then it would be on me." He shakes his head. "I had no idea what she was talking about, so of course I asked her what she meant, and she said, 'This is all your fault.'"

I grimace, trying to assimilate what that might mean. "But I don't think she meant that," he says, and I stare at him in disbelief. I remind myself that he doesn't know Lexy is on her way from London to Seattle, and if he's hiding something, he'd better come clean for his own sake. But before I can say anything, the familiar tune of the news fills my ears.

Wayne and I fall silent, our attention drawn to the reporters. The anchorman is sitting next to a blonde who has the countenance that only a runway model can possess. She proceeds by giving us the news: "Donald Trump didn't appear at last night's Miss USA pageant, which he cosponsors, because he was 'campaigning in Phoenix.'" On the screen, a Tweet expands with a typical picture of Trump in which his lips are slightly puckered, his eyebrows lowered.

The view switches back to the studio, where the anchorman continues. "NBC has severed ties with Donald Trump because of remarks he has made about Mexican immigrants. NBC made a statement, quote: 'Donald Trump's opinions do not represent those of NBC, and we do not agree with his positions on several issues, including his recent comments on immigration.'"

I turn my attention to Sam, whose eyes are falling shut. "Wayne."

"Yeah," he says.

"I'm going to put Sam in his stroller. Then I should probably go."

He turns to me. "Don't you think that's…risky?"

"What do you mean?"

"To drive under the influence…especially when you're trying to get custody of Sam." He fails to hide his bewilderment.

I sigh, and my shoulders drop. He's right. Even though it was only one drink, it was a strong one. I can't take any chances. At least I have everything I need: diapers, baby food, Sam's toys, clean clothes, wipes, and his portable crib, which is in the car (yes, I take it everywhere I go).

"So…where should I sleep?" I ask, rocking Sam in my arms.

"In my bed," he says, and I give him a dazed look. "I'll sleep on the couch, of course."

Our eyes meet and he looks at me a little longer than usual, and then our heads jerk up at the familiar sound of Eric's voice on the TV. A microphone maneuvers unbearably close to his mouth, clutched in a reporter's hand.

"Craig Davis has been released without charge," he says, motioning his head from one side to the other, speaking toward the eager crowd encircling him. Everyone anxiously waits for him to continue, but then he nods, indicating that he's done. He tries to make his way down the steps of what appears to be the police station, but I'm not sure. Several reporters block his way. "Sir, sir!" one woman shouts from behind him, frantically waving the microphone in his face. "Is he still your prime suspect?"

"That's all for now," Eric says, then successfully pushes his way through the horde.

I don't hear the TV after that. I just stare at the floor, my thoughts swirling out of control. I glance at Wayne, who's still watching the news carefully. "Maybe they're looking for you now," I say and snort, but he's not smiling. *It was just a text message,* I think, *but then again, it was just a spare key.* I stare at him for a moment longer, and then I decide to lock the bedroom door when we go to sleep tonight.

Tuesday, July 14, 2015
Afternoon

The first thought that struck me this morning was *Lexy must have arrived in Seattle by now*. I decided to send her a message on Facebook. I told her I've been following the case closely, that I might give her more than the detectives will, and that I'll be home tonight if she wants to come over. Then, out of nowhere, the thought surfaced that she might know every little detail of what happened that night. Even so, I pushed my luck because the detectives won't tell me shit, and I need to talk to her.

As I folded Sam's blankets and stuffed them into a bag, the smell of greasy bacon swirled up my nose. My stomach churned, begging me to eat. I gently pressed the door open to find Wayne's feet anchored in front of the stove. He was flipping bacon and sausage and stirring scrambled eggs. He glanced over his shoulder. "Good morning!" he said jubilantly.

It was clear that he'd already had his morning shower. His dark-brown hair was neatly styled, his face smoothed by a razor, and he was dressed like he had a job interview.

I smiled, wondering how Lexy had messed this up—what her deal was with Roy and how stupid she is. But then again, I don't know Wayne very well. He might be a jerk for all I know.

"Please," he said, wobbling the spatula sideways, "have a seat."

"You do this every morning?" I asked, sliding the chair out from underneath the kitchen table.

He lifted his chin and peered at me. "Not really," he said, moving the pan back and forth. "Only for guests…special guests."

I gave him a polite smile, and something voracious gnawed at the pit of my stomach, making it growl. "I'll be on my way soon," I said, ceasing the idea of spending the day together. Not that he implied that, but whenever someone does little favors for me—even from the kindness of their heart—I can't help see a hidden agenda, even though they might not have one.

Casting me a smile, he tossed a couple of bacon strips onto my plate. "All good," he said, planting the dish in front of me.

After I devoured my meal, I thanked him and left with Sam. I had something to do, something important.

Now I'm at the Elysium Hotel, where Craig lives. Yes, that's right, Martha won't let him back into his own house. Ridiculous. All last night, I kept rolling around. I couldn't figure out if it was because I was sleeping in Wayne's bed or because something was bothering me about Craig, about his attitude whenever I've questioned him.

I reasoned there's only one thing I can do, and that's to confront him again. But this time I'm not backing down.

"So," I say, walking around the well-made, queen-size bed, "I know why your DNA was really in Lexy's car." I'm bluffing, of course, but it's all I've got.

Craig clenches his teeth as his eyes drop to the floor. "How?"

I think fast. "Aliya told me."

His eyelids droop as the life draws out of him. "I fucked up," he says.

My face falls slack; I was completely unprepared for such a response. I try to find my voice, but I can't.

"No," he says, a hand raised in the air. "You don't have to say anything. I figured you'd find out soon anyway." He walks up to me, and my back straightens. "El, I couldn't…" He pauses, and then he meets my eye. "I just couldn't admit it."

I try to play along. "Which part?" I ask, a little too desperate. His eyes fall to the floor.

"That I cheated?" It comes out as a question.

"You cheated on Martha?"

"Wait, you said Ali—"

"Well, fuck it. I lied."

He lets out a long breath. "That's fucked up, El."

"That *is* fucked up. *You* are fucked up…and besides, this will make the headlines soon anyway." I pause. "With who?"

"Lexy."

"Jesus!" I exclaim, shaking my head, my teeth exposed as I bite my lower lip. I almost kick the first object in sight, but then I realize it's Sam's car seat.

"She came on to me," he says. "Before I knew it, she had her hands down there."

"Why admit this *now?* After all the times I confronted you?"

"The police retrieved the records from her old phone. They found an increase in the number of interactions between Lexy and me. And like you said, she's on her way to Seattle. Would've come out anyway."

I give him a chuckle, my eyes fixed on him. "Pathetic," I say, shaking my head. "You're the embodiment of a fucking cliché."

Lexy

Saturday, May 16, 2015
Afternoon - 1 ¼ Months Before Disappearance

I figured the phone vibrated in Wayne's hand right before he asked me who Vicky was—God, I still cringe when I think about it—because the battery was about to die. Or a message came through, and he deleted it; I'm not sure. But I guess it doesn't matter anymore.

I waited till Wednesday for Roy to respond to me. I felt he owed me a reply. At least an acknowledgement that he had received my message, even though my phone showed that he'd read the text. I just wanted to hear from him. So I sent him another one, saying, "I did it." It took him another day, and then he replied:

I need some space.

That's it. That's fucking it. After I stared at the message for a minute or two, I decided I wouldn't text him again until he contacted me, and this would be the last time, his last chance. Because he'd done this before. He asked for space, and I gave it to him. Even though I needed him more than ever, I tried to put his needs first. Then he ran off with another girl, cheated on me, asked his friends to lie to me, and treated me like shit. Yet here I am, giving him another chance, another shot at this. If I had a friend like myself, I would've broken my fist on her face and told her how stupid she is. But of course, there's always more to it than we let on.

Evening

I'm back at the Woods Motel Inn in Sammamish. The same one we drove to a few weeks ago.

"Lexy," he says, walking up to me, and then he cups his hands around my cheeks. "No one can know about this."

"I have no intention of telling anyone," I say, and before he can say anything, I plant my lips on his. He swings me around and shoves me onto the bed. I turn to look at him as he unbuttons his shirt. *Why?* I ask myself. *Why am I doing this?* I ought to know the answer, but I keep denying it. I keep telling myself that it's okay to sleep around, but I know I'm doing it to feel accepted, wanted, or worthy. It all started a year ago, when Roy left me, because I was *impossible to be around.*

He hunches forward, takes my arm, and flips me onto my stomach. My chin rests on the mattress, the springs weighing down as he crawls over me.

I close my eyes as I tell myself why I'm so promiscuous: because I want to believe I'm wanted—but I'm not worthy of love; I don't deserve it. I mean, what makes me so special? So I take bits and pieces of people to fill the parts that have been ripped out of me. It's an endless cycle of give-and-take, even though there's no love to it. It's all an illusion. An illusion of requited love, for the moment, for the time being.

Ella

Tuesday, July 14, 2015
Afternoon - 18 Days After Disappearance

"Does Martha know?" I ask.

"No," he says, head lowered, arms stretched out to his sides as they rest on the mattress.

"How sure are you?" I ask, pacing the room.

"Very sure."

I can't help wonder if she pretended not to know, but we're talking about *Martha.* If that woman has something on her mind, it comes right out of her mouth. No fucking filter whatsoever. So that seems implausible. "Detective Baldwin will probably inform her, don't you think?"

"Well, as long as I don't have to break it to her," he says, and swallows.

"Maybe you should man up and take responsibility, Craig. Why can't you just tell a woman you screwed her over? You have enough balls for the world to suck, but when you really need them, they're gone. Stop being a coward. That's fucking weak."

His mouth snaps shut. I bet no woman has ever spoken to him like this before. "When are you planning on telling her?" I ask, but he remains silent, unmoving. "You'd better do it soon," I say, "or I will."

Lexy

Tuesday July 14, 2015
Afternoon - 18 Days After Disappearance

Seattle feels as foreign as it did the first day I set foot in it. The ten-hour flight felt like days, and this drive feels like forever.

The rattle of the window unnerves me as we make our way to the police station. The officer who's driving doesn't say much, nor does the one sitting next to me, who hasn't taken his eyes off me since I got in the car. Guess they were advised to keep their mouths shut while escorting me.

I look at the trees passing me, at the cars changing lanes, its drivers eager to get home, everyone moving about with a goal, a destination to reach.

The asphalt on the road makes the car clatter, the vibration reverberating in my chest. I take deep, steady breaths. *Everything will be okay,* I keep thinking, convincing myself that I did nothing wrong…well, if only that were the case.

As the car comes to a halt, I glance to my right. Steps lead to the front door, where a bold sign with blue letters reads, REDMOND POLICE STATION. It feels like my heart is giving out as the driver walks around the car to open my door. My legs tremble, and I force a watery smile. I look up at him as he waves me toward the main entrance. Each step feels higher than the one before, each tread heavier than the previous one. The entrance is at spitting distance, but it feels miles away.

In my mind, I try to rehearse what I'm about to tell the police, and then I wonder if I should've brought a lawyer. But my mother, who knows nothing but lies, said we don't have that kind of money. She believes I'm merely here to aid with the investigation and then I'll return home. Hell, she's even getting the baby room ready for her grandchild, which she's surprisingly thrilled about.

A tall bald man nods to me as I enter the station. He doesn't say a word as he stretches his hand out and takes me by my elbow. He leads me up another set of stairs, down a hallway, and into an interrogation room. Here a woman awaits me, who seems to have neglected her face altogether. Something tells me she always wears her stealth-force boots. I imagine her sitting at home, her legs propped up on the coffee table, as she stuffs her mouth with greasy fries.

"Detective Aliya Winters," she says, fiddling with a pen. My eyes trace back to the bald man in the doorway.

"And I'm Detective Eric Baldwin," he says, gesturing me to sit.

The room is freezing cold, and the pen, which Aliya now taps on the table, sends crisp quivers down my back. It's just us, three bodies propped onto three chairs, and a silverish-grey light cone, hovering just low enough to expose every twitch and facial expression.

The two detectives prop their elbows on the table like rehearsed puppets, and then they fold their hands in unison. Eric leans in, his eyes glaring through me. Aliya glances at the papers in front of her, and I dread for this interrogation to begin.

Eric jerks himself upright, making me gasp for air, my eyes wider than before. He reaches into his pocket and takes out a remote. "Almost forgot," he says, and chuckles. He presses a thumb down, and a red light flickers on a mounted camera.

Say something wrong, and you're screwed, I think. *Now it'll be like carving words into stone.*

"Right," Aliya says, then clears her throat. "Please state your full name, date of birth, and where you're from."

I do as told, sinking into my chair, knowing deep down why she asked. *For the court case.*

Now it's Eric's turn to speak. He states the time, date, and the names of persons present. He doesn't take his eyes off me, and neither does Aliya.

"Lexy," she says, "why did you tell us over the phone, before coming here, that you 'feel responsible for everything' and that 'you lied'?"

It sinks in how bad that must've sounded and the terrible position I placed myself in. My eyes rapidly shift between them. My heart quickens; my body tenses; and the hair on the nape of my neck prickles. Suddenly my shoes feel small, too tight, and I realise I need to speak; I need to say something. I open my mouth, but I close it just as fast.

"Do you want me to repeat my question?" Aliya asks, annoyance smeared across her face.

I shake my head slightly and clutch the sides of my chair. I hold my breath, and then I blurt it out: "Because I did."

Lexy

Saturday, May 16, 2015
Evening - 1 ¼ Months Before Disappearance

He finishes inside me, exhaling in relief, his neck exposed. He falls down to my left. "Wow," he says, resting a hand on his forehead. "Why is it that when you do something wrong, it feels so much…better?"

I prop myself onto my elbows and turn my head toward him. "It's not really *that* wrong," I say, staring at him as he pants slightly, his eyes closed. "I left Wayne, remember? I'm not seeing anyone."

The corners of his lips lift a bit. "It doesn't make it any less wrong," he says, opening his eyes.

"What?" I sit up and frown. "Because I work for your mum?"

"And my dad."

There's silence. The hum of cars outside suddenly fills my ears, along with the *tap tap tap* of a faulty valve somewhere in the bathroom. He doesn't move, nor do I. Both of us just stare at each other, wondering what would happen if Lorraine found out that her au pair is sleeping with her son.

Saturday, May 30, 2015
Afternoon

I heard from Wayne again. He told me exactly what he thinks of me. *I deserve it*, I thought as I read his texts. I decided not to reply, not to fire him up, so I let him rant. Then, amid the messages fuelled with resentment, Roy reached out to me:

Do you want to come over so we can talk things through?

I immediately relaxed. For a while I thought he hated me. For a while I gave up hope. *Talk things through*—that didn't work out too well last time. Even though we're up and down, we've loved each other since the day we met. I know that. He knows that. I guess everyone who knows us does.

We met on a busy night in London while I was dancing with two of my friends. Everyone was moving to the beat, guys trying to get our attention. But Roy didn't; he was stock-still even though he was in a wild, rowdy crowd. He stood out like a cock on a female statue. His eyes were on mine, and he refused to look away. He had one hand tucked deep in his jeans pocket while he occasionally lifted his other hand as he drank his beer. Another song passed, and I couldn't stop myself from approaching him. We didn't exchange a single word. No hesitation. No second-guessing. He just curved a hand around the back of my neck and pulled me in. It was the most memorable kiss I've ever had, and instantly I knew—*somehow* I just knew.

Now, in the parking lot, I look at him as he walks up to me from his apartment complex. His steps are wide, strong, his massive shoulders pulled back. I haven't seen him in two and a half months.

As he gives me a hug, calmness drifts through me, a sense of security. We let go simultaneously, exchanging smiles. "Pizza?" he says, his face lighting up.

I nod, and he winks. He walks out in front of me, guiding the way to his place, even though I know where to go: two lefts, into the elevator, level five, down the corridor, number 53. "My brother just left," he says, as he closes the door behind us.

"When's he coming back?" I ask, taking off my leather jacket.

"Sunday evening."

"When will you tell him?" I ask, but he ignores my question. Instead he preheats the oven.

His brother, Dean, doesn't like me. Last time I heard, he referred to me as an "inconvenience." He made his own assumptions about Roy and me since I begged Roy to keep what really made us drift apart between us. Dean wanted him to start anew. He thought that if he could take Roy away from London, away from his frat friends, away from me, they could work together and have a successful law practice. Yet here I am, and Dean will most certainly not have any of it.

Roy takes a pizza out of the freezer, still not answering my question. "When will you tell him?" I repeat. "About us? You know…that I'm in Seattle."

"It's not that easy, Lexy."

I eye him, wondering if the truth would make Dean reevaluate his opinion of me. Good or bad, whatever. Not that my standing with him could be any worse. "I guess you can tell him what happened," I say, but the words hitch in my throat.

He pauses. "What?"

"I told Wayne."

He stares at the floor, shaking his head. "Wow…now that's some hypocritical bullshit."

"It was pretty easy for you when you told your mother," I say, fuming with resentment.

"I told you I was sorry about it!" he says, apologising for the hundredth time. Only if I could take it as one, see that he means it.

"Roy," I start to say but fall silent as he sharply exhales through his nose.

"Do what you want," he says, waving me off, determined to hide his hurt. "In any case, it's always been about you."

"I know," I say, and his face goes blank; he's clearly unprepared for such a response. "I'm sorry for blaming you," I say, "for almost everything." Roy doesn't move, nor does he speak; he just stares at me. "I want *us* to work," I continue, taking a step forward. "I screwed up. You screwed up. We totally fucked up…and it's time we shared responsibility for what we did."

He snorts, conveying a clear message of *Look who's talking*. He clears his throat and lowers his head. "You know, I've tried for months to forgive myself for what I've done," he says, his voice trailing off. "I fucking panicked! And you made it so hard to love you. You were *impossible* to be around." He swallows. "I already felt responsible, Lexy…and you made sure I thought about it *every fucking second* of the goddamn day." His eyebrows are drawn, and his eyes well up with tears.

I want to say that he pressured me to terminate my pregnancy, but I already reminded him plenty of times. *I did it for you,* he'd say. *Your bloody life depended on it—can't you see that?* I do see that, and that's what gets to me. *What makes me so special?* I ask myself that every day since we made the decision.

The doctor's exact words were: "There's an eighty percent chance that you won't make it, a twenty percent chance that you and your baby will." So many questions flashed through my mind: *You…or your baby? You…or your baby? Is she worth the twenty percent? Are you worth the eighty?* "Your condition can go from mild preeclampsia to severe preeclampsia very quickly," the doctor said. "And since you're in the middle of your exams, the stress will increase the likelihood that it will." I still didn't want to give up my baby. Roy uncomfortably shifted in his seat, eyeing me as the doctor continued. "Your kidneys and/or liver can fail unexpectedly. There's already been a drop in your red blood platelets, and you're only eighteen weeks pregnant."

Roy couldn't deal with the thought of losing me, and I couldn't bear the thought of giving up my child. We fought day and night. He reassured me that one day we could start a family when we were ready. After weeks of arguing, I made my decision. My *selfish* decision.

At night we'd go to bed, and he'd cuddle up from behind, his hand resting on my belly, on our baby. I'd lie there knowing that in a few days, my baby would be gone, even though her daddy's arm was holding us safely…but only for the night.

When we went out on the town, everyone swilled drink after drink. My friends would buy me cocktails, and I'd throw them into the toilet, hoping things would change. *You're in no position to have a child*, I'd convince myself, *and your mother would disown you. You'd lose everything else—your education and Roy too.*

A few days before the surgery to terminate my pregnancy, when the days felt like months, Roy would go out with his mates and get hammered, while I'd be at my apartment completely sober. One night I took a drink from a friend and sipped it. My heart scattered with every swallow. I knew what I was doing, but I told myself it might be the first step to accepting what was going to happen. I thought if I could do that, I could force an *I don't care* mantra into my mind. Perhaps I'd believe that; perhaps I'd cope that way. I thought, *If you can't deal with it, force yourself to deal with it.*

After I terminated the pregnancy, Roy couldn't cope with it, since I blamed him for pressuring me. He felt responsible, and he tried to distance himself from me, which didn't help at all.

I think the saddest thing in the world is loving someone who used to love you or loving something you never really had, like my child. That's when the depression began, and I've hated myself ever since.

I break eye contact with Roy and stare at the floor. "You left me," I say. He doesn't respond. The pain I've been burying all year long creeps up my throat. "Why did you leave me?" I ask, but I don't recognise my voice; it's strained and hoarse. I direct my gaze back to him, but my vision is blurred.

"Because I couldn't fucking look at you!" His voice blasts through me, resonating across the kitchen, making my shoulders jolt up. "I couldn't look at you for one second," he says, this time softer. "Your face was a reminder, a glimpse into hell. I couldn't be around you! You were fucking…impossible! As much as I love you, that's how much I wanted you to disappear."

I don't know what to say because I know he's right. I was hard to be around, but he made it harder. I felt like a monster, unworthy of anything, of anyone's love. Ending my pregnancy was the most difficult decision I've ever made. I lost not only our child but also myself.

"I love you," I tell him, "and I'm sorry. But if we can't put this behind us, we can't move forward…even though it feels like we don't deserve that."

Roy looks at me for a moment longer, and then he pulls me in. He holds me tight, kissing down on my hair. "I promise I'll never make you do anything like that again. I'm sorry, Lexy. If I could do it all over, I would."

Right here in this moment, I realised two things: 1) if you know what love is—parental, spousal, or any type for that matter—it's the worst punishment, because you won't be able to live the same life you did after it's gone; 2) there's no need to throw around blame, because it'll only ruin you.

But now, if I want things to work out between Roy and me, I need to do one thing. I need to tell him I'm pregnant…again.

Ella

Tuesday, July 14, 2015
Afternoon - 18 Days After Disappearance

"Okay, okay." Craig walks up to the window, his back turned to me. "Will you come with me when I tell Martha what happened between Lexy and me?"

I almost choke on my spit. "What? Are you twelve?" I eye him for a moment. "Now that you mention it, I don't think you're man enough to tell her."

"Please," he says, his chin almost resting on his shoulder as he stares at the floor, "don't make this worse than it already is."

"I don't think anyone has the skills to do that. You've fucked this up so hard that no one can make this any worse." He remains silent, and I roll my eyes. "Oh, for Christ's sake," I say, "You're such a coward." I wave him off, but he's not pleased. "Next time clean up your own shit."

He gives me a look, his eyes revitalized.

"So…tonight then?" I ask.

He nods, staring at the carpet. "Guess so," he murmurs. "If she can make it on such short notice." He seems to ruminate for a while before he finally takes his phone out of his pocket. His fingers pounce at the screen, and then he puts it away. "Okay. I asked her to meet us at Lorraine's place."

"Why there?"

"If we meet at my house, who leaves?" He lets the question hang in the air for a second. "I'd have to throw her out. At Lorraine's that won't matter. I just can't see you and me having to leave my *own* house."

I sigh, agitated at how he's trying to disperse the blame. "You mean *you'd* get thrown out, and I'd walk out with my head held high, with no fucks to give."

Craig manages a smile, but it disappears as soon as his phone chimes. He taps the screen, his eyes scanning across it. "Martha will be waiting outside my house in twenty minutes," he says. "She needs us to pick her up."

I throw my hands in the air. "You didn't tell her the drive will take us at least thirty?"

"It will?" he asks, and then he sees Sam, who's been sleeping peacefully through it all. "Oh, of course…baby on board," he says, nodding.

After he texts her back, he gathers his things and offers to carry Sam's car seat, as these days my forearms constantly have a red line running across them. "Why couldn't Martha drive to Lorraine's herself?" I ask him.

The door clicks behind us. "She's had a few drinks."

"Well, that's just perfect," I say, as we trudge down the corridor and into the elevator. "How is she when she's drunk?"

He presses a button to his side, "G" for ground level. "Unpredictable," he says. "There's a side to Martha that no one has seen but me. Or at least that's how it feels."

The elevator glides downward. "She's extremely territorial, and when things don't go her way, she acts out." I remain silent as the dread sets in. "Two days after Lorraine confronted me on my fortieth birthday, Martha lost it. I had to buy a new set of plates." The elevator comes to a halt, and the doors slide open. I gape at him as he walks out in front of me to the reception desk. He offers the busty woman behind the desk a polite smile as he returns his key, and then he grabs his bag and follows me to Lorraine's van.

"Did Logan ever see her like that?" I ask, as I unlock the car.

Craig leans in to click Sam's seat into its base then closes the door and stares at me. "Not that I know of. Well, maybe once, but I'm not sure he heard us. At the lake house, Martha and I had plans. We were supposed to go for a walk together. I forgot about it and told Logan I'd go target shooting with him. I told him to go outside and I'd join him in a few minutes. He had his earmuffs on. Martha was furious that I blew her off to spend time with Logan. She grabbed a glass and threw it at me and cut her hand in the process."

I look at him for a moment as I shake my head. "Fucking hell. Now I get why you want me there tonight." I scan the parking lot. "Where's your car?"

"The police have it."

"What? I thought they were done with you."

"Seems not," he says, walking over to the passenger's side. "Hope it's okay if we go together."

I nod, and we get into the van, the doors shutting one by one. "I guess you had your fair share with the detectives when they arrested you," I say. "What do you know about this new development?"

"You mean Lexy being alive?" he asks, swinging his head from side to side, making sure I'm not about to reverse in front of a car.

"Yes," I say, driving out of the parking lot. "Did you know she's been fine all this time?"

He twists in the passenger seat and glares straight at me. "No, I didn't."

I change lanes to merge onto I-5 North. "Did you sleep with Lexy in your house up in the Olympic Peninsula?" I glance at him from the corner of my eye.

"No."

"Did Wayne ever give you the impression that he suspected something?"

"No," he repeats, fiddling with the bottom of his jacket. "I swear to God, I don't know anything more than you do."

I regard him for a moment longer, and then I flick the indicator to take the ramp toward Redmond. He swings his head around again as though I'm his daughter driving for the first time, except he's only concerned about his own safety.

"Stop fucking doing that!" I say, raking him with contempt. He sinks into his seat. "You know what, Craig?" I say, taking a right, "I'm absolutely thrilled to know that once this investigation ends, I'll never have to see you again."

He turns his head away far enough so I can't read his face. Moments later, I pull up to his house, where Martha's standing on the cobblestone driveway, her arms crossed over her chest. A defensive stance, or maybe she's agitated or just piss cold. I'm not sure, and I don't care. Peering at Sam, she gets into the van without saying a word. Her seat belt clicks in place, and then I back out of the driveway and head to Lorraine's house. No one speaks the entire time. All I can hear is the tires humming along the road, Sam snoring, and the occasional tick of the indicators.

I park the van in front of Lorraine's garage. The passenger door slides open as Martha gets out. She walks right up to me, throws her arms around my shoulders, and squeezes me tightly. I stand there frozen, my arms glued to my sides. Martha turns to Craig, nods, then hastily turns to walk toward the house.

Craig helps me with Sam, and I grab the diaper bag. The keys jingle as I flip one of them over on the chain to open the front door. They follow me inside and down the hallway. I gesture for them to sit down at the kitchen table before I take Sam to his room, where I place him in his crib, hoping he won't wake up anytime soon.

Back in the kitchen, I flick the lever of the teakettle, trying to be as cordial as possible. Craig and Martha sit opposite each other, still not saying a word. I turn my back on them, wondering how Logan's murder case has anything to do with this, and how they're, once again, making this all about themselves.

Lexy

Monday, June 4, 2015
Morning - 3 Weeks Before Disappearance

I wipe the dark textured countertops, one by one, as I work my way through the kitchen. I hear footsteps on the landing upstairs. A click of a door. It must be Martha. She's late. Usually she leaves by now. I imagine her stumbling into class, the professor awkwardly trying to proceed with his lecture as the attention of his students shifts to the blonde at the entrance. I wonder if she likes the attention, if she ever pretends to be younger than she is. Not that she's old, but some of her classmates still live with Mummy and Daddy, and she's married to an almost-forty-year-old businessman who has a sixteen-year-old son.

Martha's footsteps in the kitchen bring me back to the present. She swings open the fridge door, grabs a yoghurt and runs out. It happened so fast. I'm not sure if she decided not to acknowledge me, or if she didn't see me. I shrug at the thought and continue to labour the morning away. The plates glide from between the racks as I unpack the dishwasher, storing them where they belong.

Logan's alarm goes off, and then there's a distant shuffle of bedcovers, and now four feet stomping on the landing. First Craig comes down, nodding toward me. I give him a pasted-on smile as he grabs the newspaper, unfolds it, and makes his way to the couch.

Then Logan romps down the steps, grinning. He winks at me right before moving from behind the wall, where his dad can see him. My face twitches at his incautious behaviour.

He walks up to me, not seeing his dad to his left, who's glued to the couch and peering at us over the rim of his glasses. I stiffen my neck and slightly widen my eyes to make Logan stop, but he doesn't pick up on it. He strides on with a goal, and a wave of nausea hits me. I clasp the edge of the countertop. He's so close that I can smell his aftershave. My eyes dart to his arm, which he lifts to take a hold of me, or pull me in—I don't know. I glance at my mug on the counter. Without a second thought, I push it to the floor.

"Oh, shit!" I say, falling to my knees, hidden from Craig's sight. The sudden whisk of the newspaper makes Logan's head jerk to his left. I'm glaring at him from below, shaking my head. He gives a step back, his face smeared with an expression that's hard to place. Disbelief? Shock? Perhaps both.

Craig clears his throat as he makes his way into the kitchen. "You okay?" he asks, unsmiling.

"Yeah, yeah. Sorry," I say.

Logan glances at his watch. "Dad, why aren't you at work?"

"I have a conference call I want to take from home," he says, pushing his glasses up the bridge of his nose. He's lying. I know because I asked him to stay so we could talk. We're just waiting for Logan to leave, who's now sitting on a barstool, still startled.

I cautiously assemble the chunks of glass scattered across the tiles. Craig goes back to the living room and plunges down on the couch, tugging the newspaper back open.

The glass clinks into the garbage bin, and then I clap my hands together as I purse my lips. "Logan, you'll be late. Get a move on."

He sighs, his energy shocked right out of him. He gives me a polite smile that transforms into a smirk. I squint while slightly shaking my head, and then he grins.

"Off you go," I say, and he gets to his feet. He winks once more, and I clench my teeth. "Bye," I say, waving him off before he can do anything foolish.

The door shuts behind me. Craig lowers his elbows as he drops the paper on his lap. "Is he gone?" he asks, but before I can peek out the window, he makes his way over to have a look for himself.

He closes the curtains and motions for me to follow him to the living room. I sit opposite him, my fingers entwined, my hands stiff.

"So," he says, leaning back into the cushions, his right foot bolstered by his left knee, "what is it?"

I try to decipher him. Is he annoyed? In a hurry? Worried? My breathing accelerates, and then I say it. "I'm pregnant."

I squeeze my eyes shut because suddenly I'm back in London when I said those exact words: "I'm pregnant." I was unsure whether I should smile or appear distraught. Roy was hunched forward, his hands holding the edge of the counter, his back flat and arms stretched out. That image is ingrained in my mind. I couldn't read his face, what he thought or felt. It became apparent when he slowly straightened his back, and then he struck the wall with his fist. Blood spiraled down his palm. He was beyond livid. I couldn't tell if he was angry with me or with the situation, but that lucid moment haunts me to this day.

I open my eyes, studying his face. Now he's leaning forward, elbows resting on his knees. He bites his lower lip, glaring. "Congratulations," he says, pretending as though he never had sex with me.

"It's yours," I add, unwavering.

Craig blinks fast, like he's trying to assimilate what I just said, then he squints. "Are you sure?"

"Yes."

"How far?"

"Two and a half months. Around there."

"Well, it could be anyone's child," he says, almost relieved, chuckling.

"But it's yours."

He glares at me. "What do you want?" he sneers.

"I *need* money. Medical bills, financial support…the works."

He snorts. "Not without a paternity test."

"You can't make me."

"A judge can."

I smirk. "You really want Martha to know about this?"

There's silence. He breaks out in a sweat, his knuckles a pale yellow as he tightens a fist.

"We can keep this between us," I offer. "They'll never know."

"Get rid of it," he says, spitting the words out. It's Craig's voice, but I see Roy's face.

"No!" I scream, leaning forward. "I won't do that!" His eyes dance around the room as my face flushes. "Don't you dare say that again!"

"Don't threaten me then," he says in a placating tone.

We hold each other's glare as I try to control my breathing. "If you go to court, Craig, what are the chances that Martha won't find out?" His head drops, his eyes searching for options. "No one has to know," I say, and the crease between his brows weakens.

"Except us?" he asks.

"Except us," I say, and he looks as though he's considering my offer.

Lexy

Tuesday, July 14, 2015
Afternoon - 18 Days After Disappearance

"So you had sexual intercourse with Craig Davis." Aliya says, trying to get a clear statement.

"Yes," I reply, staring at the red light flickering on the wall.

"You're certain it's Craig's child?"

My eyes drop to my hands. "No."

"Then why did you tell him it was?" Eric asks, his eyebrows raised.

"I needed the money," I admit, making them exchange glances.

"Please list the names of the potential fathers of your unborn child," he continues.

My eyes move between the two detectives as I start, "Wayne, Craig…" I swallow. "Roy or Logan."

The skin on Aliya's forehead pulls back. She's probably thinking, *Slut.*

"So let me get this straight," Eric says. "Roy rejected you, and then you sought approval from other men?"

I shamefully nod.

"How many sexual encounters did you have with Roy?"

"Since I came to Seattle…one."

Aliya shifts her weight on her chair. "Who knew about your affair?" she asks.

"Which one?"

They both chuckle disdainfully. I would have had the same reaction once. Before my university days. Before *everything.* I've become the girl I thought I'd never be, the one I despised back in high school. The attention whore.

"Let's start with Roy," Eric says, his eyes piercing mine. "So you used the name 'Vicky' whenever you referred to him in Wayne's presence, am I right?"

"No," I say, and his head flicks up from his notes. "I used the name 'Vicky' whenever I met with any of them."

Eric nods. "What were you doing at his brother's law firm?"

I swallow hard. "I visited Roy. Asked him for legal advice. I'm sure you know why by now."

"We need to hear it from you," Aliya says, folding her arms.

"To understand why I sought his legal advice, you need to know what happened before that."

They exchange glances again, seeming more intrigued than ever.

Ella

Tuesday, July 14, 2015
Evening - 18 Days After Disappearance

I take cautious steps toward them, two tea mugs clutched in my hands. Craig and Martha take them and lower them to the table, each one offering me a polite smile.

As the sun sets, the colors in the room fade, transforming into shades of gray and indigo blue. It softens Martha's skin, diminishing any imperfections, making her appear almost vulnerable. Craig's back is turned to the sliding door, his face shadowed.

I flick the light on. Both of them flinch. "Sorry," I say, taking a seat at the end of the table. Now we're sitting in a triangle: Craig to my left, Martha to my right.

My eyes move slowly between them, waiting for someone to break the silence. My mind traces back to the message I sent Lexy on Facebook. Am I obliged to listen to every word they say? Perhaps I can check to see if she replied.

My hands rummage through my handbag, but before I can grab my phone, Craig starts to speak. I pause, preparing myself for Martha's reaction.

"Martha," he starts, stretching an arm out. She doesn't resist; she lets him rest his hand on hers. "Honey…I made a mistake." She looks at him as though he's about to say he dropped a jar of sesame seeds.

"Go on," she says, in a cringe-worthy, solicitous tone. She straightens her back, the chair creaking beneath her. My hand presses against the mess in my bag, motionless.

"Honey…I know I said I wouldn't do the same thing to you, but this time was different." There's a pause. "I promise."

Her skin bunches around her eyes, and she grits her teeth, making me wince. Her eyes shoot at me, radiating abhorrence. My eyebrows flick up and down in an *I have nothing to do with this* gesture.

Craig continues, and Martha's head jerks back toward him. "Remember when Lorraine showed up at our house a few months ago?" he says, waiting for her to respond. She merely nods. "You didn't talk to me for days, and well…you wouldn't even let me touch you."

"With reason," she says.

"Yes…well, no, not really, because I didn't send her those texts, but I can see how it could've made you feel."

I think of what Dr. Rowe said—that Lorraine could read headlines and short sentences. But I decide not to interfere.

"Well, darling, around the time of my fortieth birthday, I…" He slightly cringes, his face wincing at what he's about to say. "Honey, I cheated on you."

Martha pulls her hand away, and her eyebrows knit together as her eyes fill with tears. "What?" There's a moment of silence. A tear escapes her left eye, the fold line around her mouth guiding it toward her chin, which is trembling. "You did what?" she repeats, this time with an incredulous expression etched across her face.

Craig's eyes jitter around, and then he leans in toward Martha, swallowing. "I slept with Lexy," he says, and he catches my eye as I purposely frown at him to cut it the fuck out. He juts his shoulders forward in a *What else should I do?* shrug. Martha's eyes are fixed on the table, her chin tucked to her chest, and I hear a tremble in her breathing.

And then I wait for her to throw a fucking scene…I can see Craig is anticipating it too. It's almost impossible for a woman like her not to. I can hear the *tick tick tick* in her head: a tripwire ready to explode in fury. And then, in my mind, I start to count down from ten.

Any moment now.

Lexy

Tuesday, June 16, 2015
Morning - 10 Days Before Disappearance

Logan shuts the door behind him as he leaves for school. I sink into the couch, inhaling the scent of overcooked bacon, but it's overpowered by the acrid taste of gastric juice crawling up my throat. I run to the bathroom and hover over the toilet. My stomach tightens as I heave, but nothing comes. I stand there for a moment longer, waiting to be sick, but then I turn to pee for the second time in ten minutes.

I'll have to tell Lorraine about my pregnancy. Of course, I'll tell her Wayne is the father. Maybe she'll let me rest from time to time; perhaps I'll get a much-needed break.

I catch a glimpse of myself in the mirror. My eyes trace down to my belly. I stand sideways, lifting my top. I chuckle for thinking there'd be a gentle mound. The only sign so far is my fuller breasts, which I had to wedge into my bra this morning. I'll press them down by wearing a tight crop top, then hide them under a loose blouse. At times like this, I wish it were winter.

I saunter upstairs to Logan's room, thinking, *Hopefully I won't have to make my child's bed when he—or she—is sixteen.* Something tells me it's a boy, but it doesn't really matter. At least I'll be well prepared since I've been practically raising Sam.

I tuck the sheets underneath the mattress, wipe the wrinkles out of the duvet, and grab the sides of the pillow. I squeeze my hands together before I pull them back out again—it's almost like playing an accordion. Then I pick up the overloaded laundry basket and make my way downstairs.

At the bottom of the steps, I turn left and go to the laundry room. I toss the clothes into the machine, pour some detergent in, and set the timer so it'll start right before Logan gets home from school. I'll send him a text to remind him to throw his clothes into the dryer.

With a sigh, I make my way to the kitchen to grab my bag from the counter and leave, but as soon as it comes into view, I pause. My stomach flips. *Perhaps she forgot something*, I think. But then I see it.

Martha's leaning forward on her elbows with my phone up to her face. Her expression is blank as her eyes scan the screen. The hair on the nape of my neck stands up, sending a chill down my spine. She acknowledges my presence by chuckling bitterly, her eyes still on my phone.

I gather all my energy and blurt it out: "What are you doing?" She doesn't budge. Now she's pressing the keys, lifting her weight off her elbow to lean on her arm. "Martha!"

She chuckles again, but this time with her lips twist into a sour smile. I eye the door, weighing my options, calculating. She snorts once more, and then she rolls her eyes up to me. In a disturbingly sharp manner, she cocks her head to the side, her ear almost touching her shoulder. We hold each other's stare, and then she gives me a *poor girl* look as she curves the corners of her lips downward, widening her eyes. I try my best not to move, not to convey any signs of weakness or fear.

A few seconds of silence pass, and then an unsettling explosion of maniacal laughter fills the house. Martha's nostrils flare atop exposed gums, her teeth flashing between her curled lips. She slams the counter with her palm once, twice…and then a third time, making me flinch each time.

"You fucking whore!" Veins bulge in her face as her eyes turn dark. "You fucking whore!" It's a guttural roar, her voice lingering over the word *whore.* Her fingers tremble as her neck stiffens.

I try to lighten my tone—"What are you talking about?"—but my voice cracks. Thoughts rage through my mind: *What does she know? How much does she know? Fuck!*

Martha disappears behind the wall, making her way around the counter. The first thing that comes to my mind is my baby's safety. *Does she know I'm pregnant? Did Craig tell her? Did I forget to delete a message? Did a message come through at the last minute? Fuck!*

I glance at the door again, willing my legs to kick out and run, but I can't move. Before I can look back at her, she swings a fist at me. She strikes my jaw with tremendous force, causing my teeth to pierce into my tongue, making me shriek in pain. Before I can register that blood is dripping from my mouth, she grabs me by my face, curling her fingers into my cheeks. She looks down at me along her nose, spitting as she says, "Now you listen to me, you little fucking cunt."

She jerks my face forward, making me lurch closer to her. I frown, trying to bear the throbbing in my jaw. She twists my head sideways, bringing her mouth to my ear. "This is what's going to happen. You *will* leave this goddamn country within the next week, or I'll make sure everyone knows about your little secret. You're a fucking murderer."

I jam my fist into her chest, propelling her away from me. "Fuck you!" I scream, pointing a finger at her. "You know nothing. It'll be my word against yours."

"Oh, really?" she says, sneering. "It's a shame you felt you had to document all your feelings in a memo on your phone, which, by the way, has already been delivered to my e-mail. God, you're stupid." She laughs again. "Oh, and Wayne told me all about it. You know, about the abortion."

A dagger twists in my heart as her words echo through me. "So," she continues, "you're going to leave this country, and we can keep it our little secret," she says, widening her eyes. There's silence. I stare at the floor, wiping the blood from my chin. "Oh, my God," she says, forcing a laugh from her throat, "imagine Lorraine's reaction when I tell her you fucked Craig."

My throat tightens. "You won't do that," I say, and Martha's eyes sweep from my toes to my head. "You have too much pride to throw yourself into the same boat she's in."

"Oh, sweetie," she says, her face breaking into a smile, one that doesn't reach her eyes, "either way, you'll be kicked out of the au pair program. Whether it's me telling the world about your abortion or sharing the foreseeable news that you're a whore, you'll be on a plane home in no time."

"It wasn't an abortion!"

She curls the corners of her lips down, smirking. "Oh, that's right. You murdered your child to save your own life. Was it worth it, Lexy? Did she die in vain?" She narrows her eyes, waiting for me to react, but I know better than to give her the satisfaction.

My heart races, ready to explode in my chest, and my fingers ache, ready to scratch the smile off her face. "How long?" I ask.

"How long *what*?" She clenches her teeth.

"How long have you…known?"

Martha takes a step forward. "For quite a fucking while now. You think whenever you skipped upstairs to fuck my husband that I left for class. I sensed something was wrong when I…" She pauses, her eyes frantically scanning me, her nostrils flaring again, her face twisted in a pained expression.

She charges back to the kitchen, where her hands rummage through the top drawer. She comes back into my line of view as my eyes focus on the scissors in her hands. She bobs them in the air, her mouth opening to say something, but it shuts just as quickly. She throws the scissors to the floor, and then she yanks my head back by my hair. "*This*…" she hisses. "*This* is what I found on my goddamn bed," she says, tightening her grip as my hair pulls at the skin on my skull, making me wince.

"Martha…Martha…please," I beg, as my scalp burns. "I'll leave! I'll leave!"

She releases her grip and turns around to grab my phone from the counter. My hand goes to my head as I try to rub the ache away. She glides my SIM card out from the metal chips and bends it until it snaps. Then she hurls the phone against the wall, the pieces scattering across the floor.

She turns back to me. "If you ever tell anyone about this, you'll regret it for the rest of your life," she warns. "And once you're home," she adds, "you won't call here. You won't send any texts. *Nothing*! Do you understand me?"

"Yes…yes, I do." Martha's eyes trace down my stomach, and I cross my arms over it, trying to protect my baby. She gives me a disgusted look, snorting as she shakes her head slightly. "Don't even dare fucking mentioning my name to anyone."

I stare at her, thinking, *You're no better than me.* She once did this to another woman, and perhaps the wheel does turn. I guess Wayne was right about karma, just like he turned the wheel on me…but I don't blame him; I can't.

Lexy

Tuesday, July 14, 2015
Evening - 18 Days After Disappearance

"So that's why your phone activity stopped about ten days before you left?" Eric asks.

"Yes, I bought a prepaid phone then. I was too embarrassed to tell Lorraine I went through another phone within two months."

Aliya shakes her head. "This doesn't add up," she says, rolling her pen between her index finger and thumb.

"Which part?" I ask.

"Martha said she had no idea about the affair. So either she's lying or you are." She drums her fingers on the table. "And I'm inclined to believe Martha." She drops the pen and runs a thumb along the stack of papers in front of her. "Do you mind explaining this?" she says, sliding a piece of paper off the top of the pile.

My eyes sweep across the document. "What about it?"

"We found these poems in your diary. The one you kept in your room."

"That's not possible. I don't...I didn't write this."

"It's your handwriting," Eric declares, letting the statement sink in.

"I took my diary to London with me." I grab my handbag and frantically search through it. Eric folds his arms as I place the journal on the table, the red cover vibrant underneath the light.

"So you have two of them," Aliya states, unwavering.

"No. This is the only one I have."

Eric flicks it open, scanning the contents. He slides the paper from underneath my nose next to the journal. "Same handwriting," he confirms, as his eyes glide up at me. He squints. "Explain."

I take the documents back from him, squeezing my eyes shut, trying to figure out how this could be. I open them again, and then it hits me. "Fuck," I say, falling back in my seat. "Yes," I tell them, blinking around the room. "Yes, I wrote this. She made me…Martha asked me to write this."

They both chuckle, evidently dismissing my statement. "She asked me to help her with an assignment. She's enrolled in college, working toward a bachelor's degree in English, and she said she didn't have the time to do it and asked me to write it for her. She clearly knew about Craig and me much earlier than I thought she did. This was all planned out!"

Eric sighs. "Well, that sounds convenient for you…and implausible."

"I swear," I say, and my eyes shoot at Aliya, waiting for her to say something. I scan through the poems, searching for something—a giveaway perhaps—but nothing comes.

"These poems are all about you…about your pregnancy too. Everything you just told us," Eric says.

I realise how far Martha pushed me into a corner, and my eyes sting with tears. "I had no idea what I was writing at the time. I had no idea what it meant. I didn't give it much thought."

They stare at me, unmoving.

"Look, she's trying to frame me! What about DNA tests? Fingerprints?"

"The journal found at Lorraine's house is covered in your prints," Eric says, making my stomach clench. He clears his throat before he continues. "How did Logan's blood end up on the backseat of your car?"

"What?"

"Answer the question," Aliya says.

I frown. "I don't know. A football injury?"

Eric chuckles again. "And what about the threats you made?"

"Threats?"

He slides a piece of paper across the table. Images of messages sent from my old number to Wayne cover the page. "I never sent these," I say, gazing at the texts. "I would never say this!" I tap a finger on one of the messages, startled. "She framed me!" I repeat, and then the similarities to Craig's case hit me.

"She did the same thing with Craig!" I exclaim. Eric seems to consider my statement. "Look, the same thing happened to Craig. We thought Lorraine was losing it, but now I get it. Martha did this. Martha is behind all of this! Talk to Lorraine again. Ask her about it."

"Well, unfortunately, we can't bring the dead back," Aliya says, her words cleaving me right through the heart as I gasp for air.

"What?" The room dims, growing out of focus. Something cold penetrates my core. "Lorraine's dead?" A warm, heavy tear rolls down my cheek. Aliya gives me a deadpan expression. "When?"

"This past Friday," Eric says, almost whispering. "I'm sorry."

They give me a moment, then Aliya reaches a hand out to take the poem back, but I slam my palm against the table. She glares at me.

"Wait!" I say, as my eye catches something. Something that might prove my innocence. I wipe away my tears before pulling it closer to make sure I'm not mistaken.

"You see," I say, "I'm British." They nod. "I wouldn't spell 'fervor' like it's written here." I press my index finger against the word, the tip growing a pale-yellow. "I'd spell it 'f-e-r-v-o-u-r.'" They glance at each other, and then they lean in to have a look for themselves. Eric raises an eyebrow, squeezing his lips flat.

"Very well, then," he says, shuffling in his chair. He glances at the camera, making sure it's still recording. He glides the paper back to him and writes a note. "Now…tell us what happened next."

I take a deep breath as another tear wets my face, and then I replay the day I left.

Lexy

Friday, June 26, 2015
Evening - Day of Disappearance

I told Martha I can't afford a flight home, that I'm short three hundred dollars. I'll have to wait for my weekly payment. Martha refused to pay for the ticket. So she decided to give me two weeks to leave. Two installments. An extra four hundred dollars.

The past ten days have been hell. Martha's been dictating my every move. I bought myself a prepaid phone, gave Logan my new number, and prayed that, in the meantime, Lorraine won't try to get a hold of me on my old one. The only times I've left the house have been to go to work at Craig's in the morning, pretending like nothing ever happened—because if I suddenly stop going over, Craig and Logan will question it—and when I visited Dean's law firm. I don't have the money to consult with a lawyer, so I asked Roy for his legal advice, since he specialises in immigration law.

I never mentioned that I'm about to leave Seattle, nor did I tell him I'm pregnant, which was harder than I'd thought it would be. I merely asked if I'm subject to 212(e), and I brought up some basic scenario questions. When he asked what my motive was, I just winked and said, "Only an excuse to see you."

Now I'm peering into Lorraine's room. She lifts her head from the pillow, her eyes swollen from sleep. "Logan wants to go to a house party. Is that okay?" She frowns. "I'll drop him off," I whisper. She nods and turns over on the bed.

I leave the door ajar, fetch Sam's monitor, and place it on her nightstand. My feet are anchored to the floor as I stare at her, knowing this is the last time I'll ever see her. Yesterday I was retching over the toilet, and she heard me from her room. When she asked if I was okay, I told her I'm pregnant. She seemed shocked, then happy when I said Wayne's the father. My throat tightens as I turn to leave, hoping she'll never find out that I slept with Craig, hoping

Martha will never tell her.

Back in my room, I grab the remnants of cash from my pink box on the dresser. I pack a few sheets of Zoloft, knowing I have my full prescription at home, and then I place my red journal in my handbag.

In my closet, I grab my camera, trying to force it in next to my dairy, but it won't fit. I search for an extra bag, something I can pack to take home, but then I pause.

What if Martha finds out?

She specifically said I can't take any of my belongings with me, and that little brats like me should be punished—that's how spiteful she is. Martha knows it'll take me years to earn back what my belongings are worth, but all that matters is my baby. My fingers splay over my stomach, and I decide not to take the risk. Once I'm in London, we'll be safe. Once I'm out of America, everything will be okay.

My pulse quickens as I place my camera back in the box, taking only the things that will fit into my handbag. My head spins as I make my way downstairs, where Logan awaits me on the couch.

"Ready to go?"

"She said it's okay?"

I nod, and his face breaks into a grin as he brings a clenched fist up to his face, mouthing, "Yes."

I shake my head slightly, managing a faint smile. "Right. Let's go. I don't have a lot of time."

He winks. "How come? You don't have any friends to meet up with."

I flick a hand at him. "Fuck off," I say, chuckling.

Logan follows me outside, still smirking, as I fish the keys from my bag. I catch his eye. "Whatever you do tonight," I tell him, "don't get drunk."

He winks at me again before we both get into the car. I twist in the seat toward him. "Where am I taking you?"

"Carmen's."

"I thought you were going to a party." My hand slightly tightens on the wheel.

"I am, but first I'm meeting with Carmen."

"I thought you two were over?"

He gives me a mischievous smile. "You want us to be over?"

"No…Logan." My hand drops from the keys in the ignition. "We shouldn't have slept together. It was wrong, and I'm really sorry."

"You shouldn't say that out loud," he says. "You could get locked up for it."

I glare at him, unsmiling. In London the age of consent is sixteen. What is it in Washington? Sixteen? Eighteen? But never mind that. I'm his au pair…I'm in a position of trust, which makes it…immoral.

"I didn't *sexually abuse* you, Logan."

"I know, but not in the eyes of the law."

I break eye contact as I stare at the gear lever. I beg him to keep this between us. And then I wonder if Martha knows. I swallow hard as adrenaline spikes through my system.

"Lexy," he says, touching my shoulder. "Don't worry. I won't do that to you."

"Logan, I'm serious."

He presses his lips together, his eyes filled with concern. "You'll be okay."

I take a deep breath, wondering if I should tell him what I've done…and what's about to happen, but I'm not sure I can trust him. And how would he react if he knew I slept with his dad? So instead I say nothing. I turn the key in the ignition, and we drive off.

As I'm driving, thoughts rage through my mind. *What if he tells his friends? Brags about it? What if they lock me up? Take my child away from me? Register me as a sex offender?* I glance at him, mulling over my options. *What can I do to prevent that from happening?* My stomach seizes, and my fingers feel cold against the steering wheel. My mind shifts to Roy, and I wonder if I'll ever see him again. I try to swallow the lump in my throat, but I can't. The ghostly glow of Logan's phone on the windshield reveals the countenance of my face. I blink hard, trying to hide my anxiety.

I take a right into the parking lot of a 7-Eleven and park the car next to a gas pump. "Why are we stopping?" Logan asks as I turn off the engine.

"Maybe if you took your eyes off your phone, you'd see why." He lifts his head but drops it just as fast. "Here," I say. "Get yourself something to eat. You shouldn't go over to Carmen's on an empty stomach."

He grabs the ten dollars and steps outside the car. I follow him as he enters the 7-Eleven, and then I tell him I need to make a quick call to a friend. He nods and turns to browse the aisles. I exit the shop, my feet heavy on the gravel as they amble toward the pay phone. The coins slide through the slot, clinking their way down the machine. I dial the number Martha gave me, and it rings for a few seconds before she answers.

"Where are you?" she asks with a forced calmness.

"At the 7-Eleven. The one you said I need to call you from."

There's silence. "Oh…good. So you're on track," she says, like a manager would when they check in with their employees. "Now remember to leave the car at Seahurst Park. I'll get it from there."

She explains for two minutes too long why I need to do so because she can't drive all the way to the airport. She says she'll bring the car back to Lorraine's place since she has the spare key I gave her this week.

"I've given it some thought," she says. "After you've been home for a few days, send Lorraine an e-mail, saying you hated working for her."

I glance through the shop window, trying to see where Logan is. "I can't do that," I say, and a breathy laugh shoots through my ear.

"You'd be fucking stupid not to," she says. "You do what I say." I remain silent as I urge myself to keep it together. "I wonder what your mother would do if she found out you killed her first grandchild."

I take a deep breath, craning my neck. Logan's making his way to the cashier, but he stops midway. "Logan's with me," I say.

"What?"

"I have to drop him off at a party…well, then he changed his mind. I'm taking him to Carmen's house."

She sighs. "Fucking hell," I hear a door close, and I imagine her walking through the house, trying to hide our conversation from Craig. "Okay, I'll get your car when Craig picks him up tonight."

There's a moment of silence, and then I ask again, "Why can't I take my belongings with me?" Logan's at the cash register, handing the money over.

"Because you don't fucking deserve it," she says, and my body trembles. "You deserve *nothing*."

She hangs up, but I still clutch the phone against my ear for a few seconds, trying to suppress the impulse of smashing the receiver against the glass. My hand slowly clicks the handset back into the holder, and I try to keep my composure as I exit the box.

I stride over to the car, where Logan's waiting for me, and I fake a smile that requires every ounce of effort I can gather.

Lexy

Tuesday, July 14, 2015
Evening - 18 Days After Disappearance

"You didn't think for a moment that it was an odd thing for her to ask?" Eric asks.

"Leave?"

"No, to park the car at Seahurst Park…and not take your belongings with you," he says, frowning in disbelief.

"Yeah, I thought it was weird. I was sceptical about it, but what could I do? Call the cops? Tell them—*you*—that I had sex with a sixteen-year-old…as his au pair? Disappoint my mother once more? Dropping out of university was quite enough, thank you. I didn't dare ask Martha any questions. I couldn't dare risk my child's safety. I owed it…to my baby. To…everyone. Including myself."

My eyes shift between them. "I had two options: refuse to leave, consequently paying the price by Martha revealing my affair with Craig as well as my terminating my pregnancy. Being shamed in public, losing my job, not being allowed back into America for breaking my contract, and eventually being deported back home. Or I could leave by myself without causing any more drama, grief, and disappointment."

Aliya scratches the back of her head, nodding, and then she clears her throat. "What happened after you left the 7-Eleven?"

"I dropped Logan off at Carmen's house."

"And Martha said Craig would pick Logan up that night?"

"Yes."

"Okay," she says, folding her arms. "And after you dropped Logan off?"

"I left the car at Seahurst Park as Martha instructed me. After that, I used my phone to call a cab."

"We have no records proving this," Aliya states, arching an eyebrow. "Your phone activity stopped about a week and a half before you left."

"Yes. Like I said, Martha broke the old phone Lorraine gave me. So I bought myself a cheap prepaid phone."

"So why didn't you use the prepaid phone to call Martha at the 7-Eleven?" Aliya asks.

"She was paranoid that her number might get traced to the phone I had. So she asked me to call her from the pay phone. She didn't want Craig to know she told me to leave."

"Again…you didn't think that was suspicious?" Eric asks.

I chuckle, throwing my hands in the air. "I'm sorry…yeah, I must've known Logan was going to get murdered. Jesus, who the hell would've thought that? I didn't grow up in Hollywood."

"I guess some people just have more common sense than others," he says, taking notes. "It's called instincts."

"Well, sorry for not thinking about that when I had a lot on my mind…things you clearly don't understand."

He shrugs. "I'm a detective, not a psychologist. I'm doing my job. I don't have to sympathise with your petty shit," he says, and Aliya's eyes shoot at him.

I fall silent, and then a tear trickles down my nose. "That's why I said I feel guilty…and responsible." I break down in uncontrollable sobs. "I didn't think anything like this would happen."

Neither of them moves. The room fills with an uncomfortable silence, my sobs breaking it rhythmically. "So," Aliya says, "is there anything else you'd like to add?" I shake my head. "Okay, well, that's enough for now." She reaches for the remote. She states the time and ends the recording. "Do you want to request protective services?"

"No." It comes out in a whisper. "I'll be fine." Earlier I received a message from Ella on Facebook. I want to hear what she has to say because I have no idea what happened to Logan that night. The last time I saw him was when I dropped him off at Carmen's house.

"Book yourself into a hotel, and call us with your location. Keep your whereabouts to yourself." Eric leans back in his chair. "And don't even try to leave the country," he says. "We're not done with you." I wonder if he's referring to the statutory rape—as they would refer to it. Or if I'm still one of their main suspects; perhaps they don't believe me.

"You're not done with me?" I feel my heart sinking. "Because I slept with

Logan?"

Eric clears his throat. "As a parent, I'd like to see you punished for that, but the age of consent is sixteen in Washington. So what you've done isn't illegal—it's just wrong."

I let out a long breath then think about all my belongings, wondering if I can retrieve them. Thousands of dollars' worth of clothes…and my camera, among all the other things I left behind. I contemplate whether I should swing by Lorraine's house before going to a hotel.

But first I'll reply to Ella's message.

Ella

Tuesday, July 14, 2015
Evening - 18 Days After Disappearance

Martha lifts her head, looking neither of us in the eye, as she stares out the glass door. "I hope that whore died."

My eyes meet Craig's as I realize she has no idea that Lexy is still alive. Not to mention that she's in Seattle. I intentionally frown at him, and he slightly shakes his head, signaling me not to tell her. I excuse myself from the table so I can check my Facebook inbox. Martha's sniffs grow inaudible as I distance myself from them.

A circle-cropped photo of Lexy is positioned in the upper corner of my phone. A white number 1 extends to the side, centered on a red block. I tap the image, which makes my inbox expand across the screen.

> Hi, Ella, I'm on my way to quickly pick up some of my belongings from Lorraine's house. I'd like to hear what you have to say. The detectives just finished their interrogation. Martha tried to frame me. I don't want to stay too long, in case someone sees me.

My fingers frantically dance over the keyboard, warning her that Martha's here. I hit "send," but I don't get a notification that she's read my message. My head spins. Her phone probably only works with Wi-Fi, since she's on a British network. I hurry back to the kitchen.

"You two need to leave," I say, faster than intended. I try to look away, but I can't help glare at Martha, thinking about all the shit she's spun. How she pretended to search for Logan's body, how she fucked us all over. But then suddenly I realize that Lexy could be lying, trying to cover her own tracks.

"I'm not leaving with him," Martha says, pulling her brows in.

"I'll drop you off," I say, desperate for her to leave. Her index finger jerks down her thumb as she picks the skin next to the nail.

"Guess I'll stay here tonight," Craig says, slowly standing up.

"No," I tell him. "Find somewhere else to stay."

Martha clutches her upper arms, and I glance at the clock. The message came through twenty minutes ago. Lexy will be here any minute.

"I never want to see you again," Martha says, jumping to her feet and leaning toward Craig.

"Then I suggest you move the fuck out of my house," he says.

Their voices become a distant distortion as the gravel outside lights up. I gaze at the yellow oval shape on the road, which levels and gradually disappears as a car drives into view then comes to a halt.

I sneak away from Craig and Martha to the main entrance, but the bickering behind me diminishes as I see them turn to me in the reflection of the window next to the door.

The door where a faint, hazy figure moves behind it, ready to knock.

Lexy

Tuesday, July 14, 2015
Evening - 18 Days After Disappearance

I stare at Lorraine's van. The only vehicle in the driveway. My heart sinks at the sight of it, but the sensation is interrupted by the door swinging wide open in front of me.

Ella positions her body to block the entrance. Her posture is stiff, her eyes wide. She mouths something, and I squint my eyes, focusing on her lips, trying to make out what she's saying.

"Go! Fucking run!" she whispers, but before I can react, Martha's head pops out from behind her shoulder, pulling Ella from the door.

I turn to run, but as I take my first step, Martha grabs my hair and tugs me into the house. Before I can find my balance, she kicks me in my stomach, propelling my back against the wall. I curl up in pain, gasping for air, my fingers splayed across my belly. Craig runs toward us from behind the kitchen table as Ella stumbles to her feet, holding her hand for me to pull myself up, but before I can grab it, I hear a sound that makes my heart stop.

The cock of a gun.

Martha stands at the end of the room, waving a pistol around. "Move!" she demands, flicking her wrist as she gestures us to the living room.

She locks the front door before following our every step. "Sit," she says, and we do what she says, except for Craig.

"Darling," he says, "you don't have to do this. Please, honey. It was just…once or twice." Her hand starts to shake as she aims at him. Craig takes a step toward her. "I love you," he says, and the next thing I know, blood sprays across my face, making me squeal in terror. My voice scrapes through my throat, sending a deafening shrill through the house. Craig's body drops to the floor, blood seeping from his head.

Martha swings her gun at my stomach, and my body starts to tremble as I scream, my veins protruding from my neck.

"No! Please don't! No!"

Ella

Tuesday, July 14, 2015
Evening - 18 Days After Disappearance

Lexy is hysterical, and rightfully so. For some reason, I felt numb to the bone but only up until Sam woke up from the gunshot. The sound of his cries readjusted my thoughts, inducing an undeniable urge to protect him.

Lexy's voice pierces my ears as she pulls her legs up to her stomach, preparing herself for Martha to pull the trigger. If I haven't seen terror before, I'm seeing it now, smeared across this poor girl's face. My eyes move to the floor, tracing the line of blood seeping from Craig's head, and I lift my feet to prevent it from soaking into my shoes.

"Get up!" Martha yells, flicking the pistol upward. I do as told, taking Lexy's hand to help her stand. Whimpering, she curls her shoulders forward, her head tucked to her chest.

"Put your hands in the air," she says. "Both of you." I try my best to control my breathing, trying to think of coherent ways to handle this. My eyes move to my right. There's an armchair one or two feet from the wall. I scan the room for objects, but there's nothing light enough to pick up and swing quickly.

Martha slides a chair over from the kitchen, waving the gun as she signals Lexy to sit. She keeps the pistol directed at us as she pulls drawers open, searching for something. Her hands rummage through the contents, throwing papers, pencils, and keys to the floor. She holds a length of dirty brown rope to her face, and then she tosses it at me. "Tie her up."

I bend over to pick it up, glancing at Craig. His eyes are lifeless, his jaw slack. I know a dead body when I see one, and there's not a breath left in his lungs. I look at him for a moment longer before I straighten my back.

"If you don't tie her up properly, you'll both join Craig," she says. I walk around the chair to kneel behind it. Lexy's already pressing her wrists together for me to tie them. The rope trembles as her fists do, while Sam still shrieks from upstairs. I slowly let the rope rest on her hands, pinning them in an unmovable position as I fasten the knot. I take a step back and move to the side.

Martha tugs at the rope, making sure it's tight. "Thanks," she says, sending a wave of nausea through me.

Thanks?

She takes four steps back and swings the gun out from her side. "No!" Lexy screams, frantically trying to jump from her seat.

Martha pulls the trigger. The shell casing drops to the floor, rolling in a half circle, then a second, a third, and a fourth. Instantly I leap behind the armchair, crawling as fast I can toward the opening on the other side to escape down the hallway to the front door. Lexy's voice suddenly fades, and then the firing stops. There's silence; the air reeks of chemicals. I can't hear Sam anymore since my ears are ringing. I pause on all fours. The hardwood floor creaks, snatching the breath from my lungs. One step…then two in my direction. I bow my head as the anticipation rips me from within. The gun cocks once more, and I squeeze my eyes shut, readying myself for the blow.

"Bah!" Martha screams, making me fall flat on my stomach, gasping for air. Her laughter reaches my ear. I direct my gaze from the floor to her, looking into the muzzle of the pistol. She pulls the gun back, widening her eyes.

"Now why would I hurt you?" she asks, her face breaking into a grin. Her expression suddenly goes blank, her eyes vacant. "Unless you have something to tell me," she says, jerking the gun back to my face.

"No," I say. "No, I don't."

She pulls the pistol back again. "Good." She darts her free hand out for me to grab. Startled, I place my hand in hers, pulling myself up. My eyes sweep across the room, and the sight of Lexy makes me swallow a lungful of air.

Her head and shoulders are drooping forward, her buttocks slightly elevated from the chair as her arms are still fastened to it.

"What?" Martha utters, as I eye the blood coiling down Lexy's legs. "You feel sorry for the whore?"

I say nothing, and she snorts. Sam cries louder, his tone becoming more frantic. Martha inches toward the stairs, her eyes rolling aloft. "Oh, for fuck's sake," she says, her head lifting toward the ceiling.

"Don't even think about it," I say.

She turns to face me. "Aww, you came to love the bastard." Her feet are rooted before the first step, one she's clearly eager to take. "Do you know what Craig told me?"

I shake my head.

"He said if I didn't get my tubes tied, he wouldn't marry me. He said he's *done* with kids." She pauses. "I did it for him…and this is how he repays me?" Her eyes sparkle as her jaw juts forward.

"Sam isn't Craig's child," I say in a placating tone. "He has nothing to do with you, Craig, or Lexy." I pause as Martha regards me for a moment. "Is that why you killed Logan? To get back at Craig?"

She holds my gaze for a few seconds. Her face twists into a grimace, and then she turns her back on me, taking the first leap up the stairs. Suddenly my doubt, hesitancy, and fear are overpowered by a wave of rage.

My legs shoot out from beneath me as I run after her. I grab her by the ankles, hauling her feet from underneath her body, her torso smashing against the steps. A loud grunt emerges from above as the stairs tremble. Martha grabs the railing to her right, trying to twist her body to aim the pistol at me, but before she can, I dive for the gun. With both hands I smack her wrist repeatedly against the edge of the step. She grabs my hair with her free hand, trying to drag me down, but I don't even budge. She tries to kick me off her, but I press my knee into her stomach, pinning her down. "You fucking bitch!" I bellow.

Martha's fingers lose their grip, and the pistol tumbles down the stairs. She scuffles a few steps down, but I stop her by grabbing her blouse at the nape of her neck. I drag her to the second floor as she kicks out frantically, choking as her blouse closes in underneath her chin.

I hear three loud thuds against the front door, and then it blows off its hinges. Ignoring the officers swarming into the house, I throw her onto her back, and then I plow my fist into her face.

With every strike, I see their faces: Logan, Craig, Lexy, Lorraine. "You fucking home wrecker!" I scream, as her eyes roll back into her skull, blood spattering across her face. Someone's pounding up the steps behind me, and I plant a final blow against her nose, making her fall unconscious.

Two hands grasp me by the shoulders, heaving me off her. I fly into Eric's arms, and he holds me tightly. "You're safe! You're safe now!" he says, as I break down in tears, screaming at the thought of Martha touching Sam.

Danielle Esplin

Ella

Friday, May 6, 2016

Afternoon - 10 ½ Months After Disappearance

I take a framed photo from the last box and place the picture of Lorraine and her two boys on my desk. Nine months have passed since that horrible night at Lorraine's house, and ever since, the events have replayed over and over in my mind.

I see Martha's eyes rolling back into her skull—the moment I'd thought I'd killed her. I probably would have if it weren't for the neighbor calling 911 after hearing the gunshots. I see the paramedics resuscitating her, then the four strong hands carrying a stretcher down the stairs. The streets filled with red-faced joggers, mothers with splayed hands held against their children, and journalists peering at the scene.

Photos surfaced in the newspaper the next day. One of them was of me—my eyes glazed, my knuckles lacerated, my fists bruised.

I turn to look at my study. Empty boxes are spread across the carpet. I've just moved into a house after having rented an apartment for a few months. Lorraine's house is still on the market. "Buyers are hesitant," the realtor said.

I decided to stay in Seattle so Sam can have a relationship with his father, but I haven't heard from Robert in eight months.

He attended Lorraine's funeral, though. It was tragically beautiful. We held it in a quiet, serene cemetery in Bothell. Not that many people attended. I recognized a face here or there, but I wasn't sure how they were connected to my sister. *A neighbor? A schoolteacher? Someone from work? A stranger?*

They played one of her favorite instrumental pieces, "Cold" by Jorge Méndez. I plucked some of her much-loved red and white geraniums from her yard and scattered them across her coffin as they lowered her into the ground. I fell on my knees and sat on my haunches next to the rectangular pit. Wayne came to hold me while everyone else stared with despondent eyes. I didn't look at them for long because my face was buried in my hands. When they shoveled dirt onto her coffin, I wailed uncontrollably, wishing I could bring her back. I can't remember anything after that really. I don't remember getting in the car or driving home.

A few days later, we held funerals for Craig and Logan. They were laid to rest next to Lorraine's grave. Lexy's body was flown to London so her mother could get closure and properly say good-bye to her daughter and unborn grandchild.

Shortly after the funerals, Roy contacted me, offering his legal help for free. Dean wasn't thrilled about the idea, but together they helped lock Martha up for good.

When they brought up new evidence I didn't know about at the time, the jury had no choice but to find her guilty. They found Logan's clothes in a bag buried in the woods, along with a few strands of Martha's hair.

She refused to cooperate, and the prosecutors concluded it was premeditated murder. Martha said she told Lexy that Craig would pick up Logan from Carmen's house while she quickly returned Lexy's car to Lorraine's residence. She stuck to that version of events, claiming she called Craig, and he agreed to pick Logan up at Carmen's. Easy to blame it on the dead, right?

But Craig had an alibi, and that's why he was suddenly released without charge back then; he was out with friends in a pub. Martha's statements were also proven wrong when phone records were retrieved. It showed on Craig's phone that Martha did call him, but the call never went through. It was just a missed call. Carmen testified that she didn't see who picked Logan up on the night of his disappearance. Prosecutors then concluded that Martha picked up Logan while Craig was out with his friends in a pub from 5:33 p.m. to 1:45 a.m. the next morning, ultimately giving Martha no alibi. She never spoke to Craig on the phone, and then she pretended to have no knowledge of Logan being at Carmen's in the first place.

Because Martha refused to speak, prosecutors were left to draw up a possible scenario based on the evidence they had. They deduced that she lured Logan into believing they were going away for the weekend, so he never went to the party he was planning on attending. Perhaps Martha even said his father was already there. She must've stopped beside the road—maybe said she was worried about a flat tire or some other kind of car trouble—and then she shot him twice. Thanks to ballistics, they proved this was the same gun she used a month later to murder Craig and Lexy. Craig's pistol from the lake house tested negative for Logan's murder. Martha used an unregistered weapon—a class C felony for possession of a handgun without a required permit, license, or certificate. She also refused to say where she obtained the pistol, and tracing the weapon back to a seller led to a dead end.

The prosecutors believe she wanted Logan's body to be found in order to frame Lexy, but she wanted to be subtle about it, so she hid it underneath some debris. His phone was never recovered, but his phone records also showed no interaction with Martha the night of his death. They also concluded that Martha wanted Lexy to leave her belongings, ultimately making it look like she fled the country as fast she could after supposedly murdering Logan.

When asked to explain Logan's blood in Lexy's car, the prosecutors argued that Martha must've planted it, just like she planted the diary in Lexy's room. They reasoned that with Lorraine in the hospital and no one at her house, it was easy for Martha to use Logan's house key, which she took from him the night of his disappearance, and enter the premises, ultimately planting the diary in Lexy's closet.

Martha's lawyer then said, "But it's Lexy's handwriting," and the prosecutors hit back by saying Martha had asked her to help out with an English assignment months before, evidently supporting the prosecutors' claims of premeditation. "Why didn't Lexy pick up on it?" Martha's attorney asked, and the prosecutors simply replied, "If the meaning of the poems were so obvious, why did the detectives have to print them in the newspaper, asking for the public's help?"

When the poems were read aloud in court, they suddenly made sense. Martha knew much more about Lexy than anyone else. Video footage of Lexy's testimony revealed that Martha had read her private messages and memos on her phone. Wayne also had confided in Martha, which made it impossible for her to claim that she knew nothing about Lexy.

Then the shocker came out, which made headlines across the country: "Nanny Slept with Boss's Murdered Sixteen-Year-Old Son." Reporters bombarded Wayne, asking if he knew she was cheating on him with Logan or if he had picked up on anything when they'd gone to Olympic National Park for the weekend with Craig and his family.

The trial for the murders of Lexy and Craig started shortly after. The medical examiners testified that Martha had suffered a severe concussion that night. Martha claimed she was innocent, but she didn't fool the jurors.

Wayne testified against her. He said he received a message from Lexy early in the relationship that "didn't sound like her." He asked who it was, and when she didn't reply, he asked if she sent the message to the wrong number. She came back saying he should save his numbers, so he shrugged it off because he was busy bartending, not wanting to stir up a fight. When the detectives retrieved the messages, they realized Wayne didn't use a question mark in his "wrong number" text, making Lexy think he had sent "who is this" to the wrong number. A poisonous misunderstanding. *The importance of a question mark.*

Martha then confessed to snatching Craig's and Lexy's phones while they were "busy upstairs" or whenever they were partying. She said it was easy, since Craig was prone to having blackouts after drinking, so she'd just delete the messages she sent Lorraine, and when being confronted (like the night of Craig's fortieth), she'd play the victim she supposedly was.

I was their star witness, but Martha's lawyer hammered on the fact that the detectives had found *me* on *her* and claimed I was responsible for Lexy's and Craig's deaths. When the rumors surfaced that Craig had abused my sister and that I wanted revenge for Lorraine, Martha's lawyer read a passage aloud from my sister's journal. The rumors were based on old text messages, which were referenced in one of her diary entries, where she described what happened:

> We were fooling around like old times when we moved to Seattle. After Craig had come back from a business trip, our love rekindled. Logan was off at summer camp with friends, so it was just the two of us.
>
> I paraded in front of him in my new Victoria's Secret lingerie when I noticed his lack of interest. By now he had drunk too much, and I thought he was probably tired from traveling. I left him on the bed and went to the bathroom. That's when I saw the string of condoms protruding from his travel bag. Of course he denied cheating on me, but I wouldn't let it go. Both of us were intoxicated, and for the first time in my life, I really lost my composure. I slapped him across the face and screamed hysterically at him. He stared at me with a blank expression, shocked by my behavior. It was as though I'd

> sucked the life out of him. I pounded my hands against his chest, and that's when he punched me in the shoulder. It didn't hurt as much as I thought it would; he must've restrained himself. I think he just wanted to scare me. I didn't have a bruise, and I couldn't even feel it the next day. I was hungover, though, and he said he couldn't remember what had happened the previous night. That's when I showed him the texts he sent me after he stormed out to a pub. He wrote that I was a "stupid fucking bitch" and that "I made him do it," referring to him hitting me. Craig was apologetic for weeks after that. Well, if only I knew he was feeling guilty about sleeping with Martha.

I couldn't help question how Lorraine could love such a fuckup, but I knew better than to say that aloud. Prosecutors then said that Martha's fingerprints were on the gun, and she also had gunpowder residue on her hands the night Craig and Lexy were murdered. So the jury couldn't see a motive or probable cause relating to the accusations made against me, and Martha was found guilty on all charges. She received three life sentences without the possibility of parole.

Since then I've seen Wayne a few times. He really loved Lexy, and he's having a hard time moving on. A month ago, he got a job in sales at a pharmaceutical research organization. I hope things work out for him and that we'll keep in touch.

My gaze breaks as Sam toddles into the room. He scurries in a circle, bending over each box to see if they're empty. With a smile, he looks up and yells, "Ice cream time!"

I promised to take him after I'm done unpacking. I give him a faint smile, trying to hide the despair my memories just produced. I take his hand as he grins.

"Let's go!" I say, bouncing him on my hip, and we leave our new house, ready to start anew.

At the ice cream shop, Sam can't hide his excitement. I gleam from the inside just looking at his smile. I tighten my hand around his as I push the door open. We enter the shop, where teenagers are leaning in for the latest gossip, mothers are eating waffle cones with their babies next to them in strollers, and baristas are weaving between one another, trying to keep up with the horde.

After five minutes, we reach the front of the line, and Sam starts to jump excitedly as I place his order. With a smile, the cashier hands me my receipt, his trimmed mustache curling upward.

We stand aside, waiting for Sam's ice cream. I watch him as he eyes the man holding the cone underneath the dispenser, the swirls snaking out at the bottom.

Sam hasn't asked about his parents yet, and I dread the day he comes to understand what happened. The day he questions everything. The day I'll have to explain that his mother died of cancer, alone. The day he'll ask what happened to his father, for which I won't have an answer. How do you sugarcoat abandonment? He…disappeared? One day he'll ask about the muscular teen in his baby photos, and I'll have to tell him his half brother was murdered by his mother's ex-husband's wife. When will he realize that we're living in a tragic world?

As he begins to devour his ice cream, getting it all over his face—his nose, cheeks, even in his hair—I hear a familiar voice behind me and swing around.

"Aliya," I say, oddly glad to see her. Even though I've been in Seattle for almost a year, I haven't gotten out much.

I expect a formal nod of the head, but instead she hugs me. "Ella, so nice to see you," she says, taking a step back. There's a moment of silence as we smile at each other, embracing the serendipitous moment. "How are you?"

"Good. Good. Thanks," I say, as we inch toward the side of the shop.

She takes a sip of her coffee as her eyes widen at the sight of Sam. "Wow," she says, gesturing toward him. "Time flies."

I nod as we sit down at a table. "If only it could fly faster," I say, squeezing Sam to my side. "It feels like it happened yesterday."

She nods as she licks the froth from her lips. "It must feel like a never-ending story since that hideous book came out."

I squint my eyes, tilting my head as my brows knit together. "Come again?"

"My God, haven't you heard?" She leans forward. "Our phones have been ringing nonstop. Journalists and reporters have been trying to get information about your case."

"You didn't—"

"Of course not," she says. "No one got a hold of you?"

"No." There's silence. "About what?"

"Martha published a book about that night…and the events leading up to it. It's causing quite an uproar. There are lunatics out there with petitions going around. She's trying to file for an appeal."

I wince, and then my eyes scan the room, trying to see if anyone's staring, but no one is. "Are you fucking with me?"

She shakes her head before she fishes for something in her jacket. She takes out a notebook, click her pen, and writes something down. "Here." She slides the paper toward me. "This is the title of the book. Google it at home and read it."

"All of it?" I ask.

"Preferably."

"How much does the book cost?"

"It's a free download," she says. "A convicted criminal can't benefit financially from his or her crimes in the US." She places the paper cup on the table. "Call us if anyone starts to bother you," she says, which makes me turn and look at Sam. "You've got our number, right?"

"On speed dial," I say, making her chuckle.

She gulps down the last bit of coffee before she gets to her feet. "I have a case to get to," she says, inching out to the side.

I stare at the note for a moment before I look up at her. "Thanks," I say, waving it in the air. She double taps the table with her fist, winks at Sam, then flings a scarf around her neck. "Call me," she says, pointing at me like I always did before I left her office. I shake my head, laughing at how ridiculously hostile I was back then, and then she heads out with a smile planted on her face.

I zip up Sam's jacket before we move out into the unseasonably brisk May afternoon. I take his hand and swing the door open, eager to get home and see what Martha's up to.

Evening

I stride into the house, stepping around boxes, wrapped frames, and furniture. I put one of Sam's favorite TV shows on and leave the room. In my study, I drop the mail on the desk and open my Internet browser. I type "Give It Back" and press "enter." A few articles pop up. One, in particular, catches my eye: "Is Ella Jensen Truly Innocent? Martha Davis, Who Was Convicted for the Murders of

Craig Davis, Logan Davis, and Lexy Wright, Speaks Out."

I urge myself not to click on it, but I can't resist. The article expands over the screen. I read it—not once or twice, but three times. Then I open Amazon and search for the book. I flinch as I click to download it.

The e-book loads, slowly coming into view. I scan through the pages, and then I restlessly click on the arrow to get to the last page.

> *When Lexy came over one afternoon, she said Lorraine couldn't read anymore. I knew she was wrong, because I sent the text messages to Lorraine from Craig's phone—usually when he'd drink at night and wasn't paying any attention to me. I did the same with Lexy. I sent Wayne a message or two while she was fucking my husband upstairs. They thought I was off at class. She thought no one could hear them. But I did. I heard every grunt and moan coming from my bedroom. I heard every bit of my husband's infidelity.*
>
> *I guess unrequited love makes you go nuts. Lorraine died with one life wish. Guess what that was? My husband. Why? Because he didn't want her.*
>
> *It's funny, though, because I almost joined her in that dark pit, where it's too dark to distinguish between love and pain, where everything's incomprehensible. Where the line gets blurred by a sense of desperation. And where it all turns into a deep obsession.*
>
> *Why did that whore au pair come to Seattle? Oh, that's easy: an old flame.*
>
> *Now let's turn to Ella, who has some serious daddy and mommy issues. No one ever loved or wanted her. She's a damaged soul. She killed them, and she's pinning everything on me. Yes, I'm not perfect, but I didn't murder Craig and Lexy. She did. She murdered them because they treated her only family member—the only thing she has in life—like shit. Guess who's roaming your streets, Seattle? A psychotic killer. It's not fair that Ella Jensen gets to live her life without being punished.*

A cold sensation sweeps down my back. Then I chuckle. *Surely no one believes this.* I check for customer reviews, and surprisingly there are more than forty. It's sad how people feed off the misery of others.

I sigh in relief as I read the first few reviews, all of which say her book is bullshit. They cite the evidence found against Martha, reminding the public what she did. I scroll down. There are three five-star reviews. Probably three idiots who are always trying to set themselves apart from the mainstream. It's fools like them who'll believe anything they want, despite the evidence.

I lean back into the chair, and then my eyes dart to the mail, realizing there's nothing written on one of the envelopes. My pulse quickens as I realize someone had to walk up to the house and place the letter in my mailbox. I take a deep breath, and then I grab the envelope and tear it open. Inside is a sheet of paper with one sentence typed on it. My eyes scan it. I read it again, unsure what to think, but then fear sets in.

You deserve what's coming for you.

My heartbeat slows to an unsettling degree as the hairs on my arms rise. I slowly get to my feet, almost losing my balance, to draw the curtains so no one can see me from outside.

I hurry to the living room, where the TV is still blaring. I can see the transitioning of lights cast on the carpet. I yell Sam's name as I walk faster, striding down the hall. My heart keeps pounding, almost as though it's giving out. He appears around the corner, wide-eyed, frightened. I press him against my body as he whimpers.

Without letting another second pass, I hoist him up to my hip and hurry back to the study. I grab the receiver from its base and call the police. There's silence. I try again, and then I break out in a cold sweat.

Someone had to have cut the house line.

I turn to Sam, trying my best to hide my fear. "Honey, I want you to hide in the closet for me." He resists, not wanting to be left alone.

"I promise you three ice creams," I say, managing to force a smile.

His face lights up, and then he dashes to the closet with a grin. "Okay, now…don't come out until I come get you." He nods. "Promise me you won't make a sound."

"Promise," he says, and I give him a kiss on the forehead before I close the door behind me.

In the kitchen, I grab my cell phone and pound a finger against the screen.

After what seems like forever, someone picks up. I explain my situation, and they immediately dispatch an officer to my house.

I quietly open one of the drawers and grab a butcher knife. My fingers tighten around the handle. My wrist shivers. I take a step back, tucking myself into the corner of my living room as far as I can.

And then I wait. *Tick. Tick. Tick.*

This nightmare never ends.

About Author

Danielle Esplin is from South Africa, and she lives in Los Angeles. She's currently writing her second psychological thriller while working in the entertainment industry. She's the founder of The Bulletproof Club, where she provides a brand new approach to the dynamics of toxic relationships and situations. In her free time she writes songs, sings, and reads. *Give It Back* is her first novel.

Visit Danielle at:
www.danielleesplin.com
www.thebulletproofclub.com

About Author

BLACK ROSE
writing™

www.ingramcontent.com/pod-product-compliance
Lightning Source LLC
Chambersburg PA
CBHW010445100726
47904CB00008B/2482
* 9 7 8 1 6 1 2 9 6 8 3 2 2 *